A Broad, A Brawl, and A Broken Jaw

"Excuse me, miss . . ."

Eileen looked around in surprise. "I wonder what he wants."

Longarm stopped and turned. "Something I can do for you, old son?"

An arrogant sneer twisted the man's thick lips. "I wasn't talking to you, cowboy. I want to speak to the lady."

"Could be the lady don't want to talk to you." Longarm moved between Eileen and the man, who started to shove past him.

Longarm stopped the man with a hand on his chest, and he was none too gentle about it.

The rancher flushed with anger. "Why, you—"

He tried to bring the butt of his gun down on Longarm's head. Longarm stepped in quickly so the blow missed his skull, but the gun butt thudded against the back of his left shoulder so hard that his arm went numb.

Luckily, there was nothing wrong with Longarm's right arm. He drove a fist into the man's belly. Hot, sour breath gusted in Longarm's face from the man's lungs. Longarm stepped back, cocked his fist, and smashed it into the rancher's jaw. The man went over backward and landed in the gutter.

"I just wanted to talk to the lady . . . she looks like somebody I used to know."

Longarm glanced at Eileen. "You ever seen this gent before?"

A shudder went through her as she shook her head. "Never."

Longarm turned his attention back to the rancher. "I reckon you made

TABOR EVANS

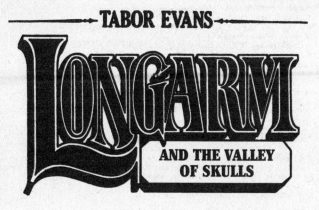

LONGARM

AND THE VALLEY OF SKULLS

JOVE BOOKS, NEW YORK

THE BERKLEY PUBLISHING GROUP
Published by the Penguin Group
Penguin Group (USA) Inc.
375 Hudson Street, New York, New York 10014, USA
Penguin Group (Canada), 90 Eglinton Avenue East, Suite 700, Toronto, Ontario M4P 2Y3, Canada
(a division of Pearson Penguin Canada Inc.)
Penguin Books Ltd., 80 Strand, London WC2R 0RL, England
Penguin Group Ireland, 25 St. Stephen's Green, Dublin 2, Ireland (a division of Penguin Books Ltd.)
Penguin Group (Australia), 250 Camberwell Road, Camberwell, Victoria 3124, Australia
(a division of Pearson Australia Group Pty. Ltd.)
Penguin Books India Pvt. Ltd., 11 Community Centre, Panchsheel Park, New Delhi—110 017, India
Penguin Group (NZ), 67 Apollo Drive, Rosedale, North Shore 0632, New Zealand
(a division of Pearson New Zealand Ltd.)
Penguin Books (South Africa) (Pty.) Ltd., 24 Sturdee Avenue, Rosebank, Johannesburg 2196,
South Africa

Penguin Books Ltd., Registered Offices: 80 Strand, London WC2R 0RL, England

This is a work of fiction. Names, characters, places, and incidents either are the product of the author's imagination or are used fictitiously, and any resemblance to actual persons, living or dead, business establishments, events, or locales is entirely coincidental.

LONGARM AND THE VALLEY OF SKULLS

A Jove Book / published by arrangement with the author

PRINTING HISTORY
Jove edition / October 2008

Copyright © 2008 by Penguin Group (USA) Inc.
Cover illustration by Miro Sinovcic.

ISBN: 978-0-515-14538-0

JOVE®
Jove Books are published by The Berkley Publishing Group,
a division of Penguin Group (USA) Inc.,
375 Hudson Street, New York, New York 10014.
JOVE is a registered trademark of Penguin Group (USA) Inc.
The "J" design is a trademark belonging to Penguin Group (USA) Inc.

PRINTED IN THE UNITED STATES OF AMERICA

10 9 8 7 6 5 4 3 2 1

Chapter 1

Peace was better than war. Living was better than dying. A warrior's honor was important, but was it more important than waking in the morning next to one's wife and feeling the curved softness of her rump pressed against one's manhood?

These were simple things indeed, but it was astounding how many men failed to grasp them. Perhaps it took years to gain such wisdom, and years were something that Falls from the Sky, the chief of this band of Cheyenne, had in abundance.

He had convinced his people that the time for fighting the whites had come and gone. Others might continue the struggle, but Falls from the Sky saw the futility in it. There were only so many Cheyenne, but evidently there were as many whites as there were stars in the heavens, because they just kept coming and coming . . .

Even now the settlers had moved into the valley near the Cheyenne hunting ground and started a town. They brought with them oxen and plows so that they could farm the land. That seemed incredibly foolish to Falls from the Sky, but they were white. Incredibly foolish was to be expected from them.

Even now, as the Cheyenne chieftain left his lodge and peered west toward the mouth of the valley, he seemed to hear the sound of hammers as the whites worked to erect more buildings in their town, which had no name that Falls from the Sky had ever heard. He was probably just imagining things; the valley was a couple of miles away, as the white men measured distances. It was unlikely he could actually hear the hammers. But not impossible, because sound carried well in the clear air of the Wyoming Territory high country.

The sun had not been up for long, and a shiver went through Falls from the Sky as he saw the way the slanting, reddish rays painted the two big rocks flanking the entrance to the valley. Those rocks were massive, their curved tops rising high over the valley mouth. Time and weather had pitted the rocks' surfaces, forming dark indentations on each that looked like eyes, a nose, a grinning mouth . . .

The settlers called their new home Happy Valley. Fools. To the Cheyenne it had another name, a more fitting name considering its reputation as a cursed place.

The Valley of Skulls.

Falls from the Sky shook his head as he turned back toward his lodge. Before he could push aside the buffalo-hide flap over the entrance, he heard something else. This was no figment of his imagination. This was real, and it sounded like thunder.

But the morning sky was clear of clouds. The rumble had to be something else.

Hoofbeats, Falls from the Sky realized. Many horses were coming, and their approach was swift. Somewhere in the village, a woman cried out in panic.

Then came the gunshots.

The sudden crackle of revolvers sent Falls from the Sky leaping back into his lodge. Even as his wife asked him

2

what was wrong, he snatched up the old rifle that he had carried when he rode against the yellowlegs many years before. Since that time, it had been used mostly for hunting.

But Falls from the Sky could still use it to kill an enemy if he had to. If he and his people were threatened with violence here in their own home. He ran from the lodge and saw the riders sweeping through the village.

White men!

Not soldiers, though. These invaders wore long coats and hoods pulled over their heads so that only their eyes were visible below the hats crammed down over the hoods. Their hands were filled with guns that spat flame. The air was filled with smoke and dust and screams.

Only old men and women and children were in the village right now. The young men had gone out to hunt the day before and had not yet returned. Otter That Glides, the son of Falls from the Sky, was leading them on the hunt.

The chief wished that his son were here right now to fight at his side. But since that was not the case, Falls from the Sky would have to do what he could without Otter's help. He flung the rifle to his shoulder and tried to draw a bead on one of the invaders galloping through the village, whooping and shooting.

One of the white men spotted the old Cheyenne and veered toward him. The marauder fired, sending a bullet whistling over Falls from the Sky's head just as the chief pulled the trigger. The white man's shot didn't hurt him, but it came close enough to make him flinch and that threw his aim off. The shot fired by Falls from the Sky whined harmlessly into the air.

Before he could even attempt to reload the old single-shot rifle, the white man charged him, and Falls from the Sky had to leap out of the way of the horse. He stumbled and fell, old muscles betraying him. His spirit was still young, but his body had too many years for this. By the time Falls from the Sky climbed to his feet again, the white men had raced all

3

the way through the village and were riding off, still yelling and firing their guns into the air. They didn't turn back and were soon out of sight.

Falls from the Sky hurried through the village to see how many of his people had been killed in the attack. To his surprise, although several of the old men had been hurt when they were knocked down by the horses, no one was dead. The Great Spirit had smiled on them this morning, Falls from the Sky thought. Either that, or the white men hadn't intended to kill anyone.

In that case, the attack on the village must have been for sport. That was just the sort of thing some white men would do, Falls from the Sky thought as he attempted to calm his people, who were understandably shaken and upset. Some whites considered it *fun* to terrorize those weaker than them.

The Great White Father in Washington had sent an Indian agent to Happy Valley. Falls from the Sky resolved then and there to visit the man and complain about this attack on the peaceful village. Perhaps the agent could do something about it. Perhaps he could even find out who was responsible and have them punished. Falls from the Sky hoped so, because if anything like this happened again, he might have to reconsider what he had been thinking about earlier.

Perhaps peace was not better than war after all.

"Keep a close eye out, Jack. We ain't far from where those varmints held up the stage a couple o' weeks ago."

The young man who clutched a double-barreled Greener in his hands leaned forward, excitement on his face and in his voice. "You think they're gonna try to rob us, Pete?"

"Ain't no way o' knowin'." The wiry driver slapped the reins against the backs of the six horses pulling the stagecoach. "I wouldn't be a bit surprised, though."

The coach rocked and swayed as it followed the rough

road west toward Happy Valley. The one-eyed old-timer handling the six-horse hitch was called Blind Pete, even though he wasn't blind except in one eye. The other one still worked just fine. Next to him on the box was a fresh-faced youngster named Jack Boggs. Blind Pete had been driving stagecoaches off and on for twenty years, but this was young Jack's first time to serve as shotgun guard.

This particular stage had been making regular runs to Happy Valley for about four months now. For a while, there hadn't been any trouble. The Indians in the area were friendly for the most part, and no road agents had come along to hold up the stage.

All that had changed a month or so earlier. Masked bandits had stopped the stage on three occasions, busting open the box and taking the mail pouch, and also robbing the passengers of any valuables they were carrying. The last time, the guard had tried to put up a fight and gotten ventilated for his trouble. The outlaws had blown him right off the seat and damned near hit Blind Pete in the process. Pete had explained to young Jack that he didn't want that happening again.

"If you get a chance to let fly at 'em without gettin' both of us killed, go to it. But if they got the drop on us, for God's sake don't do nothin' stupid. We'll give 'em the mail pouch and live to get drunk when we get to Happy Valley."

Jack had nodded as if he understood, but Pete worried anyway. The boy was only twenty years old, and kids sometimes got caught up in the heat of the moment and forgot all about what they'd been told to do.

Maybe the outlaws weren't anywhere around this time. It was only a few more miles to Happy Valley. Maybe they were gonna make it without any problems . . .

Those thoughts going through Blind Pete's head were rudely interrupted by more than a dozen masked hombres who spurred their horses out of a thick stand of aspen and blocked the road. They pointed their guns at the stagecoach as Pete hauled back on the reins, and even with one good eye, the muzzles of those Colts looked as big around as the mouths of a bunch of damned cannons.

Beside him on the seat, Jack Boggs started to lift the shotgun. Pete twisted, grabbed the twin barrels, and forced them back down. "Are you loco, boy? You're gonna get us killed!"

"But, Pete . . . they're road agents!"

"Doggone right they are. They killed a fella who was sittin' right beside me a couple o' weeks ago, and I don't want you to end up the same way." Pete looked at the outlaws, who sat their saddles in silence, and raised his hands. "Take it easy, fellas. You can have whatever you want. No passengers today, though. Sorry."

"You're *apologizing* to them because we don't have any passengers for them to rob?" Jack was aghast at the idea.

Pete wasn't through, though. He reached down to unlock the box under the seat. "No need to bust the box open neither. Here's the mail pouch." He pulled out the canvas bag and tossed it into the road. "Don't blame me if there ain't nothin' valuable in it. I got nothin' to do with that. Can we go now?"

What sounded like a chuckle came from one of the masked outlaws. They wore hoods under their hats that concealed their faces except for the eyes, and long dusters buttoned to the throat hid their clothing. The hombres who had carried out the other holdups had been dressed the same way, and Pete had no doubt this was the same bunch.

The owlhoot who had laughed swung down from his saddle, walked forward to pick up the mail pouch, then gestured with his gun. The rest of the gang split into two groups, moving off the road so that the stagecoach could pass between them. They kept their guns pointed at the two men on the box as Pete got the team moving again.

"I think I can get a couple of 'em." The harsh whisper came from Jack as the stage started to roll through the gap between the two groups of bandits.

"You try it and I'm liable to shoot you my own damn self. Keep that scattergun *down*."

As soon as Pete was past the outlaws, he whipped up the

team and hollered at them, causing the horses to strain against their harness and break into a run. The coach bounced and swayed even more as its speed increased. Jack had to grab hold to keep from being jolted off the seat, which was just what Pete intended. The boy couldn't do anything foolish if he was hanging on for dear life.

Pete risked a glance over his shoulder and saw that the outlaws were galloping off in the other direction, putting more distance between them and the coach with each passing second. That was just fine with Blind Pete.

He was of a good mind to quit this job when they got to Happy Valley. He was too old for this shit, had too few years left to waste wondering if he was gonna get blown to hell by some masked owlhoots.

A few minutes later, the big rocks marking the entrance to the valley came into view, looming over the trail like a pair of leering skulls. A shiver went through Pete as he saw them. Every time he drove between them, he felt a little like he was driving right into Hades itself. The air even had a faint whiff of brimstone to it.

Not for the first time, Pete thought that whoever had come up with the name Happy Valley must have been plumb loco!

Chapter 2

"Happy Valley, eh?" Longarm snapped a lucifer into life with an iron-hard thumbnail and held the flame to the tip of the three-for-a-nickel cheroot clamped between his teeth. "I got a feeling that if it was really all that happy, you wouldn't be sending me there, Billy."

From the other side of the desk, Chief Marshal Billy Vail harumphed. "Don't let it go to your head, Custis, but you're right." He picked up a document from the welter of papers on the desk and leaned forward to hand it to Longarm. "Take a gander at that."

The big, rangy deputy marshal leaned back in the red leather chair in front of the desk, cocked his right ankle on his left knee, and puffed on the cheroot as he read the report. As usual, there were no spelling or grammatical mistakes anywhere in it. Vail's clerk, a pasty-faced, four-eyed young gent named Henry, took great pride in his ability to play the typewriter.

That accuracy didn't make the words themselves any more appealing.

Longarm looked up from the paper. "This makes it sound like they've got a heap of trouble up there. A gang of masked varmints holding up stagecoaches and attacking Indian villages . . . reckon that drops the mess in our laps in two different ways."

Vail nodded. "That's right. Those outlaws have interfered with the United States mail, and we've got a complaint from the local Indian agent that's been forwarded to us by the BIA as well."

"You think the same bunch is responsible for all of it?"

"The descriptions match. I'd say it's pretty likely."

"What about the local law?"

Vail's pink, mostly bald head moved from side to side. "There isn't any. Happy Valley is up in the Owl Creek Mountains and is fairly isolated. There's a stage from Casper a couple of times a week, but that's it. It was only opened to settlement a few months ago. There's a settlement, but no town marshal. Those folks are pretty much on their own."

"Which is why they called on Uncle Sam for help."

"Yeah. I'd send half a dozen deputy marshals if I could spare them, Custis, you know that, but I just don't have the manpower."

"So I get the job all by my lonesome."

"Yeah. All by your lonesome."

Longarm could tell that bothered Vail. Cherubic appearance aside, Billy Vail had once been a hard-riding lawman himself. Age had chained him to a desk in an office in Denver, from which he sent out deputies to handle the sorts of chores that once he would have taken care of himself. Sometimes those deputies didn't come back, and that grim possibility gnawed at Vail's guts, even though such dangers were just part of the job for a federal lawman—or any other sort of star packer.

Longarm was Vail's top deputy and had handled a lot of perilous assignments during a long, adventuresome career.

9

He had been beaten up, shot, nearly drowned, left to roast in the blazing desert, and come close to freezing to death on more than one occasion. Somehow, though, he had always pulled through and brought his cases to reasonably satisfactory conclusions. He didn't see any reason why things should change now.

"Don't worry, Billy. This probably won't amount to much. I'll chase those varmints down and see that they get what's coming to them one way or the other. Be back before you know it."

Vail grunted. "Pick up your travel vouchers from Henry. And good luck, Custis."

Longarm nodded and got to his feet. He didn't say anything about it, but he preferred not to rely too much on luck. Luck could—and always did—run out sooner or later.

But as long as it was willing to remain on his side . . . he'd damned sure take it.

Henry didn't look up from his typing when Longarm paused in the outer office to pick up those travel vouchers Vail had mentioned.

"Where are you going this time?" Henry asked.

"Place called Happy Valley." Longarm grinned around the cheroot in his mouth. "Want to come with me? Sounds like your sort of place, Henry."

"I don't think so." The usually dour young man didn't get the joke. He just handed over the vouchers with the customary warning not to try to pad any of the expenses. Henry was a veritable hawk when it came to expense reports.

Longarm was about to leave the office when Henry spoke again, proving that maybe he did have a little bit of a sense of humor after all.

"One thing, Marshal . . ."

"What's that?"

"If events follow their usual course, once you get to Happy Valley . . ."

Longarm raised his eyebrows. "Yeah?"

"It won't be very happy anymore."

Longarm was still chuckling over Henry's gibe when he got back to his rented room in a boardinghouse on the other side of Cherry Creek from downtown Denver. It wasn't quite noon, and there was a train leaving for Wyoming Territory at two. That gave him plenty of time to throw some gear into his war bag and get a bite to eat before leaving.

His packing didn't take long. When he was done, he left his war bag, saddle, and Winchester on the bed and went to the door, intending to stroll down the street to a little café that served decent food and had a plump, pretty, blond waitress who enjoyed flirting with him. He opened the door to step out into the hallway on the boardinghouse's second floor.

And stopped short because a woman stood there, fist upraised as if she'd been about to knock on the door.

"Oh!" The startled exclamation came from full red lips. "I'm sorry. Marshal Long?"

Longarm nodded and took off the flat-crowned, snuff brown Stetson. "That's me."

The woman lowered her hand. "They told me at Chief Marshal Vail's office that I could find you here."

"Well, I reckon I owe 'em a debt of gratitude then."

She smiled and blushed, which made her even prettier. She wore a dark green traveling outfit that clung tightly enough to reveal the enticing curves of her body. Thick, auburn curls cascaded from under a neat little hat that matched the dress. Her complexion was creamy except for a scattering of very faint freckles across her nose. She had a dimple in her chin and brilliant green eyes. Longarm had seen women who were more classically beautiful, but seldom had he run across a gal who was more appealing than this one. It must have been Billy Vail who had told her where

11

to find him, he decided. He doubted if Henry would have wanted to do him such a favor.

"My name is Eileen Brewer."

Something about the name struck Longarm as familiar, but he couldn't figure out what it was. He took a step back and gestured with the hat in his hand.

"Please come in, Mrs. Brewer, if you don't consider such an invitation improper."

"It's *Miss* Brewer, and I suppose the question of propriety rests solely on your intentions, Marshal."

Longarm laughed. "We'll leave the door open. The landlady insists on that anyway. She ain't much on her boarders having callers of the opposite sex."

"Well, my purposes here are strictly business." Miss Eileen Brewer came into the room. She glanced around, but it didn't take her long to see everything there was to see. The place was sparsely furnished. Longarm slept here while he was in Denver, and that was about all.

"What can I do for you?"

She looked directly at him. "I'm told that you're headed for Happy Valley, Wyoming. I'd like to travel with you, if I could."

Longarm snapped his fingers as he realized why her name had sounded familiar to him. "You must be related to the Indian agent up there. I saw his name on some paperwork a while ago."

"That's right. Allen is my brother. He sent for me. I'm going to be living with him."

"At the Indian agency?"

"That's right." She frowned a little and, just like blushing, that didn't make her any less pretty either. "Why? Is there some reason I shouldn't?"

Longarm shrugged. "Well, not really, I reckon. They've been having some trouble up in those parts—that's why Marshal Vail's sending me up there—but as far as I know the Indians in the area are all friendly and you ought to be pretty safe."

"Yes, Allen has told me that none of his charges are hostile. That's why he sent for me after our mother passed away in St. Louis. She was the only other family we had left, and I'd been caring for her."

"I'm sorry to hear about your loss."

Eileen smiled. "Thank you, Marshal."

An idea occurred to Longarm. "I was just on my way out to eat before catching the train for Cheyenne this afternoon. Maybe you'd like to join me?"

"Why, that would be lovely! We can discuss the arrangements for the trip."

"I reckon so." Longarm just liked the idea of sharing a meal with a woman as pretty as Eileen Brewer.

The café where he'd intended to go was not good enough, though, he decided as he took her arm and left the boardinghouse with her. The company of a lady like her deserved a nicer place than the Red Top. It would be better if they went back across Cherry Creek to one of the restaurants downtown.

Longarm settled on one called Trammell's, which was nice enough without being overly fancy. They sat down at a table with a snowy white linen tablecloth and set with good silverware and china. This was the sort of place where Longarm ate maybe once or twice a month, always during the week after he'd received his wages. The further it got from payday, though, the more likely he was to eat in hash houses like the Red Top.

Eileen smiled across at him. "This is very nice. Do you come here often, Marshal?"

"All the time."

"I don't suppose there'll be many places like this where we're going."

"Probably not. From what I've heard, Happy Valley is still sort of primitive. There's a settlement, but it's only been there for a few months. Probably hasn't grown up very much yet."

"That's the way Allen's letters to me made it sound, too.

The Indian agency is fairly new, too. The Bureau of Indian Affairs decided to station an agent there when the valley was opened for settlement. They thought there might be some clashes between the settlers and the nearby tribes. All the trouble has come from the whites, though, not the Indians."

That jibed with what Longarm had read in the brief report Billy Vail had shown him. It was a good thing he had run into Eileen. Maybe she could give him more details about what was going on up there, since she had been in touch recently with her brother. One thing puzzled him, though.

"You said you came to Marshal Vail's office looking for me . . ."

"Well, not for you specifically. Allen mentioned in his last letter he had requested that a marshal be sent to look into the trouble, and he suggested that I might be able to travel with whoever was assigned to the job. He thought it would be safer that way." She smiled. "You know how older brothers are. They always worry about their little sisters . . . even when we're perfectly capable of taking care of ourselves."

That answered Longarm's question. "Yes, ma'am, I reckon so."

"Oh, don't call me ma'am." She reached across the table and rested her hand briefly on the back of Longarm's hand. "Since we're going to be traveling together, you might as well call me Eileen."

"All right. I'm Custis."

"That's a fine old Southern name, isn't it?"

"I suppose so. I'm not really from the South, though. Born and raised in West-by-God Virginia."

"Well, I'm sure we'll have a fine trip, Custis . . . and I hope you don't find *too* much trouble waiting for you in Happy Valley."

Longarm had high hopes for the journey, too, given Eileen Brewer's auburn hair, green eyes, and sweet smile.

He wasn't going to get his hopes up about the other sentiment she had expressed, though.

One thing he had learned over the years . . . whenever Billy Vail sent him somewhere, trouble was nearly always waiting for him—and usually a whole heap of it, too!

Chapter 3

For once, Private Max Malone wasn't actually looking for trouble.

But damned if it didn't find him anyway.

A couple of hundred miles north-northwest of Denver, the brawny, black-haired Malone stood at the bar in a dingy saloon and glared at a burly, bearded man in a buffalo coat. "If you've got somethin' to say about Ireland, why don't you say it to me face?"

As usual when Malone was mad—or drinking—or both—his Irish brogue had grown thicker. The blue-uniformed soldier's hands were clenched into knobby-knuckled fists. He was obviously spoiling for a fight, but so was the man in the buffalo coat, who had a trace of an English accent in his voice.

"I just said that Ireland was full of drunken barbarians . . . and you're not proving me wrong, are you?"

Malone might have taken a swing at the man then and there if a big hand hadn't come down on his shoulder from behind. "Better take it easy, Malone. You know Sergeant Cohen said he was fed up with your brawlin'. If you get in a fight, he's liable to have you on latrine duty for a month o' Sundays."

Malone glanced back at the tall, gangling form of Stretch Dobbs, one of his fellow privates from Outpost Number Nine, the army post a couple of miles up the road from this rough settlement. Dobbsy was right. Sergeant Ben Cohen had laid down the law when Malone, Dobbs, Rafferty, and Holzer had gone to the orderly room to get permission to come to town.

"I'm tired of havin' to bail your ass outta jail, Malone." The first shirt was built like a grizzly bear and had a voice to match. It filled the orderly room outside Captain Conway's office. "You get thrown behind bars again and I might just leave you there to rot. And if I don't, you might wish I had when I get you back here!"

That seemed mighty unfair to Malone. Every time a fracas broke out, some of the other soldiers were mixed up in it, too. Of course, the fight usually started because Malone took offense at something some dumb son of a bitch said . . .

A growl escaped from Malone's lips. "All right, let's get outta here. We'll go find somewhere's else to drink."

The four soldiers turned away from the bar. They were about to leave the saloon when an arrogant laugh came from behind them.

"Just like an Irishman to cut and run. They're all a cowardly lot."

Malone stopped and stiffened. Before he could turn around and once again confront the man in the buffalo coat, though, Private Wolfgang Holzer stepped past him. Holzer was a big, blond Prussian who had stepped off an immigrant ship in New York and been bamboozled by an unscrupulous recruiter into signing enlistment papers. Unable to speak any English, he had found himself a member of the mounted infantry on his way to Wyoming Territory quicker than you could say "Katzenjammer."

The English language was still quite a challenge for

17

Holzer, but not loyalty to his friends. "Coward not Malone. Buffalo coat man much hot air full of." A hard poke of Holzer's finger to the man's chest punctuated every other word.

The man's face contorted furiously. "Why, you big dumb Dutchie!" He swung a fist, and Holzer was too slow to get out of the way. The punch crashed into the side of his head and knocked him against the bar.

Well, that did it, thought Malone. With a shouted curse, he threw himself at the bastard in the buffalo coat, who, judging by his accent, was one of those worthless remittance men, second or third sons who could never inherit the family estate because of British law. Most of them joined the British army and were sent to India or places like that, but the ones who were cashiered out of the service for one reason or another often wound up in the States.

Malone didn't know this hombre's history, and didn't give a damn about it either. All he cared about at the moment was the satisfying jolt that shivered up his arm when his fist plowed into the man's bearded jaw.

All of Malone's considerable strength was behind the blow. It sent Buffalo Coat stumbling backward, out of control, toward a table where a poker game was going on. The players scrambled to get out of the way. They had time to do that but not to grab their money off the table before the man came crashing down on it. The table's legs snapped and it collapsed. Coins and bills went flying.

That brought angry shouts from the cardplayers. One of them yelled at Malone, "You did that on purpose, bluebelly!"

Malone heard the Southern accent in the words. "Bluebelly is it? Would you be one o' those damned Johnny Rebs?"

In the heat of the moment it totally slipped Malone's mind that one of his best friends, Reb McBride, Easy Company's bugler, was a former Confederate, too. He was too caught up in his anger to be thinking about anything like that.

"Least I ain't Yankee scum!"

As a matter of fact, Malone hadn't taken part in the War Between the States and had no real stake in it. He would have taken offense even if the hotly spoken words had carried just the opposite message. His fists cocked to deal out more damage, he rushed toward the man who had just challenged him.

Malone never got there because a chair came crashing down on his back, knocking him to the floor. He pushed himself up on hands and knees and shook his head groggily.

"Come on, Rafferty! We gotta help Malone and Wolfie!"

That shout came from Stretch Dobbs. As Malone looked up, the towering private waded into the men who had been playing poker. Malletlike fists on the end of long arms struck left and right. Malone supposed that one of the men had been the varmint who walloped him with the chair. From his knees, he threw himself forward in a diving tackle, catching one of the other men around the knees and bringing him down with a startled yell.

Within seconds, a full-scale brawl had erupted in the entire saloon as men who hadn't had any part in the original trouble slugged away at each other for no apparent reason. Malone and Dobbs were in the thick of it, as was Wolfgang Holzer, who had recovered from the blow that had knocked him against the bar. The fourth member of the group from Outpost Number Nine, Private Rafferty, was the only one not taking part in the fight.

That was because Rafferty was crawling around on the floor, scooping up coins and greenbacks from the poker game that had been scattered when the table collapsed. The layer of sawdust on the planks was damp and disgusting from tobacco juice, spilled beer, and God knows what else, but the *dinero* Rafferty was snatching up would still spend just fine.

The sleeves of Malone's blue uniform shirt were rolled up over brawny forearms. Those arms pistoned back and forth like parts of a smoothly functioning machine as the

Irishman battled. He didn't care who he hit. Whoever popped up in front of him, he knocked them down. It might mean a month of latrine duty, but this was a glorious fight!

Suddenly, he felt his feet leaving the floor. Someone had hold of him from behind and had heaved him right into the air. Malone let out a startled yell as he saw one of the saloon's front windows rushing at him. Actually, of course, he was going toward the window, and he barely had time to curl his arms around his head to protect his face before he crashed into and through the glass.

The window shattered in a silvery, tinkling shower of a million shards under Malone's weight. He slammed down on the boardwalk outside, and his momentum carried him right on across it and into the street. Dust filled his nose and mouth and choked him. Every inch of exposed skin stung from the myriad tiny cuts inflicted by the broken glass. For a moment, Malone couldn't hear anything except echoes of his own startled yell and the crash of shattering glass.

Then he realized that somebody else was yelling, too, and guns began to roar. Were they shooting it out inside the saloon? Had the brawl turned deadly?

Dobbs and Holzer and Rafferty were still in there!

Malone blinked dust out of his eyes and struggled to his feet. He wasn't too steady, and staggered a little before he caught his balance. He realized now that the shots weren't originating inside the saloon after all. They came from farther down the street, along with most of the yelling. People ran past him on the boardwalk, and he heard a man shout, "Look out, mister!"

It took Malone a second to realize that the warning was directed at him. He swung around, still shaky, and saw to his shock that a couple of men on horseback were charging right at him.

The danger registered instantly and galvanized Malone's muscles. He dived toward the boardwalk, frantically trying to get out of the way of the horses. They swept past him, missing him by mere inches. As Malone landed on the planks again and rolled over, something else he had seen in that brief glimpse finally sunk in on his stunned brain.

The men on the horses wore buckskins and feathers and had paint on their faces.

The town was under attack from Indians!

That point was driven home an instant later as an arrow struck the boardwalk right next to Malone and stood there with its shaft still quivering from the impact. He looked up and saw that the street was filled with hostiles. Two or three dozen of them at least. Some were armed only with bows and arrows, but many had rifles they had stolen from white victims in previous battles. The rifles cracked wickedly as gray clouds of powder smoke rolled along the street.

The townspeople were trying to fight back, but clearly they had been taken by surprise. Malone was surprised, too. Mister Lo had been quiet lately, and Malone, like everybody else, had begun to hope that the worst of the Indian troubles were over.

Not today. Not here. This was a pitched battle, and the settlers were getting the worst of it.

Like the townie who suddenly collapsed practically in Malone's lap. An arrow had caught him in the throat, and blood gushed out around it. Malone would have felt sorry for the poor bastard if there was time for such things, but he was more interested in the holstered gun on the man's hip. Malone grabbed the revolver and wrenched it out of leather. When he raised the gun, he saw one of the savages drawing a bead on him with another arrow.

The gun bucked in Malone's hand as he fired. The bullet was just a little quicker than the Indian's reflexes. It punched into the man's chest and drove him backward on his pony so that when he released the arrow, it flew well over Malone's head and hit the saloon's false front instead.

Crouched on one knee, Malone shifted his aim and fired

again and again and again, not stopping until the gun's hammer clicked on an empty chamber. His fusillade was rewarded by the sight of two more renegades toppling off their ponies as they raced past in the street, whooping and shooting.

Hands grabbed him and lifted him to his feet. "Malone! Are you hit?"

The anxious question came from Stretch Dobbs. Malone looked down and saw that his uniform was speckled with blood, but the stains had come from all the little cuts he had gotten from the broken glass.

"I'm fine. Where's Holzer and Rafferty?"

The other two privates appeared on the boardwalk, carrying rifles that they must have gotten hold of inside the saloon. The four soldiers hadn't been armed when they rode into town from the outpost. Holzer and Rafferty brought the weapons to their shoulders and began firing.

They were professional fighting men and their shots took a toll, downing another Indian and wounding several more. The renegades didn't linger. Still yelling like banshees, they charged on out of the settlement, never looking back. The attack had lasted only a few minutes, but it had done considerable damage. Most of the windows along the street were broken. Of course, the one Malone had been thrown through didn't really count against the Indians. On a more sobering note, Malone saw half a dozen or more bodies lying in the street or on the boardwalks. None of the Indians who were killed or wounded had been left behind, so all the bodies belonged to unfortunate settlers.

Rafferty looked after the dust cloud that marked the war party's route. "What the hell was *that* all about?"

Malone shook his head as he heard the sound of a bugle coming from the direction of Outpost Number Nine. The rest of Easy Company would have heard the shots and would be galloping toward the settlement to find out what was going on. They were too late to help, of course, but this wouldn't be the end of it. Malone felt sure of that.

Captain Conway was going to want to know what had happened here and why . . . and that meant at least part of Easy Company would soon be hitting the trail after those blasted Indians.

Chapter 4

Eileen Brewer proved to be charming company, just as Longarm expected she would. After they finished their meal at the restaurant, he walked her back to her hotel so she could make arrangements to have her bags delivered to the train station.

Then they parted company for the time being, agreeing to meet again at the station. Eileen put out a gloved hand before Longarm left.

"I'm so glad we met, Custis. I think sharing each other's company is going to make the journey much more pleasant."

Longarm took her hand. "I hope so. See you in a little while."

He didn't waste any time getting back to his rented room and gathering his gear for the trip. He had already gotten to the train station and loaded his war bag, saddle, and rifle in the baggage car by the time Eileen appeared, trailed by a porter wheeling along a cart with a couple of bags on it. It appeared that Eileen traveled fairly light for a gal, and Longarm liked that.

They found a couple of empty seats side by side, and Eileen told Longarm to sit next to the window. She settled down beside him, and a few minutes later, with a shrill whistle of steam from the locomotive and a slight lurch, the train began to roll northward.

"Allen said in his letter that I would have to change trains in Cheyenne and go from there to Laramie. I can catch a stagecoach there that will take me to Casper and from there on to Happy Valley."

Longarm nodded. "That's right. The westbound doesn't leave Cheyenne until tomorrow morning, so we'll lay over there tonight. Then we'll be a couple of days on the stagecoach before we get to Happy Valley."

"I've never traveled on a stagecoach before. Are they comfortable?"

Longarm chuckled. "Depends on whether you call bouncing around and breathing a lot of dust comfortable. They're easier and faster than riding the whole way on horseback, though."

Eileen's dark red eyebrows rose. "You don't paint a very appealing picture of it, Custis, I must say."

"Oh, it really ain't that bad. A little rough, but you'll get used to it."

"Well, I'll be glad when we get there."

So would Longarm, other than the fact that when they arrived in Happy Valley, it would mean that he wouldn't be traveling with Eileen anymore. He thoroughly enjoyed having a pretty woman at his side.

The motion of the train and the rhythmic clicking of the wheels on the rails took their toll on Eileen. She was soon yawning, and when her head dipped toward Longarm's shoulder, he didn't discourage it. She finally muttered something about giving up and leaned into him. As she rested her head on his shoulder, he felt the warm, firm pressure of her left breast against his right arm. That was mighty enjoyable, too.

He dozed for a while as well, until some instinct woke

him. Opening his eyes, he turned his head and saw a man across the aisle and one seat back staring at Eileen. The hombre looked away quickly, but not before Longarm saw what he was doing. The man was stocky and well-dressed in a gray suit and cream-colored Stetson. He looked like the sort of man who might be a fairly well-to-do cattleman.

Longarm didn't blame the fella for looking at Eileen with open admiration. She was worthy of admiring. He didn't need to make a habit of staring, though. Longarm decided that he wouldn't say anything about it to the man just yet, as long as the hombre didn't make a pest of himself.

Eileen woke up after a while and gave a cute little yawn, patting her open mouth with a gloved hand. "I'm sorry, Custis. I didn't mean to turn your shoulder into a pillow."

"I didn't mind a bit. Feel better now?"

"Yes, I do. This Western travel is fatiguing, isn't it?"

Longarm shrugged. "Most places west of the Mississippi, it takes a long time to get where you're going. I reckon folks get used to it. I did."

"You said you were from West Virginia. Have you lived out here for very long?"

"Fifteen years or so. Drifted out to the frontier after the, uh, Late Unpleasantness 'twixt North and South."

"You were in the war?"

Longarm nodded. "Yeah, but don't ask me on which side. Been so long, I sort of disremember."

"I barely remember the war myself. I was fairly young at the time."

"Yeah, I expect so. Anyway, I did a little cowboying when I got out here, but it didn't take me long to figure out that I wanted to look at something besides the south end of a northbound cow. Wound up pinning on a badge, and eventually went to work for Uncle Sam and Billy Vail."

"The chief marshal?"

"Yep."

"He seems like a nice man. Like someone's kindly old grandfather."

That comment brought another laugh from Longarm. "Don't let him fool you. That old fella was a real hell-roarer in his time. I still wouldn't want to rile him up too much."

They continued to chat about Longarm's career as a lawman. He asked a few questions about Eileen's background, but she turned them aside with a smile, saying that there was nothing even remotely interesting about her life. She had never done much of anything except care for her widowed mother, she claimed.

A couple of times during the afternoon, Longarm caught the fella in the gray suit staring at Eileen again, and it was starting to get his dander up. Before he could say anything, though, the train rolled into Cheyenne. Longarm and Eileen would be getting off here to wait for the westbound train the next morning, and Longarm hoped the rancher, if that was what he was, would be traveling on.

That didn't prove to be the case. The hombre disembarked from the train after Longarm and Eileen had gotten off. Longarm saw him being greeted by a couple of hard-faced men in range clothes, a further indication that the fella was a cattleman. The two men who met him probably worked on his ranch.

Longarm had been through Cheyenne many times before, so he was able to advise Eileen on what to do next. "There's a good hotel just a couple of blocks from here. I plan to stay there tonight."

"Then I do, too, by all means, Custis. Lead the way."

He told a porter where to send Eileen's bags, then claimed his own gear from the baggage car and carried it as they walked the two blocks to the hotel. A soft, warm dusk was settling down over the town, as the sky shaded from deep blue in the east to gold and red in the west, a spectacular display left over from the recent setting of the sun. Eileen exclaimed over its beauty.

"If every sunset is this lovely, I think I'm going to like living out here."

There was a lot about the frontier that *wasn't* beautiful, thought Longarm, but it had its appealing qualities, too.

Instinct made the hair on the back of his neck prickle again, and when he glanced back he saw the hombre from the train following them, trailed by the two men who had met him at the station. The man was taking long strides as if he were trying to catch up to them. A second later he hailed them, confirming Longarm's guess.

"Excuse me, miss . . . ?"

Eileen looked around in surprise and asked Longarm a low-voiced question. "Is that man talking to me?"

Longarm's reply was curt with annoyance. "I reckon he is."

"I wonder what he wants."

"Might as well find out." Longarm stopped and turned, fastening an intent look on the man coming toward them. "Something I can do for you, old son?"

An arrogant sneer twisted the man's thick lips. "I wasn't talking to you, cowboy. I want to speak to the lady."

"Could be the lady don't want to talk to you." Longarm moved so that he was between Eileen and the man.

He started to shove past Longarm. "Why don't we let her decide about that?"

Longarm stopped the man with a hand on his chest, and he was none too gentle about it as he shoved the hombre back a step.

"I don't think so."

Eileen's worried voice came from behind him. "Custis, I don't want any trouble . . ."

The man's voice flushed with anger. "Why, you—" He jerked a hand at the two hard cases with him. "Teach this bastard a lesson while I talk to the lady."

28

Ugly grins appeared on the beard-stubbled faces. "Sure, Boss." The men moved toward Longarm.

One of them suddenly leaped forward, swinging a fist at the big lawman's head. Longarm knew he might have been able to avoid this fight if he had shown them his badge; chances were they would have decided not to tangle with a deputy U.S. marshal. But he instinctively didn't like the rancher, and the other two varmints rubbed him the wrong way, too.

So it felt pretty good to block the punch and drive his own fist into the middle of his attacker's face. Blood spurted over Longarm's knuckles as the man's nose broke. He howled in pain and stumbled back a step, clapping both hands to his bloody nose.

That didn't give Longarm much of a respite, though, because the other man was right behind the first one. He got a punch in that caught Longarm on the jaw. Longarm shrugged it off and hooked a left into the gent's midsection. His right came across in a slashing blow that landed solidly on the man's chin and jerked his head to the side. The man staggered back and dropped to a knee.

The fella with the busted nose had recovered some in those few seconds, though, and he plowed in again, arms swinging. Longarm parried as many of the blows as he could, but he had to absorb some of the punishment. Meanwhile, he dealt out as much as he received if not more.

He rocked his opponent back with a jab, set himself, and delivered an uppercut that lifted the hard case off his feet. The man flew backward and crashed into his companion, who was still struggling to get up. Both men sprawled in the street, no longer interested in continuing the fight.

"Custis, look out!"

The warning came from Eileen, of course. Longarm whirled around in time to see the rancher trying to bring the butt of a gun down on his head. He stepped in quickly so that the blow missed his skull, but the gun butt thudded

29

against the back of his left shoulder so hard that his arm went numb.

Luckily, there was nothing wrong with Longarm's right arm. He drove a fist into the man's belly so hard that it sunk almost to the wrist. Hot, sour breath gusted in Longarm's face as it was driven out of the man's lungs. Longarm stepped back, cocked his fist, and smashed it into the rancher's jaw. The man went over backward and landed in the gutter, splashing muck all over his fine suit.

Since the man still had the gun in his hand, Longarm stepped forward quickly and kicked it loose. The rancher yelled as if Longarm had broken a couple of his fingers in the process, which was entirely possible since Longarm was in no mood to be gentle about it. As the gun went skittering away, Longarm grabbed the front of the man's vest and hauled him upright, anger fueling his strength so that he managed that feat one-handed.

"Listen, you dumb son of a bitch. I'm a deputy U.S. marshal, and I've got a good mind to arrest you and your boys for assaulting a federal officer."

The man's eyes bugged out in surprise. "A . . . a marshal? I didn't know . . . I just wanted to talk to the lady . . . she looks like somebody I used to know . . ."

Longarm glanced over his shoulder at Eileen. "You ever seen this gent before?"

A shudder went through her as she shook her head. "Never."

Longarm turned his attention back to the man in his grip. "I reckon you made a mistake, old son."

"Y-yeah. I'm sorry, Marshal. Didn't mean to cause any trouble."

Longarm gave the man a shove that almost made him fall down again. "What's your name?"

"Caldwell. Bob Caldwell. I own the Rafter C spread, west of here. Biggest spread between here and Laramie."

"All right, Caldwell. I reckon you're used to being the big skookum he-wolf around here. Just remember, there's always a bigger, meaner wolf somewhere, and you never know when you're gonna run into him."

Relief came over Caldwell's face. "You're not going to arrest us?"

"Nope. I don't want to take the time or trouble. Go on back to your ranch . . . and think twice next time before you decide to run roughshod over somebody."

Caldwell straightened his clothes and brushed them off as best he could. "All right, Marshal. I appreciate it." He helped his men to their feet. They tried to glower balefully at Longarm, but were still too glassy-eyed to really carry it off. Caldwell gave them some low-voiced orders, and they shuffled off down the street. Then he turned back to Eileen. "I'm mighty sorry, ma'am. The mistake was all mine, and I regret it."

She gave him a strained smile and a nod. Caldwell picked up his hat, brushed it off, looked at Longarm again, and then followed his men back toward the train station. The ranch hands had probably brought a buckboard in to meet him at the station.

"What a dreadful incident. And right in the middle of town, too!" Eileen sounded as if she couldn't believe it. "A dozen people must have passed by during that fight, and none of them stopped to help you, Custis, or even sent for the police."

"Out here folks sort of let other people handle their own problems most of the time. If there had been any gunplay involved, the local star packers would've shown up. They can't come out for every little ruckus, though, or they'd never be doing anything else."

"You call that a *little* ruckus? I was afraid at first that they were going to beat you senseless!"

Longarm flexed the fingers of his left hand. Feeling was starting to return to it, as well as his left arm.

"I've been in plenty of bigger fights than that. This was nothing to worry about."

Eileen gave him a dubious look. "I have a feeling it's

31

going to take me some time to fully adjust to life on the frontier."

Longarm laughed. "Just wait'll you get to Happy Valley. You'll be a pioneer gal before you know it!"

Chapter 5

First Lieutenant Matt Kincaid was crossing the parade inside the walls of Outpost Number Nine when he heard the distant crackle of gunfire to the east. The settlement lay in that direction, a couple of miles away. Sound traveled well over the windswept Wyoming plains, though, and Matt had no doubt that was where the shooting was coming from.

Matt wasn't the only one who heard the shots. Private Corson was on duty in the signal tower next to the gate, and he leaned out to holler the alarm. "Sounds like trouble in town, Lieutenant!"

Tall and muscular, with crisp brown hair under his hat, Matt waved a hand to let Corson know he had heard and turned to hurry back to Captain Conway's office. On the way, he passed Corporal Wojensky and snapped an order. "Get horses ready for a patrol to the settlement, Wojensky!"

The corporal broke into a run toward the paddock as Matt continued on to the orderly room. The clerk, Four-Eyes Bradshaw, was the only one there at the moment, and seeing the urgent expression on Matt's face, he waved the lieutenant on to the door of Captain Conway's office. Matt rapped sharply on the door, and went in without waiting for Conway's response.

"Sounds like trouble in the settlement, sir." Matt paused for a second. "Actually, it sounds like a battle of some sort."

Captain Warner Conway's bushy gray brows rose in surprise. "I knew things had been too blasted peaceful around here lately! Take some men and go see what's going on, Matt."

The lieutenant snapped a brisk salute. "Yes, sir!"

He was Conway's second in command at Outpost Number Nine. Warner Conway was a highly competent officer who had served with distinction for many years, but he was also one of those unfortunate officers who, for one reason or another, had advanced only to a certain level and then seemed to get stuck there. As a result, he had been given command of this isolated outpost in Wyoming Territory, and would probably spend the rest of his days in the army here.

Conway seemed to have made his peace with that. And it wasn't like this was some backwater where nothing ever happened. Settlers were pouring into the territory, and with that growth came the threat of lawlessness, as well as the continuing danger from roving Cheyenne, Arapaho, and Pawnee war parties. In the handful of years since Custer's debacle on the Little Big Horn, much progress had been made in pacifying the hostiles, but plenty of work still remained to be done, too. It was important for Easy Company to have a good solid commander, and Captain Warner Conway fit the bill.

Matt Kincaid was content to serve under Conway—for now. He still had ambition burning inside him, though, and hoped that he never got trapped in one place like Conway. He had served at Outpost Number Nine for several years now, and he was starting to get a mite restless . . .

Matt put all of that out of his mind as he trotted toward the paddock. Second Lieutenant Fitzgerald came up to him, an eager look on his young, fresh-scrubbed face.

"I hear there's trouble in town, Matt. I took the liberty of turning out Olsen's squad."

Matt nodded. "Good work, Fitz. Get 'em mounted up and we'll go see what's what."

Over the hubbub that had broken out inside the fort as the men realized that action was imminent, Matt could still hear the distant popping of guns. The shooting had died away, though, by the time the soldiers were mounted and galloping east along the road toward the settlement.

The notes of Reb McBride's bugle floated over the prairie as the patrol neared the town. Matt saw a gray cloud hanging in the street, slowly dispersing, and recognized it as gun smoke. There had been a battle fought here, all right, but it appeared to be over now. The men of Easy Company had come too late to the ball.

Matt held up a gauntleted hand to slow the charge to a walk as the patrol entered the settlement. He saw towns-people gathered around fallen members of the community. Matt's mouth tightened into a grim line at the sight of the civilian casualties.

Spotting blue uniforms on the boardwalk in front of one of the saloons, he veered his mount toward them. He wasn't surprised to recognize one of the men as Private Max Malone. Whenever and wherever there was trouble, Malone had the knack for being right in the middle of it. Standing there with Malone were Dobbs, Holzer, and Rafferty. The big window behind them was busted out, and shards of glass lay all over the boardwalk. For that matter, most of the windows along the street were broken.

Matt reined in and looked at the Irishman. "Malone, what happened here?"

"Indians, sir. A regular war party of the red devils. They swept right through town, a-whoopin' and a-hollerin' and a-shootin'."

The news came as a shock to Matt. It had been several months since hostiles had caused trouble in these parts.

"You recognize what tribe they were from?"

Rafferty spoke up. "Markings on their faces looked like Cheyenne to me, Lieutenant. I thought I saw Blue Horse leading them."

Matt frowned. The Cheyenne war chief Blue Horse had been particularly troublesome for a while, but then he and his warriors had drifted off to the east. The last Matt had heard about him, Blue Horse was raising hell in Nebraska.

Now, evidently, he was back in Wyoming Territory. It was unusual for hostiles to attack a town like this; they generally preferred to raid isolated ranches where they could run off horse herds. Blue Horse was loco enough to do just about anything, though, and a raid such as this was a slap in the face at the white settlers, as well as at the army that was supposed to be protecting those settlers.

Matt sighed. "All right. We'll help the townspeople clean up and tend to their injured. Mr. Fitzgerald, you'll be in charge of that."

Fitz nodded.

"I'll head back to the fort and tell Captain Conway what happened, see what he wants to do about it." Matt started to turn his horse.

Malone stopped him with a question. "You think he's gonna want us to go after those savages, Lieutenant?"

"What do you think, Malone?"

"I think we're gonna be chasin' Indians again." The Irishman's hangdog expression would have been answer enough by itself.

By the time Matt got back to Outpost Number Nine, the parapets atop the walls were bristling with rifles. From the looks of it, everybody inside the fort except the handful of wives had turned out to defend the place in case it was about to be attacked by hostiles. The gates swung open before Matt got there, and when he rode in he found Captain Conway waiting for him. Next to the captain stood a lanky, hatchet-faced man in buckskins and a floppy-brimmed felt hat.

"Report, Lieutenant." Conway's tone was brisk and businesslike.

Matt dismounted. "Indians attacked the settlement, sir. It was just a quick raid, one sweep down the main street, doing as much damage as they could before they took off."

"Any idea who it was?" The question came from the buckskin-clad man. Windy Mandalian was a civilian scout and had been at Outpost Number Nine as long as Conway and Kincaid. He could have passed for an Indian himself, but his ancestors were actually from someplace in Europe called Armenia. Matt had never known anyone who was a better tracker. That was probably because Windy possessed the ability to make himself think like an Indian. He lived with the friendlies who had established a small village only a hundred yards or so from the fort.

"Private Rafferty said he thought he recognized Blue Horse."

Windy grunted and looked surprised. "Didn't know he was back in these parts. You trust Rafferty's identification?"

"He's a pretty dependable man, and he saw Blue Horse a couple of different times during skirmishes we had with him. It's hard to miss that long face of his. He really does look like a horse."

Windy nodded in agreement. "I was sort of hoping he'd get himself killed while he was off botherin' other folks. But I guess we couldn't be that lucky. I figured he'd come back this way sooner or later."

Conway turned to the scout. "Where do you think he'll go from here?"

Windy shook his head. "No way of knowing. I've heard plenty of talk about him among the friendlies. Blue Horse and his followers are kill-crazy. They've cut themselves off from the rest of the tribe. They don't have any home now. All they do is go where the wind takes 'em and kill as many whites as they can along the way."

"Then he's got to be stopped," Conway said.

"That'd be better, yeah."

"Can you pick up their trail at the settlement and follow them?"

Windy didn't hesitate in giving his laconic answer. "Yeah."

Conway nodded and turned back to the lieutenant. "All right, Matt. Put a patrol together as quickly as you can and get after Blue Horse. Take supplies for a week. And Windy will be going with you, of course."

Matt and Windy looked at each other. Both men nodded. They had worked together on numerous occasions before, and each respected the other.

"I'll take Olsen's and Wojensky's squads."

Conway nodded. "Fine. You can't have Mr. Fitzgerald, though. I'll need him here, since Mr. Taylor is already out on patrol."

"All right. I'll tell Sergeant Cohen to see to the supplies while I head back to town and round up the rest of the men. Some of the ones I'll be taking with me were still there, helping to clean up after the attack."

Conway unbent a little from his stiff demeanor. "Be careful, Matt. Like Windy said, Blue Horse is loco. He'll be even more unpredictable than the hostiles usually are."

Matt smiled faintly. "Yes, sir . . . although I reckon that if I was really worried about being too careful, I'd be in the wrong line of work, chasing Indians and all."

"You got that right," Windy Mandalian said.

Malone knew better than to hope that he wouldn't be among the men chosen by Lieutenant Kincaid to go chasing after Blue Horse. Any time there was some dirty, potentially dangerous duty, it fell to Malone. It was like that was a law of the universe. Fate, destiny, whatever the hell you wanted to call it. Sooner or later, somebody would be shooting at him again.

Knowing that didn't keep Malone from complaining about it as the patrol rode north from the settlement. Kincaid and Windy Mandalian were up in front, the civilian scout pointing out the tracks. Blue Horse and his warriors hadn't even attempted to disguise their trail, at least not at this point.

"I'd rather be back at the outpost diggin' a new latrine," Malone said, directing his grousing at Stretch Dobbs, who rode beside him.

"Not me. I hate diggin' ditches, especially ones that're just gonna get filled up with shit."

Riding behind them, Holzer nodded. "Shit ditch." Most of the time he seemed to understand only about half of what he was saying, if that much, but he clearly liked the sound of certain words. He repeated these. "Shit ditch."

Malone chuckled. "That's right, Wolfie. But we don't have to dig no latrine right now. Instead, we get to go after some crazy Injun who'd like nothin' better than to cut your throat and lift your hair."

Holzer grinned broadly. "Shit ditch!"

"Yeah." Malone wiped the back of his hand across his mouth. "That's right. One way or another we're gonna wind up in it . . . probably right up to our necks."

Chapter 6

Longarm and Eileen ate dinner in the hotel dining room after checking in and arranging for their things to be taken up
to their rooms on the second floor. The possibility of having adjoining rooms had occurred to Longarm—it never
hurt to consider all the options—but that seemed to be moving a mite too fast, so he didn't say anything about it.

Instead, they were in Rooms Ten and Eleven, which
were across the hall from each other. When they walked up
there after dinner, Eileen paused in front of the door to her
room and put a hand on Longarm's sleeve.

"Why don't you come in, Custis? I'm not really sleepy
yet, and I'd enjoy visiting with you some more."

"You sure about that? Once we get on that stagecoach in
Laramie, you're liable to wish you'd gotten all the rest you
could."

She smiled at him. "I'm certain."

"In that case . . ." Longarm shrugged. "I always make it
a rule to oblige a lady whenever I can."

Her smile took on a mischievous tilt. "I'm sure you do."

Longarm hadn't meant it *exactly* like that . . . but however she wanted to take it was fine with him. He took the key she handed him and unlocked the door, going in first so that he could snap a lucifer into life and light the lamp on the bedside table before Eileen shut the door and cut off the illumination from the hallway.

The hotel was not the fanciest in Cheyenne, but it was comfortably furnished. The room was dominated by a big four-poster with a soft mattress under a thick comforter. Longarm glanced at it and looked away, not wanting Eileen to think he was dwelling on the possibilities of using that bed.

He didn't have to worry about offending her sense of propriety. When he turned toward her, she moved closer to him and rested both hands on his chest. She was close enough that he could feel the warmth of her breath as she spoke.

"Would you think I was terribly forward if I asked you to kiss me, Custis?"

"No, ma'am. Fact of the matter is, I'd think it was a mighty fine idea."

"Why don't you go ahead and do that then?"

He followed her suggestion, slipping his left arm around her waist and pulling her tighter against him as his right hand cupped the back of her head. His mouth came down on hers in a kiss that was full of heat and passion. Eileen responded with a matching urgency. Her lips moved under his, parting and drawing him in with her sweetness.

Her hands clutched at his chest, and after a moment she began tugging at his shirt, pulling it open so that she could slip a hand inside. The weather was warm, so he wasn't wearing the upper half of his long underwear. That meant Eileen was able to stroke her fingers through the thick mat of dark brown hair that covered his muscular chest.

At the same time Longarm's left hand had slipped down to fondle the enticing curves of her backside. She pressed her pelvis harder against his groin and took her lips away from his to give a little gasp as she felt the hardness growing there.

41

"Custis, I . . . I know it's shameless of me, but I really need for you to make love to me."

Longarm moved his right hand from the back of her head to the soft swelling of her left breast, caressing the sensitive mound through her gown. He smiled.

"In that case, I reckon it'd be a good idea if we got these duds out of the way."

Her fingers began deftly unfastening the buttons of his shirt as she laughed. "I couldn't agree more!"

The next few minutes were busily taken up with the chore of undressing each other. Of course, it wasn't really much of a chore, at least not for Longarm. In fact, revealing more and more of Eileen's smooth, creamy flesh was downright pleasurable. He tried not to rush things, and even paused to lean over her breasts as he bared them so he could kiss each nipple in turn, flicking the hard, brown buds with his tongue.

For her part, she seemed to be equally entranced by his manhood, and when she lowered his underwear so that the hard, thick pole sprang free from its confinement, she grasped it with both hands and ran her palms along its impressive length and girth.

"Good Lord, Custis, I can't reach all the way around, even with both hands! How am I going to fit all of this monster inside me?"

"I reckon we'll just have to try and see how much'll go."

She laughed merrily. "Oh, we'll try, all right! More than once, unless I miss my guess."

That sounded good to Longarm. As soon as they were both naked, he steered her toward the big, fluffy bed.

Eileen sat on the edge of it and took a two-handed grip on him again, pulling him closer to her. She leaned over and ran her tongue around the tip of his shaft, circling it wetly for long, tantalizing moments before opening her lips wide and sucking the head into her mouth.

The French lesson went on until Longarm was afraid he was going to explode. He buried his fingers in her thick auburn hair and thrust back and forth between her lips, barely able to control himself. A keen pang of disappointment went through him when she finally pulled back, denying him his release.

But only for the moment. She rolled onto her back and spread her legs wide, exposing not only the V-shaped thatch of dark red hair between her thighs, but also the pouty lips of her sex. She was so wet and ready for him that droplets of moisture glistened in the forest of fine-spun hair around her opening.

"Take me now, Custis! Fill me up!"

Longarm moved onto the bed and poised over her. She reached between them and grasped his shaft, bringing the head to her drenched cleft. He was wet, too, with clear fluid seeping from the slit at the tip, but she moistened the head even more by running it up and down the fleshy folds for a moment.

Then Longarm knew the time had come. He wasn't going to wait any longer. With a thrust of his hips, he drove forward, burying half the length of his hard cock inside her. They were both so slick with need that it went in easily. Eileen gasped as she felt it filling her.

Longarm waited a couple of heartbeats, then partially withdrew only to thrust again. He went even deeper into her this time. That was just the beginning. With a series of slow, deliberate, powerful thrusts, he worked his entire length into her. She had expressed a worry about all of him being able to fit inside her, but the more excited she became, the more she opened herself to him and the deeper he went. When he had sheathed every bit of his shaft, he held it there motionless as she began to spasm around him. The hot, buttery walls of her sex clutched at him as a strong climax rippled through her.

As the shudders faded, Eileen's head sagged back on the pillow and she gasped for breath. Longarm lowered his head to hers and began kissing her forehead, her nose, her cheeks and chin. He allowed her to catch her breath before he kissed her on the mouth again and slid his tongue between her lips. She met it with her tongue, and they slid around each other in a sensuous dance as Longarm's hips began to move again.

His thrusts soon grew faster and harder as he slammed his cock deep inside her. She broke the kiss so that she could toss her head from side to side on the pillow as the fire consuming her from the inside out blazed brighter and brighter. Longarm felt his own culmination rising swiftly, practically boiling up inside him.

His climax erupted, as unstoppable as a volcano. Again and again his thick, scalding juices exploded, filling Eileen to overflowing. She jerked and shuddered as she came again underneath him. Both of them had crested the peak at the same time.

And together they luxuriated in the long, slow slide down the other side. Longarm would have rolled off her, but her arms went around him and clutched him to her, wanting to keep him there as long as she could. He stayed where he was until he finally softened enough to slip out of her. She made a small sound of loss and let him go.

He wound up lying on his back with her nestled against his side, her head pillowed on his chest. The scent of her hair filled his senses. He stroked her flank as she toyed with his now-soft member.

"I'm a wanton woman at heart, Custis. I guess I just had to behave myself for too long. It all built up inside me."

"And I was just the fella who was lucky enough to come along at the right time?"

She lifted herself on an elbow and brushed a kiss across his jaw. "No, not at all. If you weren't so special I'd still be waiting, holding it all in. But I knew as soon as I saw you that I . . . I wanted you."

Longarm kissed her lips softly. "Sounds like we were both a mite lucky."

"More than a mite." She rested her head on his chest again, and her voice was a whisper. "More than a mite . . ."

Without knowing exactly when it happened, Longarm dozed off with Eileen in his arms.

When he woke up, the lamp had gone out, leaving the room mostly in darkness. Some light from the moon and stars filtered in through the curtains over the window.

Eileen was sound asleep, curled on her side facing away from Longarm. Moving slowly and carefully so as not to disturb her, he sat up and swung his legs off the bed. He stood up and padded barefoot to the chair where Eileen had dropped his clothes as she took them off him. He felt around in the pockets of his coat until he found a cheroot and a lucifer, and then took them over to the window, which he slid up, hoping that it wouldn't squeak and wake her.

It didn't. Her breathing was still deep and rhythmic as Longarm snapped the match alight with his thumbnail and set fire to the gasper. He inhaled deeply, pushed the curtain aside, and blew a cloud of smoke out the open window.

The night was warm, and a breeze stirred the curtain as Longarm stood there looking out at Cheyenne. He didn't know what time it was, but the darkened buildings told him it was late. Most folks had turned in for the night.

That was a good idea, and he decided that when he finished the cheroot, he would get dressed and slip out to go across the hall to his own room. He didn't want to do anything to compromise Eileen's reputation before she even got where she was going.

The night was so quiet that Longarm's keen hearing picked up the faint sound of a floorboard creaking in the corridor. Somebody was coming in late. The natural wariness ingrained in him by spending years in a dangerous profession made him let the curtain fall back over the window as he turned away from it toward the door.

Suddenly, something crashed across the hall, followed almost instantly by the dull boom of a shotgun. The echoes of that roar hadn't even begun to fade away when more shots ripped out, these from handguns.

Longarm moved like a whirlwind, whipping across the room toward the chair where his clothes lay. His gun belt was draped over the back of the chair with the walnut grips of his Colt jutting up from the holster. He snagged the weapon on his way across the room to the door.

From the bed, Eileen cried out in alarm at the thunderous sounds that had jolted her out of sleep. "Custis, what—"

"Stay down! Get behind the bed!" Longarm snapped the commands at her and hoped she would follow them. The next instant, he jerked the door open and stepped out with the Colt held in front of him. He was well aware that he was naked, but there wasn't time to worry about getting dressed.

Across the hall, the rancher named Bob Caldwell stood in the doorway of Longarm's room—the room the big lawman was *supposed* to be in. He held a scattergun in his hands. Smoke curled from both barrels. Flanking him were the two hard cases who worked for him, and each man had a pistol in his hand.

One glimpse of them was enough to tell Longarm what had happened. The men hadn't left Cheyenne for Caldwell's ranch after all. Instead, they had hung around town, probably drinking, and Caldwell had worked himself up into a state where he had to have revenge for the humiliation he had endured at Longarm's hands earlier. The other two men had been more than happy to go along with him.

So Caldwell had gotten a shotgun somewhere, and they had come up here to kick open the door of Longarm's room and fill him full of lead while he was sleeping. Longarm figured the unused bed in the room across the hall was pretty much shot to pieces now.

"You boys looking for me?"

Caldwell gasped a curse as the three would-be killers twisted around. They had come up here to commit cold-blooded murder, so asking the question was just about all

46

the break Longarm was willing to give them. He opened fire as their guns swung toward him.

He took the hard case on the right first, punching a slug into the man's chest that threw him back against the wall next to the busted door. He bounced off and pitched forward on his face.

In less than an eyeblink of time, Longarm had shifted his aim and squeezed off two more shots. Those bullets tore into the hard case on the left, spinning him around. He hit the wall, too, and then slid down it, leaving a crimson smear behind him on the wallpaper.

Bob Caldwell had the shotgun leveled at Longarm, but as he tugged desperately at the triggers and nothing happened, the realization hit him that he hadn't reloaded since firing both barrels into the bed in the other room. Longarm saw that on the rancher's face, and was about to hold off on the trigger when Caldwell suddenly flung the shotgun at him.

Longarm twisted and threw up an arm to block the heavy weapon and keep it from hitting him in the head. That gave Caldwell just enough time to claw a revolver out of a holster under his coat. He fired, and the bullet chewed splinters from the doorjamb next to Longarm's head.

Longarm's Colt roared and bucked in his hand again. Caldwell stumbled backward through the open doorway behind him. He dropped his gun and pressed both hands to the hole in his chest. Blood leaked through his fingers as he collapsed.

Longarm stepped across the hall and checked both of the men who had worked for Caldwell. Dead, just as he expected. Caldwell was still alive, though, his breath wheezing raggedly. Longarm dropped to a knee beside him.

"That was a mighty dumb play, old son. You should've gone back to your ranch when you had the chance."

"You . . . son of a . . . bitch." Bloody froth accompanied the words out of Caldwell's mouth. "Don't care . . . if you are . . . a lawman . . . nobody treats me like that . . . and gets away with it."

"Appears to me you're wrong about that."

Surprisingly, Caldwell laughed. It was a harsh, ugly sound. "W-Wichita . . ." His voice was no more than a weak whisper now. "Henry . . . Henry . . ."

The words faded away into a long, rattling sigh. Longarm didn't know who the hell Henry was, other than Billy Vail's clerk in Denver, and he couldn't ask Caldwell about it because the hombre was dead.

"Custis? Oh, my God, are you all right?"

Longarm looked up to see Eileen standing in the doorway of her room with the comforter from the bed wrapped around her. That reminded him that he was naked as a jaybird, and folks would start popping out of their rooms to see what the shooting was all about any minute now. He stood up and moved to join her.

"Yeah, I'm fine. We both better get some clothes on, though. The local law's bound to show up with some questions they want answered. Sorry if it's gonna be a mite embarrassing."

"As long as you're not hurt, I don't care about anything else."

Longarm just hoped she felt the same way come morning.

And he wondered again, fleetingly, who Henry from Wichita was . . . and if he would come after Longarm to try to settle the score when he heard that Bob Caldwell was dead.

Chapter 7

The war party of renegade Cheyenne led by Blue Horse had continued almost due north for some distance, but late on the first day of the pursuit by the patrol from Outpost Number Nine, the trail began to curve to the northwest.

Windy Mandalian pointed that out to Lieutenant Matt Kincaid as they jogged their horses along at the front of the patrol. "I reckon Blue Horse finally realized he was headed straight toward Casper. He might like to attack a town of that size, but not even he's loco enough to try it with only a few dozen men. They're going to go around it instead."

"What's in the direction they're heading now?"

Windy shrugged. "Not a hell of a lot. The Shoshone Basin is that way. Not much out there, maybe a ranch or two they could raid, but that don't hardly seem worth the trouble. If they keep going, they'll come to the Owl Creek Mountains, and a ways on beyond them, the Snake River and the Tetons and the Yellowstone country."

Matt rubbed his jaw and frowned in thought. He had been through the area Windy described, but it had been a while. To the best of Matt's memory, though, there wasn't much up there to tempt a renegade like Blue Horse, who lived for killing and plunder.

"Maybe he's making a run for Canada. More and more of the hostiles have been heading up there in recent years."

"Could be. Or maybe he just don't care where he's going, as long as he keeps on the move."

"How far ahead of us are they?"

"Two hours, maybe three."

"We can run them down. Our horses are stronger and have more stamina than theirs do."

Windy nodded. "In the long run, yeah. But it's gonna take a day or two. Push these mounts any harder than that and they'll play out on you."

Matt felt frustration and impatience gnawing at his vitals like the twin demons they were, but he knew Windy was right. The important thing was that they catch up to Blue Horse and prevent the war party from killing any more settlers. It didn't matter how soon they did that, because according to Windy there weren't any towns where the Cheyenne were going, at least not anywhere close.

Because of that, Matt kept the patrol moving at the same steady rate of speed. They would cover as much ground as they could today before making camp.

"Do you think Blue Horse will stop for the night or keep going? Does he know we're back here chasing him?"

Windy laughed. "Trying to predict what a fella like Blue Horse will do, or what he knows, is just about hopeless, Lieutenant." The scout tapped the side of his head with a lean finger. "He's got voices up here, spirit voices, telling him what to do. And he's the only one who can hear them."

"You're saying he's insane."

"Not the way he sees it. And who's to say which way of looking at it is right?"

Matt didn't say anything. There were times when he wondered if Windy himself had spent too much time with the Indians. On the other hand, that familiarity with the enemy was what made him such an invaluable scout and ally. As he had many times in the past, Matt decided that it was better to put his trust in Windy.

Even if he didn't fully understand the man . . . and likely never would.

When the patrol made camp that night, they did so without building any fires. Blue Horse was canny enough, Windy Mandalian explained, to suspect that the army would be after him because of the raid on the settlement, but there was no point in confirming that suspicion for him.

Malone groused about not having any coffee or hot food, but Dobbs took a more practical stance on the matter. "I'd rather do without and keep my hair."

"Yeah, well, if the damned Injun already knows we're back here behind him, what's the point in actin' like he don't?"

"Windy knows what he's doing." The confident comment came from Corporal Wojensky, who had come up behind the complaining Malone. "If he didn't, he wouldn't have lived as long as he has. Now get busy tending to those horses, like I told you."

Elsewhere in the camp, Sergeant Gus Olsen was busy posting pickets to stand guard in the darkness. The rest of the men took care of their mounts, ate some cold rations, and washed them down with water from their canteens. It wasn't a very satisfying meal, but it would have to do. When they were finished, the men who weren't on guard duty rolled themselves in their blankets, tried to get comfortable on the hard ground, and went to sleep.

Mandalian and Lieutenant Kincaid stayed awake for a while after the other men had dozed off, talking about Blue Horse and the grim quest that had brought them out here into the middle of nowhere, but then they went to sleep as well.

* * *

51

Malone was stiff and sore when he woke up early the next morning. He hated sleeping on the ground and missed his own bunk back at the fort. As he struggled out of his blankets, he saw that the sky had barely turned gray in the east with the approach of dawn. Wojensky was moving among the men, rousing them from sleep.

"Malone, since you're already up, go relieve one of the pickets. Take Dobbs and Holzer with you and send back three of the fellas."

Malone scrubbed a weary hand over his face. "Aw, Corp, I'll bet there'll be a fire this morning. That means there'll be coffee, too."

Wojensky wasn't in the mood to listen to reason. He pointed toward a cluster of rocks in the distance. "Go."

Malone went, trailed by Dobbs and Holzer. The towering but normally good-natured Dobbs was complaining this morning, too, and even the almost preternaturally cheerful Holzer was muttering curses under his breath in his native language. Either that or clearing his throat; it was hard to tell with German.

As they approached the rocks, dangling their rifles from their hands, Malone called out softly to let the pickets know they were coming. "Hey, Harrison! It's just us. Don't shoot us, all right?"

That wasn't the way you were supposed to hail somebody when you were relieving him from guard duty, of course, but Malone never had been the sort to worry overmuch about rules and regulations. He was just a good fighting man, a natural-born soldier. That combination of qualities explained why he had been promoted to corporal and then busted back to private more times than he could remember.

It was those soldier's instincts that kicked in now and warned him when none of the men posted in the rocks replied to his call. He came to an abrupt halt and held up a hand to stop Dobbs and Holzer, too.

"Hang on a minute, boys." Malone raised his voice a little. "Harrison? Bolton? Scherzinger?" Those were the three men who were supposed to be standing guard in the rocks.

There was still no reply.

Malone's hands tightened nervously on his rifle. Could be that the three men had just fallen asleep at their post, which wasn't like them but couldn't be ruled out. Or something worse could have happened. Malone looked back over his shoulder at the camp a couple of hundred yards away. The gray light in the sky had grown stronger, and he could make out the men moving around now as the camp came to life. He heard the faint whicker of a horse in the cool, early morning air.

"Dobbs. Hotfoot it back and tell Kincaid something may be wrong."

"Send Wolfie." Dobbs and Malone had been friends for a long time. Dobbs didn't want to go.

"He's liable to get his words mixed up. The lieutenant needs to know that something might have happened to Harrison, Bolton, and Scherzinger."

"Damn it, Max—"

"Just go." Even though he couldn't seem to keep even a single stripe on his sleeve for any significant amount of time, Malone could muster up a tone of command when he needed to. This was one of those occasions.

Dobbs went, loping back toward the camp as fast as his long legs would carry him. That left Malone and Holzer to continue investigating the situation.

"Come on, Wolfie. Keep your rifle ready."

"Trouble, *ja*?"

"Damn right, yah."

The two soldiers approached the rocks carefully. Half a dozen good-sized boulders had come to rest in a slight depression, and that was where the three guards were posted. Malone put his back against the nearest rock and started edging around it. He didn't call out again. If the men hadn't answered him before, they weren't likely to now.

The shadows were thicker here, and Malone didn't see the

three forms sitting on the sandy ground and leaning back against the rocks until he almost stumbled over the closest one. Their heads were tipped forward as if they were sound asleep. Malone hoped that was all it was, even though dozing off on duty meant that the three men would be in for a heap of trouble from Captain Conway when they got back to Outpost Number Nine. He lowered his rifle and leaned down to grasp the shoulder of the closest man and give it a good shake.

"Hey, you damn fool, wake up—"

Malone jumped back as the man slumped bonelessly to the side. The poor bastard's head was tilted at an odd angle as he lay on the ground, and as Malone squinted in the dim light, he saw that was because the man's throat had been cut so deeply. The hideous wound gaped like a huge second mouth.

"Bitch of a son!"

Malone swallowed the bad taste that welled up his throat. "Yeah, what you said, Holzer." He moved around the dead man, giving the corpse a wide berth. The light was bright enough now that Malone could recognize the twisted, agonized face. It belonged to Private August Scherzinger. He was sure the other two men were Harrison and Bolton, and he was equally sure they were dead, too.

He had to make certain, though, and he did so by shaking them as he had done with Scherzinger. They toppled over, too, heads flopping grotesquely on their partially severed necks.

Malone stepped back and looked around, wild-eyed. He fully expected to hear bloodcurdling whoops at any second as Blue Horse's renegades attacked. The bastard had doubled back to wipe out any pursuit.

The air remained quiet and still, though, except for a growing commotion coming from the camp. Malone looked in that direction and saw Lieutenant Kincaid, Windy Mandalian, and several soldiers trotting toward the rocks while the rest of the patrol formed a defensive ring. They expected an attack, too.

But none came, and by the time Kincaid and the others reached the rocks, Malone was convinced that none would come. If Blue Horse was going to ambush them, he would have done it before now, while he could still take the soldiers by surprise. Malone had a feeling that by now, the war chief and his men weren't anywhere within miles of the camp.

Kincaid was hatless and grim faced in the gray light. "What happened here, Malone?"

"See for yourself, Lieutenant." Malone nodded toward the bodies of the three dead guards. "I've got a hunch that's just Blue Horse's way of saying howdy to us . . ."

Matt had never cared for Malone's lax discipline or insolent attitude, but he knew the man was a good soldier, seasoned in the ways of the frontier. Once the sun was up, it was easy to examine the scene of the killings and see that Malone had been right about what happened. Three warriors had crept up on the rocks during the night and cut the throats of the sentries, probably before the men even knew what was happening.

Matt hoped it had been that quick for them anyway.

He and Windy found the places where copious amounts of blood had spilled out onto the sand. The three pickets had been spread out through the rocks when they were attacked. Only after they were dead had they been placed together and positioned so that it looked like they were sleeping. Then the killers had disappeared back into the shadows, leaving only the faint scuff of a moccasin here and there.

Matt looked over at Windy. "Can you track the men who did this?"

"What's the point? We know they're part of Blue Horse's bunch, and we're trailing them anyway."

"How can we be sure some other Indians didn't do this?"

Windy shook his head. "I don't reckon we can, but the

odds against it are so high that they're not worth considering, Lieutenant. This is *just* the sort of thing that Blue Horse would do. He's up there ahead of us somewhere, laughing at us and feeling satisfied because he knows how bad this is gonna spook us."

"Then the best way to get back at him is to stay right on his trail and not let this bother us."

"Yeah . . . as much as we can do that."

Matt gave a curt nod. What Windy said made sense. "All right." He looked at Olsen. "Sergeant, form a burial detail. As soon as that's taken care of, we're riding out."

"Yes, sir!"

Matt and the scout walked away from the rocks. "I know it's not really professional for me to feel this way, Windy . . . but Blue Horse is adding up quite a score for us to settle when we catch up to him."

Windy spat onto the rocky ground. "You didn't stop bein' human when you put on that uniform, Matt." He patted the stock of the rifle that was cradled in his arms. "I'm sort of looking forward myself to the chance of getting that son of a bitch in my sights . . ."

Chapter 8

Longarm was right about the law showing up after the shooting, but at least he and Eileen had time to get dressed before a burly local star packer carrying a shotgun clomped up the stairs to the hotel's second floor. The corridor was crowded with hotel guests, most of them in their nightclothes, who had come out to gawk at the sprawled bodies and the bloodstains on the walls and floor. The bystanders parted to let the walrus-mustached lawman through.

"All right, somebody tell me what the blue blazes happened here! That's Bob Caldwell, damn it! How come he's dead?"

Longarm pointed through the open door of his room at the ruined bed, which had taken the brunt of the double blast from Caldwell's shotgun. "Take a look at that, Marshal. That was meant for me."

The lawman gave Longarm an owlish stare. "And who might you be?"

"Deputy U.S. Marshal Custis Long, out of the Denver office." The star packer looked familiar, and Longarm thought he had finally placed the man. "I think we've met before. You used to be a deputy under Tom Carr, didn't you?"

Thomas Jefferson Carr was the marshal who had cleaned up Cheyenne a few years earlier when it was still a haven for lawlessness. Carr's efforts had gone a long way toward making the town a civilized place. His deputies had been competent lawmen, too.

"Long, did you say? Hell, yeah, I remember you."

"I was hoping you would, Marshal."

The man shook his head. "It ain't marshal no more. I'm the chief of police."

"All right, Chief." Longarm nodded toward the bodies. "I had a run-in with Caldwell and his two men earlier this evening. Or rather, yesterday evening I reckon I should say, since it's after midnight."

Longarm had checked his watch while he was getting dressed and knew that it was after two o'clock in the morning. He continued his story while the chief of Cheyenne's police force listened intently.

"I guess what happened earlier must have rankled Caldwell enough that he decided to blow a hole in me before he went home. Those two hombres who work for him came with him. I suspect they'd all been drinking. Caldwell must've checked the register downstairs to see which room I was in, then came here, kicked the door open, and unloaded both barrels of that Greener into the bed." Longarm nudged the shotgun with the toe of his boot. "Problem was, I wasn't in the bed."

"Where were you?"

"I'd just come in myself. Was down the street having a drink in one of the saloons." Longarm had worked out the lie beforehand and explained to Eileen that he was going to tell the lie. She had told him that he could tell the truth, but bending the rules a mite in a good cause had never bothered him overmuch. "I must've come in right after them, because I got to the top of the stairs just as Caldwell busted in and opened fire. When I saw what was going on I

hollered at them, and they turned and threw down on me."
He shrugged. "Wasn't anything I could do except defend
myself."

The chief chewed his mustache for a moment before he
nodded in acceptance of Longarm's story. "Nobody can
blame you for that, I reckon."

"I hope this don't cause trouble for you, Chief. I know
Caldwell was probably an important man around here,
what with that big ranch he owned."

The lawman snorted in disgust. "You mean the ranch
that everybody figures he stocked by rustlin' his neighbors'
cows?"

Longarm's eyes rose in surprise.

"Don't worry, Marshal, Caldwell didn't have many
friends around here. Those fellas with him weren't much
more than hired guns, and I suspect they used running irons
a few times in their lives." The chief of police shook his
head. "No, there won't be any trouble about this. You won't
even have to stick around for the inquest as long as you
come by the office in the mornin' and give me a sworn statement about what happened."

Longarm nodded. "I can do that." There would be time
before the train for Laramie pulled out. And he had kept
Eileen out of the mess entirely, which was good. He had told
her to stay in her room and not come out unless he summoned her.

The chief turned to look at the curious bystanders and
curtly gestured them back into their rooms. "Nothin' more
to see here. You folks get back to your beds."

The clerk from downstairs made his way through the
dispersing crowd, looking worried and upset. Obviously,
he didn't like dead bodies lying around the second-floor
corridor and leaking blood on the carpet runner.

"Marshal Long, we'll put you in another room, of course.
What about the young lady?"

The chief looked sharply at Longarm. "What young
lady?"

59

Longarm bit back a curse. Looked like Eileen was going to get dragged into this anyway.

"Just someone I got acquainted with on the train. We happened to check in at the same time, but we're not traveling together."

"Where is she now?"

The clerk pointed at the room across the hall with his thumb. "In there."

The chief harrumphed and blew air through his mustache and looked more like a walrus than ever as he glared at Longarm. "And she didn't even stick her head out after all the shootin'?"

"She did, but I told her to go back in her room and not to worry. If you want to talk to her, I don't reckon she'd mind. Don't know what she could tell you, though. She was sound asleep when all hell broke loose."

That much was true anyway.

The chief thought it over and then shook his head. "Nah, I don't reckon I need to talk to her. She's probably upset that these killin's took place right outside her door, and I don't see any reason to make it worse for her."

"That's what I thought, too."

The hallway was clear now except for Longarm, the chief of police, the clerk, and the three dead men. The local lawman nodded at the corpses. "I'll have the undertaker hustle on up here, Dewey."

The clerk looked grateful. "The sooner the better, Chief." He turned to Longarm. "If you'll come with me, Marshal, I'll show you to another room . . ."

Longarm got his belongings from the room with the ruined bed and followed the clerk down the hall. The new room looked pretty much like the old one, except that it wasn't across the hall from Eileen's room. He supposed that was all right, since the night was more than half gone anyway.

Things settled down fairly quickly after that. The undertaker and his helpers arrived and carried the bodies downstairs. Longarm heard them talking in low voices while he undressed. Then the hotel was silent again. Wearing only the bottom half of his long underwear, he smoked another cheroot and took a nip from the silver flask he carried in his war bag. The smooth fire of the Maryland rye sent warmth through him.

He wasn't so relaxed, though, that he failed to hear the soft knock on his door.

Swinging around, he pulled his gun from its holster, which was hanging over a chair back again, and went to the door. "Who is it?" Even as he asked the question he stepped quickly to the side, just in case anybody tried to blast some buckshot through the door.

"Eileen."

Longarm turned the key in the lock, but didn't lower the gun in his hand. It was possible somebody had forced her down here at gunpoint to get him to open up. If that was the case, they were in for a surprise.

"It's open. Come on in."

Eileen was by herself. She raised her eyebrows when she saw the gun in Longarm's hand. "What's that for?"

"Just being careful." He smiled. "Habit I've gotten into because people keep trying to kill me."

"I can understand why." She got that mischievous twinkle in her green eyes again as she moved closer to him. She wore a silk robe that was partially open, revealing the creamy, lightly freckled valley between her breasts. "Imagine telling the chief of police that we're mere acquaintances!" She shrugged her shoulders, causing the robe to slide off them and bare the hard-nippled globes of flesh that rode proudly on her chest. "After everything that's gone on between us, Custis."

Longarm chuckled. Eileen had been pretty shaken right after the shooting, but obviously she had gotten over it.

"I was just trying to keep you out of it. Figured that was the way you'd want it."

She did something to the belt at her waist and the robe

61

fell off completely, the silk puddling around her feet. Nude, she stood there with the lamplight casting a golden glow over her skin.

"What I want right now, Custis . . . is you inside me again."

Longarm didn't have to be told twice.

As the chief of police had said, Longarm didn't have to stay in Cheyenne for the inquest into the deaths of Bob Caldwell and the other two men. He stopped by the chief's office the next morning, wrote out and signed a concise—if somewhat altered from the true facts—account of the incident, and then went on to the train station. By nine o'clock, the train was rolling westward, carrying Longarm and Eileen Brewer toward Laramie.

They arrived around midday, got off the train, and were directed to the stagecoach station, where they found that a coach would be leaving for Casper in a couple of hours. Once they got there, they would have to change to a different stage line for the rest of the trip to Happy Valley.

As they waited at the stage station, Eileen got a little worried. "I've never traveled by stagecoach before. Isn't it supposed to be a little dangerous, what with road agents and Indians and all?"

Longarm tried to reassure her. "Don't worry. I'll be there with you the whole way. I don't expect we'll run into any trouble."

"And there's no privacy." She smiled and lowered her voice. "How in the world will we ever . . . you know . . . with the other passengers around?"

Longarm knew what she meant, all right. He chuckled. "That *is* a problem. I reckon we'll just have to control ourselves. Either that or shock some poor traveling salesman plumb out of his shoes."

Eileen laughed and rested her head against his shoulder

for a moment. "It's going to be difficult, but I suppose we'll manage."

"Won't be much better when we get to Happy Valley either, what with you staying with your brother at the Indian agency."

She straightened, and a frown replaced her smile. "I hadn't thought about that. Custis, I don't know if I can stand not . . . being with you."

He refrained from pointing out that sooner or later his job would be done and he would be leaving Happy Valley, probably for good. There was no reason to make her feel even worse than she already did. When that day came, he would miss her, too, but he had long since come to accept the fact that in his line of work, any romances he had would be fleeting.

The Casper stage was only a few minutes behind schedule. Longarm, Eileen, and the other passengers spent the night at a relay station about halfway between the two towns. The accommodations were pretty primitive, but Longarm had stayed in plenty of places that were worse. The same couldn't be said of Eileen, who complained the next morning that she'd been forced to share her bed with what seemed like a million bugs.

She looked dusty and worn out by the time the stage reached Casper, and Longarm sort of hoped that it would be a day or two before the stage for Happy Valley left. That would give them an excuse to spend the time in a hotel, where Eileen could get a bath and sleep in a real bed.

Unfortunately, the clerk at the office of the stage line serving Happy Valley informed them that their timing was perfect: A coach was leaving in less than an hour.

"Better get your bags loaded right away, folks. As soon as a fresh team gets hitched up, the stage will be rolling out of here. Blind Pete doesn't like to waste any time."

Longarm grunted. "Blind Pete, eh? He ain't really blind, is he?"

"Only in one eye."

"Well, in that case . . ." Longarm shook his head.

He toted both of Eileen's bags in his left hand, along with his own war bag. His Winchester was tucked under his left arm, and his saddle was perched on his right shoulder. He told Eileen to sit down inside the station for the moment, and walked out to the coach, carrying their gear. Hostlers were backing fresh horses into the harness and hitching them up along the singletree under the watchful eye of a scrawny old-timer with a black eye patch. A young man with blond hair under a cuffed-back hat stood nearby, holding a shotgun.

Longarm nodded to the one-eyed man. "Reckon you'd be Blind Pete."

"That I am, mister. You a passenger?"

"That's right."

"Got a lot of baggage for one man."

Longarm inclined his head toward the station. "Some of it belongs to the lady who's traveling with me."

That perked up the young shotgun guard. "A lady?"

"Settle down, Jack." Blind Pete motioned toward the canvas-covered boot at the rear of the coach. "Stow your possibles in there and take care o' anything else you need to do. We'll be pullin' out in about ten minutes."

Longarm nodded. "We'll be ready. We're anxious to get to Happy Valley."

That brought a harsh laugh from the jehu. "Ain't never been there before, have you?"

"As a matter of fact, we haven't." Longarm frowned. "What's funny about that?"

"Not a thing, really . . . only when you get there, you'll find that it ain't so happy. Fact is, the Injun name for the place fits it a whole heap better."

This was the first Longarm had heard of the Indians having a different name for Happy Valley. "What do they call it?"

Blind Pete grinned. "Valley of Skulls."

Chapter 9

The soldiers from Easy Company were decidedly uneasy as they continued trailing Blue Horse's war party northward, after the deaths of privates Harrison, Bolton, and Scherzinger. Behind them lay the lonely graves of the three men, to be swallowed up by time and the prairie as if they had never been there.

Despite that, the task remained to the surviving members of the patrol. Blue Horse and his renegades still weren't making any attempt to hide their tracks. It was almost like the Cheyenne war chief wanted to be followed, and Matt Kincaid said as much to Windy Mandalian as they rode at the head of the patrol.

The scout nodded. "I reckon that's true. I'm not sayin' that Blue Horse could give us the slip if he wanted to, but he's not even trying."

"You think he's trying to lead us into a trap?"

Windy squinted off toward the sere, rolling hills in front of them, and as usual it seemed that he could see farther than any man ought to be able to. After a few moments, he finally nodded.

"It's possible. Could be there's an even bigger bunch of Cheyenne waiting up there somewhere for us, and Blue Horse is just drawing us on toward them. That wouldn't really be like him . . . but who's to say what he's capable of?"

"I didn't think he had that many followers these days."

"Neither did I. I figured the two or three dozen hotheads riding with him were the only ones who listen to him anymore. But again, who's to say?"

Matt looked over at the scout. "So we're either a little outnumbered . . . or a whole lot outnumbered."

That brought a grim chuckle from Windy. "That's about the size of it, Lieutenant."

Matt just shook his head and kept riding. Losing the three men was a major blow, but in the long run it didn't change anything. Matt had his orders, and he would follow them come hell or high water, as long as he was capable of doing so. Captain Conway had sent him out to pursue the hostiles, and by God he was going to pursue the hostiles!

Eventually, that attitude was going to win the West. Matt was sure of it. Unfortunately, it was going to get a lot of good fighting men killed along the way, on both sides of the conflict . . .

Around midday, Windy rode on ahead of the patrol while the soldiers stopped to rest their horses. Matt wanted someone to go with him, just as a precaution, and pointed to Private Malone.

"Go with Mr. Mandalian, Malone."

The Irishman frowned but didn't argue. Malone was a good rider and was mounted on a sturdy horse, and he was a born fighter. Even more than that, he was a survivor, Matt knew. If anything happened to Windy and somebody needed to bring important news back to the patrol, Malone stood a better chance of getting through than just about anybody else Matt could have chosen.

As the two men rode off, leaving the others behind, Windy glanced over at his companion. "I didn't ask the lieutenant to send you with me, Malone. I didn't ask for anybody to come along, as a matter of fact."

"Rather be alone, eh?"

"To tell the truth, yes. I don't like being responsible for anybody but myself." Windy shrugged. "But militarily, it makes sense, so I didn't argue with Lieutenant Kincaid."

"What is it we're doin'?"

"I want to find out just how far ahead of us Blue Horse really is." Windy urged his horse to a faster pace. "Come on!"

Malone followed doggedly, doing his best to keep up with the scout. The rest of the patrol was soon out of sight behind them, and Malone felt a shiver go through him when he glanced back and saw nothing but the rugged, windswept Wyoming landscape.

He wasn't afraid exactly. Fear didn't play a large part in Malone's life. But he was uncomfortably aware that he and Windy Mandalian were alone out here and if they ran into trouble, it would probably be all over by the time the rest of the soldiers could reach them.

The trouble would be over . . . and in all likelihood, so would the lives of the two white men.

Malone forced those thoughts out of his head and paid attention to what Windy was doing. Malone didn't particularly like the scout, but he respected him. Windy had survived a lot of years on the frontier, so he must have been doing something right.

From time to time, Windy reined his horse to a stop and swung down from the saddle to take a closer look at the tracks left behind by the Indians they were pursuing. Whenever he spotted a pile of horse apples, he inspected them closely, even going so far as to get a handful and rub it back and forth between his fingers. As Malone watched in distaste, Windy sniffed at the droppings.

"Good Lord, you're not gonna be *tastin'* that shit, are you?" Malone couldn't hold the disgusted exclamation in any longer.

Windy grinned up at him. "I would if I thought it'd help me keep my hair. Damn right I would." He wiped his hand off on the ground. "Luckily I don't have to. I can tell by how much it's dried out that it's been there less than an hour."

Malone stiffened. "We're that close to those heathens?"

"Yeah. They've slowed down over the last couple of miles. They're not running away from us anymore."

Malone looked around. He seemed to see Indians behind every rock, every little sandy hummock of ground. His voice was a whisper.

"They're waitin' to ambush us?"

"I don't think so. My gut tells me they've got something else in mind." Windy put his foot in the stirrup and swung up into the saddle. "Let's go see if we can find out what it is."

Malone trusted Windy's gut, but despite that he drew his rifle from its sheath and rode with it resting across the saddle in front of him. He was going to be ready if the damned renegades jumped them.

They had only gone another quarter of a mile or so when the sound of gunfire came floating through the air, carried to them by the endless breeze. Malone lifted his head as he heard the distant popping.

"Those are shots. Sounds like a damn battle."

"Yeah." Windy heeled his horse into a hard run, and didn't look back to see if Malone was following him.

"Charge right into hell, blast it . . ." Malone galloped after the scout, muttering as he did so.

Windy rode to the top of a long, rock-strewn ridge. On the other side it sloped down to a broad, flat expanse where grass was sparse and trees were nonexistent. About halfway across that wide-open stretch, a group of about fifteen canvas-covered immigrant wagons was stopped. Around the wagons rode the members of the Cheyenne war party, whooping and firing their rifles.

"Didn't even pull the damn wagons into a circle." Windy sounded disgusted.

"They probably didn't have time to. Injuns probably come outta nowhere."

Windy waved a hand at the open ground around the wagon train. "Out of *nowhere*? Hell, Malone, there's no cover out there. Those pilgrims should've seen Blue Horse's bunch coming a mile away!" The scout shook his head. "Doesn't change anything, though. They've still got themselves in a fix, and it's up to us to get them out of it."

"Us? You mean you and me?" Blue Horse had between thirty and forty warriors, from the looks of it. It didn't seem to Malone that he and Windy would be accomplishing anything if they charged down there, just the two of them, and got themselves killed along with those immigrants.

"Kincaid wasn't going to stay stopped for very long. He's probably not more than a mile or so behind us. Go back and get him as fast as you can."

Now that made more sense. Malone jerked his head in a nod, then paused before he wheeled his horse around. "What're you gonna do?"

Windy dismounted and pulled his Sharps rifle from its saddle scabbard. "I might be able to pick off a few of them without them realizing that I'm up here."

"But if they figure it out, some of the red devils will come up here after you."

"I'll take that chance. Get moving, Malone."

Malone started to bristle at the scout's tone. Windy Mandalian was a civilian. He shouldn't be so quick to give orders to one of Uncle Sam's mounted infantry.

On the other hand, Windy was right. Malone hauled his horse's head around and kicked the animal in the ribs, sending it racing back in the direction they had come from.

He could still hear the shots from behind him, but after a while they faded out. Malone hoped that meant they were just out of earshot rather than the battle being over. If the Indians had stopped shooting, that meant they didn't have anybody left to kill.

Malone spotted a good-sized plume of dust up ahead,

coming toward him. That had to be the patrol, and it looked like they were coming this way in a hurry. That puzzled Malone for a moment, until he realized that Lieutenant Kincaid had probably spotted the dust that *his* horse was kicking up. Kincaid was smart enough to know that one of the two men who had gone out ahead of the patrol wouldn't be returning that fast unless they had run into trouble.

In a matter of minutes, Malone saw the blue-clad riders galloping toward him. He reined in when about fifty yards separated him from the rest of the patrol, and stood up in his stirrups, waving them on. He turned his horse and started back toward the wagon train, and a few moments later Lieutenant Kincaid's mount drew abreast of his.

"What happened, Malone?" Matt lifted his voice to be heard over the pounding of hoofbeats.

"Wagon train! Blue Horse! Ambush!" Malone was a little out of breath from the hard riding he'd done, but those few short words pretty much summed up the situation satisfactorily. Matt Kincaid gave Malone a grim nod of understanding and kept going.

When they reached the ridge, the thunder of hooves was too loud for Malone to be able to tell if the fighting was still going on. But then as the patrol charged up the slope, Windy Mandalian appeared at the crest and waved them on. Malone assumed from the buckskin-clad scout's actions that the Cheyenne hadn't overrun the wagons yet.

That proved to be the case. The men of Easy Company swept over the ridge and started down the far side toward the wagon train. The canvas cover on the back of one of the vehicles was on fire, flames leaping up from it and smoke billowing into the air. Puffs of powder smoke still spurted from most of the other wagons, though. The pilgrims were still putting up a fight.

The clear notes of Reb McBride's bugle cut through the air, audible even over the hoofbeats, the shots, and the whoops from the war party. Some of the renegades heard the bugle and peeled away from the force attacking the wagons. They rode toward the patrol, firing as they came.

Easy was mounted infantry, not cavalry. Fighting from horseback was not what these soldiers normally did. Matt flung a hand in the air in a signal for them to halt. Sergeant Olsen and Corporal Wojensky took over from there, bellowing orders for the men to dismount and form a skirmish line.

With well-drilled precision, the men did so. A few of them took charge of the horses while the rest of the patrol lined up. Half of them stepped forward, dropped to a knee, and lifted their rifles to their shoulders. Olsen yelled, "Fire!" and a volley ripped out. No sooner had those shots been fired than the other half of the patrol stepped forward and knelt while the men who had just discharged their weapons stood up and moved back to reload.

Meanwhile, Matt had drawn his Schofield revolver from the flapped holster at his hip and was firing it at the hostiles, while Windy Mandalian kept taking potshots from the top of the ridge.

A couple of the renegades tumbled off their ponies as they were struck by U.S. Army lead. One of the ponies went down, throwing its rider. Blue Horse's men broke off their charge in a hurry. They picked up their fallen comrades and lit a shuck out of there, heading back to the rest of the war party as fast as they could.

The arrival of the soldiers had changed the odds. Blue Horse could have kept up the siege for as long as he wanted, wearing down the defenders, staying out of rifle range for the most part, and darting in every now and then to use fire arrows to set another wagon ablaze, picking off a few more of the settlers. The hostiles would have been victorious eventually.

But they couldn't fight the horse soldiers, too. Matt caught a glimpse of the long-faced war chief yelling orders and waving at his men, telling them to give up the fight and get the hell out of there. One of the other Indians darted in front of Blue Horse just then, and Matt blinked as the renegade's head seemed to explode. After a second, he realized that Windy must have been drawing a bead on Blue Horse, only to have the other hostile move in front of the target just as Windy squeezed off the shot. A .52-caliber round from a Sharps did some mighty ugly things to a human head, including blowing most of it clean off the shoulders of anybody unlucky enough to get in the way of the big slug.

Blue Horse must have figured out how close he had just come to dying, because he jerked his pony around and took off for the tall and uncut. The rest of the war party followed him.

Sergeant Olsen ran up to Matt. "Do we pursue, sir?"

Matt hesitated, but only for a second, before shaking his head. "The people in those wagons may need our help, Sergeant. Let's get down there. But once we're there, post some men to keep an eye out just in case the hostiles decide to double back."

"Yes, sir." Olsen looked and sounded a little disappointed, and Matt understood the feeling quite well. He wanted to go after Blue Horse, too.

But that would have to wait. Protecting those civilians came first. Matt waited for Windy to ride up and join him, and then the two men headed for the wagons to see just how much damage Blue Horse and his renegades had done this time.

Chapter 10

The young shotgun guard, who introduced himself to Eileen as Jack Boggs, was obviously smitten with her, and who could blame him? Women as attractive as her didn't show up on the frontier every day . . . although it sometimes seemed to Longarm that he was lucky enough to attract more than his share of them.

Jack held the door of the coach open for Eileen. "Here you go, ma'am. Need a hand?"

She favored him with a smile. "No, thank you, Mr. Boggs. I'll be just fine."

The youngster looked a little crestfallen, but the brightness of Eileen's smile perked him back up again pretty quickly. He left the coach door open for Longarm to climb in, too.

Blind Pete and Jack had clambered up onto the driver's box, and Longarm was about to pull the door shut, when someone called out for them to wait. From one of the coach's windows, Longarm saw a tall man in a gray suit and bowler hat hurrying along the street toward the stage station.

"You must wait. I would ride the stagecoach."

73

The man's accent marked him as a foreigner. German probably, Longarm decided. He had run into Prussians several times in the past. High-handed folks for the most part, if you asked him.

This hombre had the same sort of attitude. As he came to a stop beside the stagecoach, puffing a little because he'd been hurrying, he glared up at Pete and Jack.

"I have a ticket! Why are you about to leave without me?"

Even with just one eye, Pete returned the glare with equal intensity. "This here coach has got a schedule to keep, mister. I can't sit around all day waitin' for folks to show up if they've a mind to." He pulled a big turnip watch from his coat pocket and flipped it open. "We're already two minutes late, which means you should'a been here three minutes ago."

"I am here now." The man hefted the carpetbag he carried. "If one of you will please load my bag . . ."

"Load it yourself."

The man's face darkened with anger. He had fair, almost white hair under the bowler, and his skin had a pinkish, sunburned look even before he flushed in reaction to Pete's curt words.

Since the coach door was still open, Longarm didn't figure it would hurt anything for him to play peacemaker. He stepped out and reached for the bag. "Let me take care of that for you, old son."

The man pulled back and frowned at Longarm as if he thought the big lawman was trying to steal the carpetbag. "If you would just show me where to put it, please?"

Longarm shrugged and went to the rear of the coach. He untied the thongs that held the canvas cover over the boot and pulled it back so that the man could put his bag in with the gear belonging to the other two passengers. As Longarm tied the cover back in place, the man climbed into the stagecoach, which shifted a little on its broad leather thoroughbraces under his weight. The man was tall and broadshouldered, almost as big as Longarm.

When Longarm climbed back into the coach himself, he saw that the stranger had settled himself on the seat beside Eileen. Longarm was about to say something, but he saw the tiny shake of her head and knew she didn't want him to cause a scene. Longarm thought about it for a second, then decided to let it go. The first time the stage stopped at a relay station and the passengers got out to stretch their legs, he would make sure that he reclaimed his place beside Eileen.

"Now, if we're all ready to go . . ." Sarcasm dripped from Pete's words as he called down from the box. Without waiting for an answer, he popped the whip over the backs of the team and shouted at the horses. The stagecoach lurched into motion.

The stranger took off his bowler hat and held it primly on his knees. He didn't say anything as the stage rolled out of Casper, but after a few minutes he must have decided that introductions were in order.

"I am Dr. Wilhelm Schott."

He had turned to Eileen as he spoke, and she summoned up a polite smile in response. "My name is Eileen Brewer. And this is—"

"Custis Long." Longarm spoke before she could finish telling Wilhelm Schott who he was. He was sure she would have introduced him as a deputy U.S. marshal, and Longarm figured it might be best to keep that fact under wraps for the time being. This wasn't a case that required him to work undercover, as some did, but it wouldn't hurt anything to play his cards close to the vest, at least starting out.

Schott barely glanced at him and gave him a brief nod. Clearly, the only one of his fellow passengers the Prussian was interested in was Eileen.

She tried to make conversation as the coach rocked and swayed along the trail. "Did you say that you're a doctor?"

"*Ja,* Fräulein Brewer, but not a physician. It is a geologist I am."

"A geologist?"

Longarm supplied the information before Schott could. "He studies rocks and such."

The man frowned across at Longarm. "You know about geology?"

"Not much. But I've met a few hombres in your line of work."

"What brings you out here?" Eileen asked Schott. She sounded genuinely interested now, not as if she were just being polite.

"The University of Heidelberg has sent me to study igneous rock formations of the American West. I will write a monograph based upon my research."

"That's fascinating."

Maybe she *was* just being polite after all, because igneous rock formations of the American West didn't sound the least bit fascinating to Longarm. He'd read enough about such things in the Denver Public Library to know that all he was really interested in where rocks were concerned was that they were sometimes good to duck behind when somebody was shooting at you, and they were hell to sleep on.

Schott warmed to the subject, though, going on at such length about the things he had discovered during his sojourn on the frontier that Longarm started to get drowsy. After a while, he tipped his hat down over his eyes and leaned his head back against the front wall of the coach.

Schott continued with his lecture all the way to the first relay station, clearly oblivious to the fact that Eileen had heard all she wanted to hear about geology during the first few minutes. When the stagecoach stopped to take on a new team, she managed to pull Longarm aside as they were walking around.

"Custis, can't you just . . . I don't know . . . shoot him or something?"

"You mean shoot Schott?" He grinned.

"You're not the least bit amusing, Custis Long." Eileen gave a little moan. "But please, don't let him sit next to me again."

"I don't plan to. But you know, he'll still be able to talk to you. It's pretty close quarters in a stagecoach."

"Not if I pretend to be asleep."

Longarm patted her on the shoulder. "Yeah, you try that and see how it goes."

Eileen rolled her eyes and shook her head.

They climbed back into the coach while Schott was around back of the station, likely answering the call of nature. When he came back and found them sitting side by side in the forward-facing rear seat, he looked disappointed at first, then a little angry.

"You are in my seat, sir."

Longarm waved a hand. "Oh, seats ain't ever saved in a stagecoach, Doctor. You wouldn't know that, not being a Westerner and all."

Schott looked like he wanted to argue the point, but then his shoulders rose and fell in a sullen shrug. He muttered something in German, and then settled down on the rearward-facing seat.

Eileen didn't have to pretend to be asleep. Evidently, Schott's feelings were hurt, so he didn't say anything else. That was just fine with his fellow passengers.

They spent the night at another relay station. There were no beds, just rope bunks with thin, straw-stuffed mattresses. The only accommodation made for Eileen's gender was a threadbare blanket strung up in front of her bunk. Nor was the food—beans and fatback—very appetizing.

Longarm took the opportunity to talk to Blind Pete and ask him about something. "You said back in Casper that the folks where we're going call the place Skull Valley instead of Happy Valley. Why's that?"

The one-eyed jehu just cackled and shook his head. "Sorry, mister. Reckon you'll find out when you get there . . . if you live that long."

"What's that mean?"

"Oh, nothin', nothin'."

Longarm was sitting on the other side of a rough-hewn

table where Blind Pete was shoveling beans into his half-toothless mouth. "Listen, old-timer, I've heard that there's been a lot of trouble up here with stagecoach robbers. Is that true?"

Pete's head bobbed up and down. "It's true, all right. They've stopped the coach more'n once, stole the mail pouch, and took whatever valuables the passengers was carryin'." The driver's weathered face took on a grim expression. "Time before last when they held us up, the varmints killed my shotgun guard. I'd like to see ever' damn one of 'em strung up."

"You think they'll jump us between here and Happy Valley?"

"Who knows? You can't tell what a bunch o' no-good owlhoots'll do . . . especially that bunch!"

"What do you mean?"

Pete put his spoon down, looked around, and lowered his voice to a confidential tone. "Them bastards are downright spooky. They wear hoods over their heads so you can't see their faces—or even if they *got* faces—and they never say nothin'!"

Longarm had encountered a gang of hooded outlaws a while back, only those varmints had ridden around looking like their heads were on fire. He was in no mood to encounter anything that odd again.

"They don't talk?"

"Not that I've heard. It's like they're, I dunno, ghosts or somethin'. They make it plenty clear what they want, though, and they don't have to say nothin' for you to know that you better go along with 'em or get filled full o' lead."

Longarm filed that information away in his head and stood up. "Well, I sure as hell hope they don't take a notion to rob us tomorrow. What time will we get to Happy Valley?"

"If nothin' happens to delay us, about noon, I reckon."

Longarm nodded and stepped outside the adobe building that served as the relay station. He lit a cheroot and stood there smoking it and watching the stars twinkle into life in the sable sky overhead. As he pondered what Pete had told him, his right hand came up and tugged at his right earlobe for a moment. Then he rasped his thumbnail along the line of his jaw. Those unconscious mannerisms showed how deep in thought he was.

A soft step behind him made him turn around. Eileen stood there, her shape silhouetted by the light in the doorway behind her.

"I saw you talking to the driver. Is anything wrong, Custis?"

Longarm shook his head. "No, just finding out a little more about the gang that's been holding up the stage from time to time."

"Do you think they'll hold it up tomorrow?" More than a trace of worry could be heard in Eileen's voice.

"That's what I asked Pete. He said he didn't have any idea. You can't predict what outlaws will do."

She leaned against him, so that he felt the little shiver that went through her. "I'll be glad when we get to Happy Valley."

"Me, too." For one thing, he was mighty curious about why the Indians called the place by the much grimmer name of Valley of Skulls.

Eileen had a worn, weary look to her the next morning as they boarded the stage after a rough breakfast washed down with bitter coffee. He figured that once again she hadn't slept very well the night before. This trip had been hard on her, and he was glad it was nearly over.

Wilhelm Schott looked tired, too, and was still sulled up like an angry possum. That was fine with Longarm because it kept the Prussian quiet. Schott took out a book that looked like a journal of some sort and began scribbling in it. Probably taking note of igneous rock formations, Longarm thought.

For all the worrying everyone on board the coach had done, the rest of the trip passed smoothly, without incident or even a glimpse of masked owlhoots. Longarm noticed when the coach passed a village of Indian lodges, though, and pointed them out to Eileen.

Excitement showed on her face as she looked at the village. "The agency must be somewhere nearby. Aren't we stopping here?"

Longarm shook his head. "Doesn't look like it. The settlement must still be up ahead a ways. We'll rent a buggy or a wagon and come back out to find your brother."

"Oh." Eileen looked a little disappointed. "Well, I suppose that will be all right."

Wilhelm Schott finally spoke up again, raising his eyes from the notebook in his hand. "Your brother is the Indian agent here?"

Eileen nodded. "That's right. You don't happen to know him, do you? Allen Brewer?"

"I am sorry, fräulein, but no, I do not." Schott went back to his scribbling.

The stagecoach had rocked on only a few more yards when Blind Pete leaned over on the seat and called through the window to the passengers. "If you want to see why they call this place the Valley of Skulls, take a look!"

Longarm did so, taking off his hat and leaning over so that he could stick his head out the window. His jaw tightened as he saw the towering rock formations that flanked the entrance to the valley. They gleamed white in the midday sun, except for the pitted areas that made them resemble grinning human skulls.

Longarm had always believed in eating the apple one bite at a time, but as he looked at those grim piles of rock standing there like the gates of Hell, a chill of foreboding went through him.

Any place where you had to run a gauntlet of giant skulls to get there . . . well, it just couldn't be good.

But he sure as hell had the answer to his earlier question now.

Chapter 11

By the time Matt Kincaid and Windy Mandalian reached the wagon train, some of the pilgrims had emerged from the canvas-covered vehicles and were cheering for the soldiers and waving rifles in the air over their heads. Several men walked forward to greet the two riders.

"Hello! Thank God you men arrived when you did! Those savages would have massacred all of us."

The speaker was a tall, almost gaunt man with a graying brown beard that jutted out from his lantern jaw. He wore a brown hat with a round crown that made him look a little like a Quaker. Matt had met members of that religious persuasion before.

This man wasn't a Quaker, though. The silver whiskey flask that stuck out of his coat pocket was confirmation of that.

Matt and Windy dismounted, and Matt performed the introductions while they held the reins of their horses. "I'm Lieutenant Kincaid from Outpost Number Nine, a ways southeast of here. This is Windy Mandalian, our scout."

One of the other men spoke up. "Well, we're sure obliged

to you, Lieutenant!" This pilgrim was considerably shorter and rounder than the first man who had spoken. He was clean-shaven, too. "I'm Edgar Wilson, and this here is Nathaniel Peabody."

The tall, bearded, lantern-jawed man jerked his head in a nod.

Wilson introduced the third member of the trio. "And this other fella is Dave Lashley."

Matt nodded politely, but he didn't care much for Lashley's looks. The man had a dark, craggy face and a thick mustache. His skin was weathered and seamed, and he looked like he had spent a lot more time on the frontier than either of his companions.

"What are you folks doing out here?" Matt asked. "This isn't one of the regular immigrant trails, at least not that I know of."

Peabody responded to Matt's question. "It is now, Lieutenant. A new area has been opened for settlement recently, and that's where we're headed. It's called Happy Valley. Maybe you've heard of it."

Matt shook his head. "No, I'm afraid not."

"It's supposed to be two more days' travel northwest of here, in the Owl Creek Mountains."

Matt glanced over at Windy, who had mentioned those mountains earlier. The scout shrugged, indicating that he didn't know anything about a new settlement up that way either.

"Well, that's a little farther out than we normally patrol, so I reckon that's why we didn't know about the place." Matt studied the three men. "Which one of you's the wagon master of this train?"

"Wagon master's dead." The harsh reply came from Dave Lashley. "Horse kicked him in the head nigh a week ago."

Peabody nodded, a solemn expression on his face. "That's right. Poor Mr. Wilbanks lived about twelve hours after that, but his skull was busted and there was really nothing we could do for him."

"It's lucky that Dave was with us." Wilson grinned at Lashley. "He's been through these parts before and told us that he could lead the wagon train to Happy Valley."

"Yes, that's lucky, all right." Matt turned to Lashley. "Two day's ride northwest of here, you said?"

Lashley pointed to Peabody. "Actually, it was Nathaniel who said that, but yeah, that's right."

"Would've been nice if somebody had let the army know about that. Where did you hear of it?"

Peabody provided the explanation. "Some men from the government came to our town in Pennsylvania and held a meeting. They said that the valley had just been opened for settlement, that it had all been government land before that, and that our area had been selected for recruiting the first settlers. Everyone in those parts who had been thinking about moving on west jumped at the chance."

"It's wonderful land, perfect for farming." Wilson couldn't keep the enthusiasm out of his voice, despite the close call they'd just had with the Indians. "The government men showed us all the maps and reports."

By now the rest of the patrol had ridden up to the wagon train. Matt called orders to them. "Olsen, see to the wounded. Wojensky, you and your men get out your shovels and throw some dirt on that burning wagon. We don't want the fire to spread to any of the other wagons. And Olsen . . . form a burial detail if needed."

The sergeant nodded in stoic acceptance of that grim task. This would be the second time today he and the men of his squad would have performed it, if it proved necessary again.

Matt turned back to Peabody, Wilson, and Lashley, who seemed to be the leaders of these immigrants. "Did you have to pay for this land you're going to?"

Peabody nodded. "Well, of course. Just because it belonged to the government doesn't mean we were going to get it for nothing. And there were other fees involved, too, for handling the paperwork and everything."

Matt didn't say anything for a moment, then decided that it might be wiser to change the subject. "Mr. Lashley, you're not from Pennsylvania, are you?"

"No, I ran into these folks in Kansas City and decided to come with them. Good thing I did, too. I was able to help 'em organize a defense when those Cheyenne jumped us."

Lashley was boasting a little. He hadn't done a very good job of it since the wagons hadn't even been pulled into a circle. None of the immigrants could have been paying much attention to allow the Indians to get that close.

"You recognized them as Cheyenne?" The question came from Windy.

"Damn right I did. I've fought Injuns before. More'n once, in fact. Those redskins took us by surprise. We'd heard back up the trail that things were pretty peaceable in these parts right now."

"They have been. That was a bunch of renegades led by Blue Horse."

The look on Lashley's face showed that he recognized the name. "He's supposed to be a pretty bad Injun."

"We've been on his trail since yesterday when he raided the settlement down by Outpost Number Nine, where we're stationed. He seems to be working his way northwest."

"Toward Happy Valley?" Wilson had lost his jolly attitude and seemed alarmed.

"Could be."

Wilson turned to Peabody. "Nathaniel, we didn't figure on having to fight Indians. Those government men didn't say anything about that."

"You didn't expect things to just be handed to you on a silver platter, did you, Edgar?" Peabody shook his head. "I'm sorry to hear about it, but this comes as no surprise to me. I knew we might have to fight for our land sooner or later."

Wilson looked anxiously at Matt again. "You and your men will escort us the rest of the way to Happy Valley, won't you, Lieutenant? I mean, it's your duty to protect civilians from the Indians, isn't it?"

Matt rubbed his jaw as he considered the request. He had realized as soon as he saw the wagon train that he had a dilemma facing him. Captain Conway had sent him after Blue Horse, and a part of Matt wanted to continue pursuing the war party just as swiftly and aggressively as he could.

On the other hand, as the commander of this patrol in the field, he had some leeway to adapt his orders in the face of changing circumstances. One of the main reasons Easy Company was stationed here in Wyoming Territory was to protect immigrants just like these and see to it that they reached their destination safely. That was the only way the settling of the West could continue.

Anyway, Blue Horse was headed in the same direction as the wagon train was going. That was the way the renegades had gone when they broke off the attack. If Matt and his men accompanied the wagons, technically they would still be in pursuit of Blue Horse; they just wouldn't be going about it as fast as Matt might have liked.

He seemed to have little choice in the matter, at least for the time being. "Yes, Mr. Wilson, we'll go with you."

Relief washed over the faces of Wilson and Peabody. It was hard to tell with Lashley. His rugged countenance stayed as stony as ever.

"Just because we're along doesn't guarantee that the Indians won't attack your wagons again, though."

"It's a lot less likely." Peabody sounded convinced of that, and Wilson nodded in agreement. "Thank you, Lieutenant. Now, I guess we'd better see to our people. Edgar and I are cocaptains of the train, you know. Duly elected before we left Pennsylvania. So I suppose we'll all be working together now until we get to Happy Valley."

"I reckon so."

Matt and Windy stood there as the other three men returned to the wagons. Neither of them said anything for a long moment, and then the scout sighed.

"Those sheep got themselves sheared, didn't they, Windy?"

"Oh, hell, yeah." Windy spat disgustedly. "Those fellas who came and put on some dog-and-pony show in their town weren't from the government. Not by a long shot."

"They were swindlers."

"Yep. The government doesn't charge for homestead land. Chances are those maps and reports they were flashin' around were fakes, too. There's no tellin' what these folks will find when they get to where they're going."

"You think there really is a place called Happy Valley?"

Windy shrugged. *"Quien sabe?* I reckon we'll find out, though, if we stick with 'em."

"I gave my word." Matt's voice was sharp.

"I know. But what are you gonna do if Blue Horse's bunch veers off in another direction?"

Right now, Matt just didn't know the answer to that question.

Surprisingly, none of the immigrants had been killed in the attack, although several of them had been wounded by rifle bullets and one man had taken an arrow in the arm. Sergeant Olsen knew how to deal with that. He gave the man a couple of drinks of whiskey, put a leather strap in his mouth for him to bite on, and shoved the arrow on through the arm so that the bloody arrowhead ripped free of the man's flesh. It was a simple matter then to break off the head and pull the shaft out, doing less damage in the long run. And the hombre had already passed out from the pain—and maybe from the whiskey—so he didn't even yelp.

The wagon that had caught on fire was a total loss, along with everything in it. It belonged to a middle-aged couple. The woman stood weeping at the loss of all her possessions, while her husband patted her awkwardly and futilely on the back. One of the other families offered to let the two of them ride with them, and promised to help them make a fresh start once they got to Happy Valley. It was small consolation, but better than nothing.

And better to lose your wagon and all your goods than to wind up dead, Matt thought. Folks could recover from a lot of things, but only one fella had ever gotten up out of the grave and walked around again. Well, two if you counted Lazarus, but that was a special case.

It was the middle of the afternoon before the wounded were all patched up and the wagon train was ready to roll again. Nathaniel Peabody had the lead wagon. While Peabody whipped up his team of mules and got them moving, Matt arranged his men in two lines, one on either side of the wagon train. Olsen's men were on the right flank, Wojensky's on the left. Windy scouted out ahead.

Two men dropped back to bring up the rear. Private Max Malone wasn't the least bit surprised that he was tabbed to be one of them. Any time there was a job that required eating dust, Malone's superiors just naturally seemed to look toward him.

Rafferty rode alongside Malone. "I'm a little surprised the lieutenant agreed to escort these wagons instead of going on after Blue Horse."

"Yeah, I didn't think anything would distract ol' Hard-Ass Kincaid from chasin' those renegades." Malone laughed. "Maybe he caught a glimpse of some of those immigrant gals. I saw one or two of 'em I wouldn't mind gettin' to know a little better, if you know what I mean."

Rafferty shook his head. "Better be careful, Max. Most of those women have husbands, and the ones who don't probably have fathers with shotguns and itchy trigger fingers. You'll get your butt filled with buckshot, you go sneakin' around those wagons at night."

"It's been so long I might just risk it. Hell, when we were in town last, I didn't even get a chance to say howdy to a soiled dove, let alone do anything else. That was when those damned renegades attacked the place."

"Well, if you hadn't wasted so much time starting that brawl . . ."

"Me? I didn't start that ruckus! It was that damned Englisher!"

They rode on, complaining as soldiers always do. The big, heavily loaded wagons couldn't move very fast, even on relatively level ground like this, so the train hadn't covered very many more miles by the time the sun began to sink behind the western horizon.

Windy Mandalian galloped back several times during the afternoon to report to Matt Kincaid that the trail left by the war party was still going in the same general direction as the wagons.

Matt was a little perplexed. "Blue Horse knows we're after him, and yet he's still not doing anything to hide his trail?"

"He doesn't *care*, Matt. He wants another fight. Oh, he'll run if things aren't going his way, like he did earlier, but that doesn't mean he wants to give us the slip. He lives to kill white men, especially white soldiers, and he can't do it if he gives us the slip."

"So sooner or later we'll have to tangle with him again."

"I reckon you can count on it."

When the wagon train came to a halt for the night, the pilgrims began pulling the big, heavy vehicles into a circle without having to be told to. That proved their late wagon master had taught them a few things before his unfortunate accident. There wasn't room for the patrol's horses inside the circle because all the livestock belonging to the immigrants was herded in there. Matt had the mounts picketed just outside the enclosure, though, and posted four men to stand guard over them. He put out other sentries as well. There was always the chance that Blue Horse would double back and hit the wagon train again, so Matt wasn't going to let his guard down.

He walked around the wagons as the immigrants built a fire inside the circle and began cooking their supper. The men of Easy Company had their own rations, of course, but if they were invited to share the meal that was being prepared, Matt was going to allow it. Hot food and coffee did wonders for morale, and the men still weren't fully over the deaths of Harrison, Bolton, and Scherzinger.

Matt had just passed one of the wagons when a short, sharp cry came from the other side of it. The noise wasn't loud, and it was possible no one else had heard it over the general hubbub going on in the camp.

But Matt had heard it plainly, and he recognized that the cry had come from a woman. She sounded like something was wrong, like she was afraid or in trouble, and Matt moved quickly around the wagon to see what was going on.

The campfire was quite a distance away on the other side of the circle, so it was shadowy here and what light there was flickered because of the dancing flames. But Matt's keen eyes could see clearly enough to make out two struggling figures, a man and a woman.

He started toward them. "Hey! Let go of her!"

The man let go, all right. He whirled around and swung a big fist, taking Matt by surprise. The blow exploded right in the lieutenant's face.

Chapter 12

Longarm wasn't the only one who noticed the grotesque appearance of the big rocks flanking the valley entrance. Wilhelm Schott stared at the rocks as the stagecoach rolled between them. He muttered something in German that Longarm supposed had something to do with skulls. Eileen also looked out the window beside her and gasped.

"I heard what the driver said, Custis, but those rocks really *do* look like skulls!"

"Your brother didn't say anything about that to you in any of his letters?"

She shook her head. "Not a word. What a dreadful-looking place." Eileen stopped and sniffed the air. "And what's that *smell?*"

Longarm had caught a whiff of the odd scent, too, mixed in with the smell of dust and horse sweat that came in through the windows. It was vaguely sulfurous, a little like the scent that lingered in the air after you lit a lucifer. But at the same time, that wasn't exactly it.

The smell also reminded Longarm a little of the stench given off by some of the geysers, hot springs, and mud pits up in the Yellowstone country, an area that had been set aside for use as a national park. He had been there several times on various assignments for Billy Vail. The place had once been known as Colter's Hell after John Colter, the first white man to visit the area, had come back with stories about how the place smelled of fire and brimstone, like the gateway to Hades.

The Valley of Skulls wasn't Hell, but it almost smelled like it could have been, Longarm decided.

Schott was writing furiously in his journal, scrawling a few lines, then lifting his head to gaze out the stagecoach window, then going back to his writing. Igneous rocks were found in areas where volcanoes had been active; Longarm dredged that fact up out of his memory. From the smell of it, there could have been volcanoes around here at one time, but surely there weren't any around here that could still blow their tops. Surely . . .

Then Longarm remembered his old friend Jessie Starbuck telling him about a volcano that had erupted and nearly buried her in lava down in Mexico, and it wasn't supposed to be there either. That thought made him frown and look out the window, searching for any mountains with smoke coming out of them.

He didn't see any. In fact, the mountains surrounding the long, wide valley were low, timber-covered, and not very impressive.

Not very impressive also described Happy Valley itself. The grass that straggled here and there alongside the stage road was mostly brown and obviously struggled to survive here. The trees were scrubby and a good number of them appeared to be dead. If the settlers who had come out here planned on farming, they must be having a rough go of it, Longarm told himself. He was no sodbuster himself, but he came from a long line of farmers and knew a little about dirt. It didn't look to him like the ground in these parts would grow much of anything except failed dreams.

Eileen shook her head. "I don't see why anyone would

want to live here, Custis. I realize we just got here, but I don't like it at all."

"Maybe the place grows on you."

She looked doubtful. "Something might grow on you here, all right, but I don't think it would be fondness."

A short time later, the stagecoach came to the settlement, which was laid out with a main street running east and west, a couple of side streets paralleling it to the north and south, and four cross streets. Several dozen buildings had been constructed, and the frameworks of others were partially erected. Some of the lots were marked off, but nothing had been built on them yet.

As the stagecoach came to a stop in front of a building with adobe walls and a plank front, Longarm heard the sound of hammering. The industrious racket told him that the people here were trying to make a go of it, but the odds might be stacked against them. Not only did it look like a piss-poor place for a town, but now the settlers had to contend with that gang of outlaws he was here to bust up.

Longarm would do his best to put those desperadoes out of business, but he couldn't do anything about the physical conditions. Folks were on their own when it came to things like that.

Someone came up and opened the stagecoach door. "Welcome to Happy Valley!" A round-faced man in a brown suit and a string tie beamed at the passengers as he held the door.

Longarm climbed out first and then turned back to help Eileen down from the coach. Wilhelm Schott emerged last and took off his hat to slap it against his clothing, brushing off some of the dust.

"I'm Richard Decker, the owner of the stage line and mayor of Happy Valley." The round-faced man looked like one of those gents who never stopped smiling.

Eileen looked puzzled. "You're the mayor of the whole valley?"

"No, just of the town here. We decided to name it after the valley, though. Are you folks new settlers?"

Longarm introduced himself without adding that he was a deputy U.S. marshal. Since Decker was the mayor, he was probably the one who had sent the letter to Billy Vail asking for help, or at least he would have known about it. Longarm would tell the man who he was, but he didn't want to do it out here in the street, especially since he'd made a point of *not* telling Schott.

He nodded toward Eileen. "This is Miss Brewer—"

Before he could go on, someone called Eileen's name from down the street. They turned to see a man in his thirties hurrying toward them. He wore a dusty black suit and had brushy red hair and freckles. A big grin was plastered across his face.

"Eileen, you're finally here!"

"Allen!"

They threw their arms around each other. Once they were side by side, the family resemblance was obvious, although Eileen was definitely lovely and the best her brother Allen could manage was being pleasantly homely. Longarm also noted that Allen Brewer was a couple of inches shorter than Eileen.

While the reunion between brother and sister was going on, Wilhelm Schott turned to Mayor Decker and asked where the nearest hotel was.

"Right across the street there, Mister . . . ?"

"Schott. Dr. Wilhelm Schott."

Decker's eyebrows rose in surprise, but Schott didn't give him a chance to say anything.

"I am not a physician. I am a scientist."

"Oh. Well, you're mighty welcome in Happy Valley anyway, Mr. Schott. I mean, Dr. Schott."

The Prussian gave him a curt nod. "I suppose there is no one here to carry my bag?"

"Well, no, I'm afraid not . . ."

Schott looked resigned to the fact that he would have to carry his own gear. He went to the back of the stagecoach, where Jack Boggs had already untied the canvas cover over the boot and pulled it back.

Decker turned to the jehu, who was taking the mail pouch from the compartment under the driver's seat. "Any trouble this time, Pete?"

The one-eyed man shook his head. "Nary a bit. Didn't see any sign o' them masked owlhoots."

Decker heaved a sigh of relief. "That's good news. Give me the mail pouch and I'll take it on over to Slidell's."

Longarm had already noticed the sign on one of the buildings that proclaimed it to be Slidell's General Merchandise Emporium and U.S. Post Office. That was the way it was in a lot of frontier towns, where the post office shared space with one of the businesses. Longarm recalled visiting one settlement where the postmaster had been not only the local undertaker but also the town barber.

Decker took the mail pouch from Blind Pete, but paused before leaving with it. "You didn't say what brings you to Happy Valley, Mr. Long."

"No, I didn't." Longarm nodded toward the emporium. "I reckon Slidell sells cheroots over there?"

"Of course."

"I'll walk with you then, Mayor. I need to pick up some more smokes."

Decker looked a little puzzled, but didn't protest as Longarm fell in step beside him. They hadn't gone very far, though, when Eileen called out from behind them.

"Custis, come and meet my brother."

Longarm glanced at Decker, shrugged, and smiled. "Reckon I'll get those cheroots later. Be seeing you, Mayor."

"Yes, of course."

Longarm returned to the boardwalk in front of the stage station where Eileen stood with her brother. She smiled as she introduced them.

94

"Allen, this is Custis Long. Custis, please meet my brother Allen Brewer."

The redheaded man gave Longarm a friendly but somewhat cautious nod and held out his hand. "It's a pleasure, Mr. Long. Eileen tells me that you befriended her on her trip out here."

"That's right." As Longarm shook Brewer's hand, he thought that the man's wariness was natural enough. Any man would be a little leery of some stranger who'd been traveling with his younger, unmarried sister.

And of course in this case, Allen Brewer had good reason to be a mite suspicious, but it wasn't like Longarm had taken advantage of Eileen or anything. She had been just as eager and willing as he was. Longarm didn't figure on trying to explain that to Brewer, though.

Anyway, Eileen didn't waste any time allaying her brother's suspicions. She leaned closer to him and spoke in a half-whisper. "Custis is the United States marshal you sent for, Allen. He's come to find out who's been causing all the trouble up here."

"Oh." Brewer's eyes, which were a startling shade of blue, opened wider. "Oh!" He grabbed Longarm's hand to pump it again. "Thank God you're here, Marshal."

"Better save your thanks until we know for sure I can run those varmints to ground."

Eileen smiled. "I have confidence in you, Custis. After all, you handled that trouble back in Cheyenne."

"Trouble?" Brewer suddenly looked concerned again. "What trouble?"

Eileen waved a hand and shook her head. "Nothing you need to worry about, Allen. Just a misunderstanding with one of the locals."

Yeah, a misunderstanding with gunplay that wound up with three hombres dead, thought Longarm. But Eileen was right about it not having anything to do with what was going on here in Happy Valley.

95

Longarm decided it would be a good idea to change the subject. "This valley don't look like a very good place for a bunch of settlers. How'd they come to be here anyway?"

"I don't know, Marshal," said Brewer. "You'd need to talk to Mayor Decker to find out more about that. My main concern is the Indians, and of course the band led by Falls from the Sky was here long before the settlers moved in."

"The report I read from the BIA said masked owlhoots had attacked the village?"

Brewer nodded. "That's right. They terrorized the place one day while all the young men were out hunting and there was no one there to defend it."

"Was anybody killed?"

"No, thank God. There were a few minor wounds, but that's all. Since then, though, potshots have been taken at several of the men when they were away from the village. It's only a matter of time until someone winds up dead, I'm afraid."

Longarm frowned. "This Falls from the Sky you mentioned, he's the chief of this bunch?"

"That's right."

"And he and his people are friendly?"

"Of course. Falls from the Sky is a wise man and has realized that fighting against the settlers and the army won't do any good in the long run."

"So there's no real reason for the gang to be causing trouble for them."

Brewer's jaw tightened in anger. "No reason except sheer meanness, Marshal, at least that I can see. That same group of outlaws has been holding up the stagecoach, and they killed the shotgun guard not long ago."

"Yeah, I heard about that. You're sure it's the same gang?"

"Unless there are two groups of outlaws and gunmen dressed exactly the same, and that seems unlikely to me."

It did to Longarm, too, although he knew better than to rule out anything at this stage of an investigation.

Eileen spoke up again. "That's enough talk about trouble for now. Custis, I want you to come out to the agency and have supper with Allen and me this evening."

Brewer nodded. "Yes, Marshal, that would be very good. We can discuss the case some more then."

Longarm thought about it for a second and then accepted the invitation. "I'll be there. Where is the agency?"

"Just follow the road back out of the valley until you get to the Indian village. There's another road that turns off to the south. It'll take you right to the agency, which is only about half a mile from the village."

Longarm nodded. "I'll be there. Much obliged for the invite."

"It's the least we can do, since you've been looking after Eileen on the way out here. I admit that I was worried about her traveling alone. That's why I suggested that she contact the marshal's office in Denver to see if perhaps she could come up here with whoever they sent."

Eileen linked her arm with her brother's. "Yes, I'm certainly glad that I was able to come with Custis." Her green eyes got that impish twinkle in them again as she smiled.

Longarm cleared his throat, glad that Allen Brewer didn't seem to notice the hidden meaning in his sister's words. "See you later then."

Eileen waved. "Come whenever you're ready."

Longarm wished she'd stop that. He fished a cheroot out of his vest pocket and watched as Brewer led Eileen to a buckboard parked not far away by a water trough. Clearly, Brewer had been expecting her to arrive today and had brought the buckboard in from the Indian agency to pick her up. As soon as he had helped her onto the seat, he fetched her bags from the stagecoach and put them in the back of the wagon.

Eileen waved merrily to Longarm as Brewer drove off. He lifted a hand in farewell as he chewed on the unlit cheroot.

Then he got his war bag, Winchester, and saddle from the coach's boot and set them on the boardwalk in front of

97

the stage station. He would carry them across the street to the hotel and check in later, but for now he wanted to talk some more to Decker, whom Longarm had spotted returning from the emporium and post office.

The lawman spoke in a low, confidential tone as Decker stepped up onto the boardwalk. "Reckon we could go into the office and talk?"

Decker looked puzzled. "Of course, Mr. Long. What can I do for you?"

Longarm's answer was blunt. "I'm the U.S. marshal you sent for."

Decker's eyes widened in surprise, but he controlled the reaction fairly quickly and led the way into the office. Outside, hostlers took the stagecoach team around back now that everything was unloaded. Longarm didn't know where Blind Pete and Jack Boggs had gotten off to. Their living quarters were probably somewhere behind the station, too.

The mayor sighed as he sat down behind a desk and waved Longarm into a chair in front of it. "Thank God you're here, Marshal. I suppose you read the report I sent to the chief marshal's office in Denver about the stagecoach robberies?"

Longarm nodded. "Yeah. Stealing the mail puts it right in Uncle Sam's bailiwick. Tell me about everything that's been going on around here."

For the next few minutes, Decker filled Longarm in on the details of the trouble. He grew heated and angry as he recounted how the previous shotgun guard had been gunned down during one of the robberies.

"But that's not all those masked bastards have been doing. They've raided several of the farms and ranches around here, rustled stock, ruined crops, shot milk cows, and even wounded a few of the settlers. It's like they've set out to make life as miserable as possible for the people who live in Happy Valley."

"Blind Pete says they never talk."

Decker nodded. "That's right. At least, I've never heard

anyone say anything about the outlaws talking. It is pretty strange, I suppose."

Longarm frowned and tugged on his earlobe. "So you can't be sure what they *really* want."

"No, I reckon not. What could they be after?"

Longarm shook his head. "You tell me, Mayor. If you ask me, Happy Valley don't look like much of a happy place even if there weren't any owlhoots raising Cain. What in the world made all you folks decide to move here and settle it, even start a town?"

Decker sighed heavily, leaned back, and rested his hands on the desk, palms down. "There you have another story entirely, Marshal. To put it plain and simple . . . we were robbed."

Chapter 13

The punch that landed on Matt Kincaid's jaw sent him staggering back a couple of steps, but he didn't lose his feet. He put a hand against the wagon to catch his balance and then pushed off, instinct sending him in a diving tackle at the shadowy figure who had just punched him.

The man was big and strong, but there was a lot of strength and power in Matt's lean, rope-muscled body, too. He crashed into the man, who seemed to be surprised that his blow hadn't ended the fight almost before it began, and both of them went down in a heap. Matt landed on top and drove a knee into the man's midsection while at the same time whipping a punch at his head.

The blow landed solidly, but it wasn't enough to subdue Matt's burly opponent. The man heaved up off the ground, sent Matt rolling to the side, and managed to scramble to his feet first to launch a kick at Matt's head.

Seeing the booted foot coming toward him, Matt flung his hands up and grabbed it. He wrenched it hard to the side and sent the man toppling over with a startled yell. Matt still didn't know who he was fighting, only that the hombre was big and tough.

But even though Private Malone had the reputation of being the best brawler in Easy Company, Matt was no slouch in that department himself. He made it to his feet in time to block another punch aimed at his head, and sent a hard right jab into his opponent's face. The man stumbled back, blood leaking from his nose. Enough of the flickering firelight reached them now so that Matt was able to recognize Dave Lashley.

Somehow, the fact that it was Lashley with whom he was fighting came as no surprise. Matt hadn't liked the man to start with, and he trusted his instincts. As Lashley grunted a curse and waded in again, Matt set his feet and prepared to give as good as he got or even better.

He was vaguely aware that the woman who had cried out as she struggled against Lashley had hurried off. He caught a glimpse over Lashley's shoulder of several men hurrying across the open space inside the circle of wagons, and figured she had gone to summon help.

That wasn't going to do him any good right now, though, because Lashley bellowed like a bull and swung sledgehammer blows at Matt's head with both fists. Matt had his hands full blocking as many of the punches as he could and trying to deal out some damage of his own as the two men stood there slugging it out. Matt landed a left hook in Lashley's belly, and would have followed it with a right cross if Lashley hadn't managed to slam a fist into his chest just then.

The two battlers were so evenly matched, there was no telling how the fight would have turned out if it had continued. But some of the other men from the wagon train showed up at that moment, followed by several of the soldiers who had been drawn by the commotion.

"Dave! Dave, stop it! Somebody get hold of him!"

The shouted order came from Nathaniel Peabody. A couple of the immigrants grabbed Lashley's arms from behind.

He yelled and struggled in their grasp but couldn't pull loose.

At the same time, Sergeant Gus Olsen put a hand on Matt's shoulder. "Take it easy, Lieutenant. Looks like the fight's over."

Matt shrugged off the noncom's hand, but he didn't lose his temper with Olsen. The sergeant was just trying to keep him from getting hurt and also to defuse any possible tension. The men of Easy Company were gathering at Matt's back, and Lashley had the immigrants around him. Even though Matt had been caught up for a moment in the heat of battle, he didn't want this fracas to escalate into a brawl between the soldiers and the pilgrims from the wagon train.

"It's all right, Olsen, I'm fine." Matt's chest was heaving from exertion, and he could tell he had some bruises starting to form in places where Lashley's hard fists had landed, but otherwise he was unhurt.

Lashley's only real injury seemed to be the bloody nose. When Peabody told the men to let him go, Lashley wiped the back of his hand across his mouth, looked at the blood smeared on it, and glared at Matt.

"What in blazes is going on here?" Peabody sounded like he took his role as cocaptain of the wagon train seriously.

Lashley poked his bloodstained paw at Matt. "Soldier boy there stuck his nose into somethin' that was none o' his damned business."

"Any time a woman is being assaulted, I make it my business, mister."

Peabody echoed Matt's statement. "A woman being assaulted! What are you talking about, Lieutenant?"

"I was taking a turn around the camp when I heard a woman cry out like she was in pain or scared." Matt nodded toward Lashley. "I came around this wagon and saw Lashley there manhandling her."

"You got it all wrong." Lashley sneered in the firelight. "I reckon a fella's got a right to have a little fun with the gal he's gonna be marryin'."

There was a stir in the crowd of immigrants that had gathered, and they parted suddenly to let a woman step through. "You're the one who has it wrong, Mr. Lashley." Her voice was clear and strong now. "You asked me to marry you, but I never agreed that I would."

She was in her mid-to-late twenties, an attractive woman in the prime of life. The blue dress she wore went well with her eyes. She wore a bonnet, but it must have slipped back while she was wrestling with Lashley, because it hung behind her head by its ties, revealing short blond curls.

Lashley protested. "That ain't true, Becky, and you know it. We come to an agreement—"

She shook her head. "Any such agreement was only in your head, Mr. Lashley. I told you straight-out that I wasn't ready to get married again."

"Yeah, but someday—"

She interrupted him again. "If I *do* get married again someday, I don't know to who it would be. That's just too far in the future."

"Can't mourn that husband o' yours forever." Lashley frowned as he muttered the words under his breath.

When Matt saw the pain that flashed in the blond woman's eyes, he wanted to step forward and wallop Lashley again. That would just start the fight all over, though, and Matt knew he couldn't do that.

Nathaniel Peabody stepped in. "If what Mrs. Hanover is saying is true, Dave, I think you owe her an apology."

Edgar Wilson, the other cocaptain of the wagon train, had joined the group and spoke up. "I agree with Nathaniel. You should tell Mrs. Hanover that you're sorry."

Lashley's jaw had a belligerent set to it, but after a moment, he jerked his head in a curt nod. Grimacing a little, he turned to the woman.

"Reckon I'm sorry, Becky. I thought there was an understandin' between us—"

"There isn't."

"Yeah, I reckon I know that now."

"All right." Becky Hanover still looked shaken and under some strain, but she nodded her acceptance of Lashley's apology.

Lashley turned toward Matt. "I ain't apologizin' to *you*, though, soldier boy."

"Wasn't asking you to." Matt's reply was equally curt.

Lashley pointed a blunt finger at him. "Fact of the matter is, we might just settle this some other time."

"Dave! We can't have that."

Lashley ignored Peabody's scolding tone and continued to glare at Matt Kincaid. Matt shook his head.

"I'm a soldier, Lashley. I don't go around fighting with civilians."

"We'll see." Lashley wheeled around and stalked away, pushing roughly through the crowd. He bumped heavily into those who didn't get out of his way quickly enough, but no one seemed to want to take offense at it. Chances were Lashley had a reputation among the immigrants as a short-tempered bruiser. That was certainly the way he seemed to Matt.

Peabody and Wilson came over. "I'm sorry about this mix-up, Lieutenant." Peabody sounded sincere, and Wilson nodded his agreement.

"Better keep an eye on Lashley," said Matt. "He's liable to try to cause more trouble."

"Oh, I doubt that. He's actually been a good companion for the most part on this journey. I'm sure it was all just a misunderstanding, as he said."

Matt glanced at Becky Hanover. The blond woman had made it pretty clear that there *hadn't* been a misunderstanding between her and Lashley. Lashley had just been looking for an excuse to manhandle her and steal a kiss— or more.

Wilson turned and motioned Becky forward. "Lieutenant, you haven't met Mrs. Hanover yet."

"I reckon there are quite a few folks on this wagon train I haven't met."

That was true enough, but Becky Hanover had to be one of the most interesting, Matt thought. She had a calm, quiet beauty about her that he found extremely appealing, even under these tense circumstances.

Wilson performed the introduction. "Becky, this is Lieutenant Kincaid."

"Matt Kincaid." He held out his hand. "It's a pleasure and an honor to meet you, Mrs. Hanover."

Her hand was warm. He felt a few calluses on it, the results of handling the reins as she drove her wagon. They didn't make her touch any less exciting.

"Lieutenant Kincaid." She smiled as she grasped his hand. "I owe you my thanks. There's no telling what Mr. Lashley would have done if you hadn't intervened."

Peabody had to speak up. "I don't think that's really fair, Mrs. Hanover. Lashley may not be what you'd call a gentleman, but I'm sure he wouldn't . . . wouldn't have . . ."

The glance she gave him was cool. "You may be sure of that, Mr. Peabody, but I'm not. And I was here, not you."

"Yes, of course." Peabody looked embarrassed and uncomfortable. "Well, I'll have a talk with Dave. I'm sure there won't be any more trouble."

Matt wasn't sure of that at all. Lashley struck him as the sort of man who would nurse a grudge. Now he had one not only against Matt but also against Becky Hanover.

Matt let go of her hand. "I can assign one of my men to keep an eye on your wagon if you'd like, ma'am."

"I don't think that will be necessary, but I appreciate the offer, Lieutenant. There are always enough people around, though, that I can call for help if I need to."

Matt hoped that was right. He wouldn't put it past Lashley to try to corner the woman again sometime, when he thought that she wouldn't be able to summon assistance.

One thing his military career had taught him, though, was not to borrow trouble. It would come along soon enough on its own.

Becky smiled. "I'd like to pay you back for coming to

my aid, Lieutenant. Would you care to have supper with me tonight?"

"We have our own supplies . . ."

"Which I'm sure aren't as good as a home-cooked meal."

Matt couldn't argue with that point. And he didn't want to, even if he could have. He smiled and nodded instead.

"That's a very kind offer, and I accept."

"Give me twenty minutes or so, and I'll have the food ready."

He turned to Sergeant Olsen, who had picked up his hat from the ground where it had fallen off during the fight with Lashley. Matt brushed it off, put it on, and then lifted a finger to the brim of it in a small salute.

"Thank you, ma'am. I'll be here." He turned away and was all business again as he spoke to Olsen. "Did you get the horses picketed, Sergeant?"

"Yes, sir."

"And guards posted?"

"They're out there and wide awake, sir."

Matt nodded. "They had better be. I don't think Blue Horse will come back, at least not tonight, but you never know."

"No, sir, not about Mister Lo." Olsen paused. "But I reckon you can be sure that after what we found waitin' for us this morning, nobody's gonna be dozing off tonight."

Matt knew the sergeant was referring to the murders of privates Harrison, Bolton, and Scherzinger while they were supposed to be standing sentry duty. Olsen was right, too. If anything, the men on guard tonight would be so overly alert that they would have to be careful not to imagine danger where there wasn't any. In the long run, though, it was better to be too cautious than to allow some renegade to sneak up on you and cut your throat.

"Very good, Sergeant, carry on." After rolling around on the ground with Lashley, Matt wanted to straighten his uniform and brush some of the dirt off it. It had been quite a while since he'd sat down to dinner with a lady—especially one as attractive as Becky Hanover—and he wanted to look as good as he could under these rugged conditions.

Not that he expected anything to happen, of course. As Lashley had mentioned, Becky was in mourning, so obviously she was a widow. Matt had no idea how long it had been since her husband passed away. Enough time had obviously gone by so that Lashley had gotten ideas about taking the man's place, but Matt didn't know how many months that translated to.

Still, it never hurt to look your best when dining with a lady. Despite the pain of his bruises, Matt was smiling as he walked away from Becky Hanover's wagon.

"Would you look at that?" Utter disgust dripped from Malone's voice. "The lieutenant's already gone and got himself a lady friend, and we only came across this wagon train a few hours ago!"

Stretch Dobbs frowned. "Are you talkin' about that widow woman, Max? All she did was ask the lieutenant to have supper with her."

The two privates were among the soldiers who had come running when the ruckus broke out between Kincaid and that big, ugly hombre called Lashley. The group had begun to disperse when it was obvious that the excitement was over, but Malone and Dobbs had lingered nearby long enough to hear most of the exchange between the lieutenant and the pretty blond widow.

"That's what you think, Dobbsy. You could see for yourself how grateful she was to Kincaid. You know how women get when they feel grateful."

Dobbs rubbed his chin and frowned. "I dunno. Any time a woman feels grateful to me, which ain't all that often, she usually just says thank you and goes on about her business."

"Well, that ain't the way this one's gonna be. You just wait and see."

"I don't think the lieutenant's gonna let us watch, Max."

Sergeant Olsen came over then and barked orders at them, telling them to go make sure the horses had water. Malone tugged his cap down tighter on his head and muttered to himself as he walked away from the wagon where the pretty blonde was starting to prepare the supper she would share with Lieutenant Kincaid.

Malone had no ambition to ever be an officer. Even the responsibilities of a corporal's stripe had proven to be too much for him on the numerous occasions when the brass had been stubborn enough to insist on promoting him.

But right now, as he thought about the supper that Kincaid was going to be having with Becky Hanover—along with who knows what else!—Malone would have given a lot to have the luck of a lieutenant on his side for a change.

Chapter 14

Longarm snapped a lucifer into life with his thumbnail and set fire to the gasper clenched between his teeth. When he had the cheroot going, he repeated what Mayor Decker had just said.

"Robbed?"

Decker nodded. "Well, not at gunpoint or anything like that. *Swindled* would be a better word, I suppose. You see, Marshal Long, I worked for a stagecoach line back in Ohio, so I knew all about coaches and horses and things like that. One day a couple of men showed up in the town where I lived. They rented a hall and plastered up fliers all over town and held a meeting. They said they were from the government, and they were looking for immigrants to move to a lush valley in Wyoming Territory that had just been opened for settlement."

Longarm winced. "And I reckon *this* is the valley they were talking about?"

"Exactly." Decker sighed. "I'm sure you've already seen for yourself, Marshal, that the country around here is hardly what you'd call lush."

"Did you have to pay these hombres for the right to come out here?"

"The way they put it, the people who decided to come out here and settle were simply reimbursing the government for certain expenses involved in opening the land for settlement. And of course there were several administrative fees that had to be paid, too . . ."

Longarm nodded. "Of course."

"I know, now it sounds like we were all fools to believe them, but they were very persuasive."

"Hadn't you ever heard of homesteading? You don't have to buy the land from the government when you do that, just prove up on it and stay there for a few years."

"They had an answer for that when someone brought it up. They said that this was different because the land that was available for homesteading wasn't nearly as good as what we would find here in Happy Valley. That was why the government had to charge us for the land and collect the fees. They said that even though we had to pay, we were getting a lot better deal." Decker spread his hands. "You know how people are when they're offered a deal, Marshal."

Longarm knew, all right. He blew a smoke ring to keep from making some comment about how gullible they could be.

The mayor continued. "Anyway, we lived back East. It's been a long time since Ohio was a frontier. We didn't really know what conditions were like out here. Those swindlers *could* have been telling the truth for all we knew. They even called the place Happy Valley. Who could resist that?"

"So a bunch of you pulled up stakes and came out here?"

"That's right. The men even provided a guide for us. We came across a lot of rugged country, and whenever anyone said anything about our destination, the guide assured us that once we got there, we'd see how much better it was." Another despairing sigh came from Decker. "Well, we got here and . . ." The way he shook his head was eloquent enough to convey what he meant.

"What happened to the guide?"

"Gone. He slipped away the first night. Some of the men wanted to go after him and string him up, or maybe force him to take us back to the thieves he worked for. But we're not trackers, and we're not gunmen. We decided not to go after him."

"I'm a mite surprised you didn't turn around and go back where you came from."

"We couldn't, Marshal. You have to realize . . . we'd all sold our homes and businesses back East and put everything we had into the trip out here. A few people did leave, but most of us simply couldn't afford to. We all talked it over and decided that we just had to try to make the best of it."

"So you started building a town, putting in farms . . ."

Decker nodded. "That's right. I started the stage line that runs between here and Casper, and other men farmed or started businesses. A few men are trying to get ranches going farther up the valley. It's been hard, of course, but we've had some small successes. Other settlers have come here from Illinois and Indiana and Iowa, places where those crooked so-called government men pulled the same trick. Most of them had to stay, too, and they joined our community. We were starting to think that we might actually make a go of it."

As Decker paused, Longarm made a guess. "Then that gang of masked owlhoots showed up."

"That's right. I tell you, Marshal, folks are starting to agree with the Indians. Happy Valley is cursed. Do you know what they call it? The Indians, I mean?"

"The Valley of Skulls."

A little shudder ran through Decker's portly frame. "It's a horrible name, but it certainly fits. I never saw anything as grotesque as those big rocks at the head of the valley."

"The smell around here ain't too good either."

"Oh, you get used to the smell after—" Decker stopped short and then shook his head. "No. No, you don't. Not really. But it gets to where it's not quite as bad."

Longarm propped his right ankle on his left knee and puffed on the cheroot for a moment before asking another question. "Are folks so shook up by what those outlaws have been doing that they're ready to leave whether they can afford it or not?"

Decker looked like he was reluctant to admit it, but he nodded. "There's been some talk. Some people say that we'll never be able to make a peaceful life for ourselves here and that we might as well cut our losses and get out. I don't believe that, though, and most of the other businessmen agree with me. That's why we decided to write to the marshal's office in Denver. I knew that since the bandits have taken the mail pouch from the stagecoach on several occasions, that brought the matter under federal jurisdiction. I thought we might be more likely to get help from the U.S. marshal, rather than appealing to the territorial authorities. When I told Allen Brewer what we were going to do, he said that he would forward a similar request through the Bureau of Indian Affairs."

Longarm thought he had a pretty clear picture of the situation now. Other than the angle concerning the swindlers who were responsible for these poor folks being in the mess they were in, Decker hadn't told Longarm anything that the big lawman didn't already know.

"What can you tell me about the outlaws?"

Decker shook his head. "Not much. You understand, I've never seen them myself. My driver Pete has, though, and he's told me all about them. So have some of the men whose farms have been attacked. The description is always the same. They wear long coats and hoods so that you can't see their faces. And they don't hesitate to shoot to kill." He leaned forward. "Do you really think you can stop them, Marshal?"

"Well, like the old hymn says, further along we'll know more about it, but I sure intend to try. I ain't in the habit of failing either."

Decker pulled a bandanna from his pocket and used it to

mop sweat from his forehead. "It would be wonderful if you could bring them to justice, Marshal. I know the odds have been stacked against us from the start here, but I honestly believe we could make something of Happy Valley if we were given half a chance."

Longarm stood up and extended his hand over the desk, "I'll try to give you folks that chance, Mayor."

The two men shook hands. Then Longarm left the stage station, picking up his rifle, saddle, and war bag as he stepped down from the boardwalk. As he started across the street toward the hotel, he thought that he wanted to talk to that chief out at the Indian village, too. He recalled the fella's name—Falls from the Sky.

Time enough for that when he went out to the agency for supper with Eileen and her brother. Thinking about the auburn-haired beauty made a smile tug at his lips under the sweeping longhorn mustaches.

He didn't know when circumstances would allow him and Eileen to spend some time together in private again . . . but whenever it was, Longarm was already looking forward to it!

After checking in at the hotel, Longarm carried his rifle and war bag upstairs and put them in the room he had been given. As he left, he wedged a match in the gap between the door and the jamb, then closed it firmly so that only a tiny bit of the match was visible. That was an old habit of his. Before he entered the room again, he would check to be sure that the match was still there. If it wasn't, he'd know that someone had been inside—and might even be waiting in there to bushwhack him.

He had left his McClellan saddle with the desk clerk while he went upstairs. He reclaimed it now and got directions to the local livery stable. Even though he didn't know how things were going to play out in Happy Valley, one thing was certain: He would need a horse to get around.

The owner of the stable was a red-faced man named Vernon. He rented to Longarm a blaze-faced bay gelding with three white stockings. The animal looked a little brittle to Longarm's experienced eye, but it was the only mount Vernon had available. Longarm paid for a week's rent and got the stable man to agree to keep his saddle in the tack room.

With that done, Longarm began walking around the settlement, giving it a good looking over.

The citizens had given the settlement the same name as the place in which it was located—Happy Valley. Longarm saw the name painted on the windows of several of the businesses, including the local newspaper, the *Happy Valley Herald*. There were two general stores, a drugstore, a café, a butcher shop, a barbershop and bathhouse, a blacksmith, a saddlemaker, two lawyers, a doctor, and three saloons. No school or church; it was a sad fact that those bastions of civilization nearly always came last when a new town was established.

None of the businesses looked to be exactly thriving. There were a few pedestrians on the boardwalks, a handful of horses tied at the hitch racks, and only a couple of wagons parked in front of the emporium. Happy Valley had the look of a settlement that might just dry up and blow away unless its fortunes changed. Its fate was still up in the air. In six months or a year it might be a ghost town.

It would be for sure unless Longarm could do something about the outlaws plaguing the area. If enough of the settlers were already talking about leaving to get the mayor and the other community leaders worried, it would be a downhill slide from here.

Longarm felt sorry for the people who had invested everything they had in this valley. When he got back to Denver, he intended to ask Billy Vail if anything could be done to track down the varmints who had posed as government officials and swindled the pilgrims who'd come here.

That was something to worry about on down the road, though. The first bite of the apple would be tracking down those owlhoots. The fact that they would strike and then disappear, only to show up again later, told Longarm that they had to have a hideout somewhere in the area.

He strolled into one of the saloons, and bought a beer when the apron told him that they didn't have any Maryland rye. The beer was warm but not too bitter.

"New in town, ain't you, mister?"

Longarm nodded in reply to the drink juggler's question. "That's right. Name's Custis Long." He didn't identify himself as a lawman. He had asked Eileen to keep that to herself, and figured she would have told her brother to do the same. He hadn't thought to tell Mayor Decker to keep quiet about his real identity. He would stop back by the stage station at his first opportunity and do so, even though such secrecy was less of a concern on this assignment than it was on some of his jobs.

"What brings you to Happy Valley?"

Longarm started to say that he was just passing through, but stopped himself when he realized that there wasn't really any place to pass on through *to*. He settled for the vague answer "Business," and kept his tone curt enough so that the bartender got the idea he didn't want to discuss it. The man went back to polishing glasses and left Longarm to nurse the beer.

A scrawny figure pushed through the batwings and came over to the bar to stand next to Longarm. Blind Pete gave him a friendly nod and ordered a beer.

"When do you start back to Casper?" Longarm indulged his curiosity by asking the question.

"Tomorrow mornin'. We make two runs a week. That's plenty, 'cause there ain't all that many passengers, usually no more'n two or three, like this time."

"Who hauls in the supplies for the stores and any other freight?"

"Mr. Decker does that, too. He's got half a dozen freight wagons that roll back and forth 'twixt here and Casper."

Longarm took a sip of his beer. "And he's the mayor, too."

"Yep. Reckon you could say he's the biggest fella in these parts." Pete shook his head. "Which means that he's got the most to lose if it all goes bust."

Longarm had thought the same thing. If the settlement failed, everyone here would be hurt, but Decker would be ruined. No wonder he was anxious for the law to come in and straighten things out.

"Where's that young fella who rides shotgun for you?"

"Jack?" Pete took a deep swallow from the mug of beer the bartender placed in front of him, grimaced, and then shook his head. "He's down to the bathhouse. Fella sometimes takes *two* baths a week! I never heard o' such a thing in all my borned days, but he does it, sure as hell. Plumb unhealthy, if you ask me."

Longarm hadn't, but he chuckled anyway.

After chatting for a few more minutes with the one-eyed stage driver, Longarm finished his beer and left the saloon. It was getting late enough in the afternoon now that he decided to get the horse from the livery stable and ride on out to the Indian agency. He went by the hotel on the way, though, and got his Winchester from his room.

With a band of outlaws roaming the countryside and liable to pop up anywhere, anytime, he didn't plan to venture too far from town without his rifle.

The road was easy to follow. As he approached the mouth of the valley, he noticed that the big rocks flanking the opening just looked like giant boulders from this side. Their sinister resemblance to skulls was only apparent when you were coming at them from the other direction.

As soon as Longarm had ridden between them, though, a little shiver went through him. He glanced back over his shoulder at the rocks. It was like the damned things were *watching* him. He didn't like the feeling.

He forgot about it a few minutes later when he spotted a cloud of dust coming toward him in a hurry. A good-sized group of riders was galloping in his direction. He reined in, frowned, and looked all around. There wasn't any decent cover nearby. He was going to have to just sit there in the road and wait to see who those hombres were and where they were going.

He drew the Winchester from the sheath strapped to the saddle and held it crossways in front of him. If he had found those owlhoots already, he planned to put up one hell of a fight.

The riders weren't outlaws. Instead of range clothes, they wore buckskins, and they carried bows and arrows instead of Colts and Winchesters. But as they galloped up on their ponies and surrounded Longarm, he looked at the grim expressions on their coppery faces and wasn't sure that he wouldn't have been better off with the outlaws.

These young warriors had to be from the nearby village, and according to everything Longarm had heard about them, they were friendly. They didn't look too friendly at the moment, though.

In fact, he would have sworn that a couple of them were eyeing his scalp with interest.

It was too late now to do anything except wait and see what they wanted. One of the fierce-looking young men edged his pony forward, bringing it to a stop directly in front of Longarm's bay. After a moment he spoke, and his words took Longarm by surprise.

"I say, old boy, what are you doing here?"

Chapter 15

Matt Kincaid cleaned himself up as best he could before returning to Becky Hanover's wagon. He even got out his razor for a quick shave. Just wanted to look respectable, he told himself again. That was all there was to it.

The wagon camp had settled down after the brief ruckus. The immigrants were eating supper or caring for their stock or getting ready to turn in. Handling a balky team all day was exhausting work, and dawn came early. Most of the men crawled into or under their wagons as soon as they had eaten, and fell into a stunned slumber.

Becky greeted Matt with a warm smile as he walked up to the wagon. She had removed her bonnet so that her blond curls shone in the glow from the fire, which cast faint reddish highlights on them.

"Hello, Lieutenant. I'm afraid I can't offer you anything fancy in the way of food. I have some biscuits I just cooked, and some good stew left over from the midday meal . . ."

Matt returned the smile. "That sounds mighty good to me, ma'am."

"Oh, don't call me ma'am." Becky laughed. "That

makes me sound so old. I'd rather you called me Becky, Lieutenant."

"And I'd rather you called me Matt."

"All right . . . Matt." She gestured toward a three-legged stool she'd set up near one of the wagon wheels. "Sit down and I'll bring you your food. I have coffee and a bit of apple pie, too."

Matt grinned as he sat down. "Sounds better and better, ma'am . . . I mean Becky."

She brought him a bowl of stew and one of the biscuits, then sat down on the lowered tailgate of the wagon to eat, too. Matt wasn't much good at making dinner conversation—life at a military outpost, with most of his time spent bossing around a bunch of ornery soldiers, didn't afford many opportunities for practicing such things—but he thought he ought to at least make an effort to do so.

"Mr. Peabody and Mr. Wilson said that your group comes from Pennsylvania?"

"That's right. My late husband and I had a farm there."

Matt made an effort not to wince. "Sorry. Didn't mean to dredge up any bad memories."

She smiled. The expression was still warm and friendly, but held a trace of bittersweet emotion. "That's all right, Lieutenant . . . Matt. It's been almost a year since Timothy passed away."

"I'm sorry for your loss." Matt didn't want to hurt her, but he couldn't restrain his curiosity. "Your husband must have died unexpectedly. As young as you are . . ."

Becky shook her head. "Timothy was considerably older than me. He was a widower, and he was looking for another wife . . . You know how things like that are."

Matt nodded. "Of course."

"He was a very kind man, very good to me. But he worked very hard, too, and his heart . . . well, I suppose it just couldn't stand the strain."

"Too bad. I'm sure he would have enjoyed going to Happy Valley with you."

"Not necessarily. Timothy was set in his ways, as most older men are. I'm not sure he ever would have budged from that farm. But once he was gone, I felt like I needed a change. I just didn't want to stay there anymore."

"Reckon I can understand that." Matt took a sip of his coffee, which wasn't overly hot but was strong and potent. "Sometimes folks just need to move on."

"What about you? What's your story, Matt?"

He smiled and shook his head. "You don't want to hear about that. It's mighty boring. Tell me about what you plan to do once you get to Happy Valley."

For a second, he thought she was going to press him about his own background, but then she complied with his request instead. "Well, the land there is supposed to be excellent for farming, but I don't think I can handle a farm by myself. That's another reason I left Pennsylvania. I'm an excellent seamstress, if I do say so myself, so I was considering opening a dress shop in the settlement."

"You made that dress you're wearing?"

"Yes, I did." She set her bowl aside and pressed her hands to the fabric below her bosom, running them down over her belly. "Do you like it?"

Moving like that sort of threw her shoulders back and lifted her breasts, and the way she pressed on the fabric tightened it, making the firm mounds stand out even more than before. Matt's gaze was drawn toward them for a second, and he had to force himself to look away and swallow before he could manage a reply.

"Yeah, it's, uh, very nice. Very nice." He knew that the repetition made him sound a little dumb, but he couldn't help it.

"Thank you. Do you think I could sell dresses like this to some of the other women in the valley?"

"I don't see why not."

The other pioneer women might buy dresses like that, Matt thought, but they still wouldn't look like Becky

Hanover. She did things for a dress that most women couldn't.

Matt concentrated on his food for a minute to get his thoughts under control, finishing off the stew and the biscuit, then draining the rest of his coffee from the tin cup. When he had agreed to have supper tonight with Becky, he hadn't really had anything romantic in mind. Sure, he had been well aware that she was an attractive young woman, and he figured that spending time with her would be enjoyable, but she was also a widow and she'd just had the upsetting experience of having Dave Lashley try to maul her. Matt had figured that romance was the last thing on her mind, and he was prepared to offer her nothing but friendship.

It was still certainly possible that was all she had in mind. She might not even be aware of the effect her beauty was having on him.

Seeing that he was finished with his food, she slipped down off the tailgate. "Let me get that pie for you."

"Do you have enough for yourself, too?"

"Well . . ."

"We'll split it." Matt's voice was firm. "I insist."

She laughed. "I suppose that would be all right." She got the small serving of pie from the pan where it had been cooked, split it into two portions, and then sat down on the tailgate again. "Join me, Matt."

Matt hesitated, but only for a second, before sitting down on the tailgate beside Becky. She handed him the wooden bowl containing his part of the dessert.

The deep-dish apple pie was wonderful, slightly sweet but still retaining the tartness of the apples. It was just as good as what Sergeant Dutch Rothausen, Easy Company's chief cook back at Outpost Number Nine, made, and that was saying quite a bit. Dutch was a fine cook.

When they were finished, Becky took the bowls and spoons and set them aside. She sighed as she tilted her head back and gazed up at the millions of stars floating overhead in the night sky.

"How beautiful the stars are." Her voice was a soft murmur.

"That they are. You talk to people out here, most of them will tell you that the night sky is one of the best things about the frontier."

Becky lowered her eyes and turned her head to look at him. "But there can be bad things out there in the night, too."

Matt shrugged. He couldn't argue with what she'd just said.

"Do you think those Indians will come back?"

"Not tonight."

"Mr. Lashley told everybody that Indians never attack at night."

That brought a skeptical grunt from Matt. "He's never heard of a Comanche moon? Take my word for it, the settlers down in Texas know all about that. No, an Indian will attack at night if he thinks it's to his benefit to do so. It's true that some of them don't *like* fighting at night, but they'll do it if they need to."

He felt a shudder go through her, and that made him realize how close she was sitting to him, practically nestled against him. He hadn't noticed until now, probably because it seemed so natural.

"So we may not be safe, even at night?"

"You're a lot safer than you were." He tried to make his tone as reassuring as he could. "You have us with you now, and I've posted guards all around the wagons. Blue Horse and his renegades are pretty tricky, but I don't think they'll be able to sneak up on us without one of my men sounding the alert."

"Blue Horse? You know the chief?"

Matt nodded. "Yeah. We've had run-ins with him before. Yesterday, he and his men raided a settlement a good ways southeast of here, near the outpost where Easy Company is stationed. We've been on his trail ever since."

"Why didn't you go after him, instead of staying here with us?"

"Well . . . our orders were to pursue and engage Blue Horse and his war party, but we also have a duty to protect civilians. It was my decision to stay here with the wagon train, and I'll stand behind it. I think we did the right thing. Anyway, it's hard to track anybody at night. We can pick up the trail in the morning."

Becky stiffened. "Then you and your men *will* be moving on. I thought . . . well, I thought you might escort us the rest of the way to Happy Valley."

Matt had spent quite a bit of time pondering that very thing. Without an experienced wagon master, these pilgrims could blunder into trouble again quite easily. They were relying on Dave Lashley to guide them, too, and Matt didn't trust the man. Lashley might claim to know the territory and be able to lead the wagons to Happy Valley, but they had only his word on that. If he was boasting or lying outright, that could land the immigrants in hot water again, too.

Anyway, the renegades had taken off toward the northwest when they abandoned their attack on the wagon train, and that was the direction in which Happy Valley lay. In one way of looking at it, if the patrol accompanied the wagons, they would still be carrying out their pursuit of Blue Horse and his warriors. That interpretation was a bit of a stretch, but not too much of one, Matt thought.

One thing was certain—if the wagon train ran into another ambush and nobody was around to help them, these pilgrims were probably doomed.

And Matt Kincaid didn't want that on his conscience, orders or no orders.

"I didn't say we weren't coming with you."

Becky lifted her head to look at him. "Really?"

"Seems to me that we're going in the same direction anyway. It can't hurt anything for us to travel together, at least for now."

A long sigh of relief came from her. "I am so glad to hear that."

Since she was sitting so close to him anyway, it seemed natural as could be for her to lean against him and rest her head on his shoulder. Her arms went around his left arm, hugging it to her. Matt was intensely aware of the soft warmth of her right breast.

It had been a while since he'd been with a woman, and being so close to one as lovely and desirable as Becky Hanover was having a pronounced effect on him. A few seconds of having her snuggled up against him like that had him as hard as a damn rock, in fact. He wanted to turn to her, pull her even tighter against him, reach up, and cup her other breast so he could find out if the nipple was as erect as his manhood was . . .

But she'd already been pawed by one man tonight. He'd be damned if he was going to subject her to something like that again.

"Lieutenant Kincaid . . . Matt." Her voice was a soft whisper, her breath a warm caress against his ear.

On the other hand, if she wanted him, he didn't have to be hit over the head with that fact more than a few times. He turned toward her and heard her whisper again.

"Please kiss me."

Matt obliged. He brought his mouth down to hers and pressed their lips together with heated urgency.

Becky let go of his arm and reached up to embrace his neck instead. Their mouths melted together, lips parting and tongues darting out to slide sensuously around each other. The passion that crackled around Matt and Becky was like the charged air of the high country when a thunderstorm was approaching. She strained against him as if trying to mold their bodies together despite the clothes that were in the way.

After a moment, though, she broke the kiss and gasped as she pulled back. "I'm sorry, Matt. You . . . you must think I'm a terrible, brazen woman. I . . . I never should have—"

He broke in before she could finish her stumbling apology. "I don't think anything of the sort. I think you're a mighty fine woman, Becky. Nobody could blame you for being a little lonely, traveling by yourself the way you are."

She rested her head against his shoulder and let out a little moan. "That's some of it, all right. I . . . I've been lonely. It's been difficult since Timothy died . . . losing him, and then all the upheaval of joining the wagon train and starting out here . . ." She lifted her head to look into his face. "But that's not all of it, Matt. It's not just a matter of . . . companionship. I knew as soon as I saw you this afternoon, before we ever met, that I . . . I . . . well, when I looked at you, I felt something that I hadn't felt in such a long time . . . I told you, Timothy was a good man, but he was older . . . most of the time, he couldn't . . . he never really made me feel like . . . like a woman."

Matt felt more than a little uncomfortable at that moment. He didn't want to hear about what had happened—or *hadn't* happened in the marriage bed between Becky and her late husband. It was none of his business. If she had a long-standing itch she wanted him to scratch, that was one thing. If she was truly attracted to him, that was fine, too, although she had to understand that he had his duty to the army, and that came first. He would even listen if she just wanted to pour her heart out to him, but this wasn't really the time or place for that.

"Listen. You have nothing to apologize for, Becky. Not for anything you said or felt or did. Life is hard, but it's all we've got and folks make their way through it the best they can. Anybody who can't understand that . . . well, those are the kind of folks you just don't need to worry about. They don't matter."

She leaned against him again, and his hand came up instinctively to stroke those blond curls. Her voice was so soft he could barely make out the words. "Thank you, Matt. I can't tell you how much that means to me."

They sat there like that for several minutes before Becky finally lifted her head again.

"But I still want you to make love to me."

Matt smiled. "I reckon we can manage that."

He glanced around the camp, which had grown quiet and still. The big cooking fire had burned down to embers. Matt didn't see anyone moving. Other than the guards he had posted, everybody was probably asleep by now.

Becky slid backward over the tailgate into the wagon and tugged him along with her. Fumbling a little because of the almost total darkness under the canvas cover, she found the buttons of his shirt and began to unfasten them. He started unbuttoning her dress at the same time. He was careful not to pop any of the buttons off or tear anything. She had made that dress and was proud of it, and justly so.

It took them several minutes to undress each other, but they enjoyed every second of the time, pausing to stroke and caress each new area of flesh that was uncovered. Matt found that her breasts were every bit as firm as he expected them to be, like fresh, ripe melons. He lowered his head to each of them in turn and sucked the hard nipples, running his tongue over the ring of pebbled flesh around them.

For her part, Becky seemed determined to explore every inch of his body with her fingers. She paused when she reached his manhood and wrapped both hands around the long, thick shaft.

"Oh, Matt . . ."

The need in her throaty exclamation made him want to plunge into her right away, but he held back. Instead, he slid his hand down the softness of her belly and stroked his fingers through the triangle of fine-spun curls that covered her mound. When he reached her opening, it was already slick with the moisture that sprang from deep within her. He found the sensitive little bud at the head of her cleft and strummed it with his finger, making desire well higher and higher inside her. She panted and her hips rolled as he continued to tantalize her with his caress.

Her hands tightened on his cock, and he knew she couldn't stand to wait any longer. Moving over her, he brought the head of his shaft to her drenched opening and sheathed it inside her with one long, powerful thrust of his hips.

Becky might have cried out in ecstasy if Matt hadn't brought his mouth down on hers at the moment of penetration. He slid his tongue between her lips and she sucked eagerly on it. Her arms and legs wrapped around him and her hips thrust back at him, and the effect was to urge him into a hard gallop as he rode her.

Within moments, spasms surged up within Becky's body. Matt felt the strong ripple as her culmination rolled through her. His own climax had been swift in its arousal. He surrendered to it, driving into her as deeply as he could before stopping there and letting his juices erupt from him. The heat of their shared peak was immense and seemed destined to consume them both.

Of course it didn't. Nobody had ever really burst into flames from a good romp, or even a great one, at least not that Matt had ever heard of. But as he slumped there on top of Becky, trying to keep his weight from crushing her as he felt the pounding of her heart almost keeping time with that of his own, he thought that if such a thing really happened, it might not be a bad way to go.

It took a while before either of them could talk. Becky regained the power of speech first.

"That was . . . incredible. Matt, I never dreamed . . . Is it possible it can be like that *every* time?"

He lifted his head and grinned down at her. "It's possible."

She hugged him even tighter. "Then you're definitely staying with us all the way to Happy Valley, because I want to do that again. As often as we can, in fact."

Matt didn't say anything, but he had come to the same conclusion. As long as Blue Horse was headed toward Happy Valley, the patrol would stay on his trail. He didn't wish any bad luck on the settlers who were already there, but he hoped like hell that the renegades didn't veer off in another direction.

Because then he would have to make a decision that he didn't want to make.

In the meantime, though, Becky had started to breathe faster, and her hips made little rotating motions underneath him. "How soon do you think . . . you can do it again?"

Matt chuckled. "What say we find out?"

Chapter 16

Even out here on the frontier, Longarm had run into enough Englishmen to recognize the accent right away when the young Indian spoke to him. It sounded incredibly out of place coming from the mouth of a coppery-faced warrior in buckskins, with a colorful headband holding back his long, raven dark hair and the feathered shafts of arrows visible where they stuck up from the quiver slung on his back. Longarm had to wonder if he had imagined the whole thing.

"What's that, old son?"

"I said, what are you doing out here? We don't get that many visitors out here."

Nope, he wasn't plumb loco, Longarm told himself. That was a British accent, and the young man it belonged to was real enough, along with his companions. None of them looked very happy to see Longarm either. In fact, they appeared to be downright suspicious. He would have been willing to bet that more than one of them was just itching to put an arrow right in his gizzard.

Under the circumstances, he figured it was better to

answer the young fella's question, even though he didn't like being surrounded and challenged like this.

"Name's Custis Long. I was invited to have dinner with Mr. and Miss Brewer at the agency."

The young warrior's stern, somewhat suspicious frown immediately turned into a warm smile of welcome. "Marshal Long! Mr. Brewer told us about you. It's an honor and a privilege to meet you, sir."

He heeled his horse forward and extended a hand to Longarm, who gripped it and shook with him.

"My name is Samuel Otter. I am the son of Falls from the Sky."

So this was the chief's boy. Longarm wondered how the young man came to have such an unusual accent, so he made a guess.

"Been away to school, haven't you?"

Samuel Otter laughed. "I suppose it's rather obvious, isn't it? Oxford actually. I suppose you're wondering how someone like me winds up at a place such as that. Come along, and I'll tell you the story while we escort you to the Indian agency."

Longarm didn't figure he really needed an escort, but outnumbered as he was, he wasn't going to argue. Samuel Otter spoke to the other young men in their own tongue, and their somewhat tense attitudes eased. Clearly, they no longer regarded Longarm as a potential threat.

Since Samuel knew that he was a deputy U.S. marshal, Longarm didn't see the need to keep his reasons for being there a secret. "You fellas figured I might be one of those owlhoots who have been raising ruckuses around here, didn't you?"

Samuel nodded as he brought his horse alongside Longarm's and they began riding toward the Indian village. "The lads and I were out hunting when those masked brigands showed up the last time. Ever since, we've been itching for a shot at them. We tried to track them, but we lost their trail up in the mountains. If you can locate them, Marshal, we'd be more than happy to pitch in and help you apprehend them."

Longarm didn't think the rest of the warriors were really interested in apprehending the outlaws who had raided their village. They looked as if something more violent and permanent was what they had in mind.

"At any rate, I promised you the story of how I came to attend Oxford, didn't I? It's quite simple really. A few years ago, my father befriended an English lord who had come over here to explore the American frontier and take part in a hunting expedition. Actually, my father saved him from a bloody buffalo stampede. Lord Ralston was very grateful and promised to repay the favor any way he could. Since my father wanted me to get a white man's education, Lord Ralston volunteered to take me back to England with him and see to it that I received the finest education possible. That was ten years ago."

"And you'd been there ever since?"

Samuel nodded. "Until a few months ago. I spoke a bit of what we called the white man's tongue when I left, but it was hardly the King's English. That's why I have this accent. I learned to speak this way, you see, and I was surrounded by nothing else for nearly a decade."

"You still speak your own folks' language, though."

"Some things one never forgets, especially those learned when one is young."

Longarm scraped a thumbnail along his jaw. "Yeah, I reckon." They rode in silence for a moment. "Is there anything you can tell me about those owlhoots we're both looking for?"

Samuel shook his head regretfully. "I wish I could. I've never laid eyes on the scoundrels."

"Any ideas why they'd raid the village like that?"

"I'm afraid not. It's not as if my people own anything that's valuable. To their way of thinking, they don't own anything except their personal belongings anyway. The earth, the water, the sky . . . all these things are merely on loan from the Creator."

Longarm nodded, well aware of the basic philosophy shared by most of the tribes. It didn't jibe with how the white men did things . . . but who was to say that it wasn't right?

"Well, I'll get to the bottom of it sooner or later. And I won't hesitate to call on you for help if I need any, Samuel."

"Splendid! There's the agency now."

They had ridden past the village and across a meadow toward a ridge. Backed up to the base of that ridge was a cluster of buildings, including a long, low structure made of logs with a shaded porch along the front of it. Cottonwood and aspen trees surrounded the agency building, the barn, and the corrals, indicating that there was a spring somewhere close by to provide water.

The door of the agency building opened as Longarm and the Indians rode up. Allen Brewer strode out, followed by his sister Eileen. Brewer raised a hand in greeting.

"Hello, Samuel. I see you've brought our visitor."

"We encountered him on the trail from Happy Valley and thought it might be a good idea to accompany him. This area isn't always safe these days."

With a solemn expression on his face, Brewer nodded agreement. "All too true." He smiled up at Longarm. "How are you, Marshal Long?"

"Fine, I reckon." Longarm swung down from the saddle. Samuel dismounted as well and said something to his companions. The others turned and rode away, headed back toward the village.

Eileen came to Longarm's side as he tied his reins to a hitching post in front of the agency building. "Samuel is going to be joining us for supper, along with his father. I hope that's all right."

Longarm nodded. "It sure is. The two of them, along with your brother, know more about what's going on around here than I do. I'll be glad for the chance to pick their brains."

The four of them went inside, where Samuel Otter's father, Falls from the Sky, was waiting. Like most of the elderly chiefs of his people, he carried himself with a simple but unmistakable dignity. Brewer introduced Longarm to the chief, who acknowledged him with a grave nod.

"You have met my son, Otter That Glides."

"Yes, I have, Chief. He seems like a fine young man."

Samuel smiled. "That's my original name, you know. I adopted the name Samuel myself, after my benefactor, Lord Ralston. That's his name as well."

The expression on the face of Falls from the Sky didn't change, but pride gleamed in his dark eyes. "My son speaks very well, like a real white man."

"Better'n most of the hombres out here." Longarm got down to business. "I'd like to talk to you about the attack on your village, Chief."

"There'll be time enough for that after we've eaten." Eileen's voice was firm. "Allen has needed a woman to take charge here, and that's what I intend to do. Supper is on the table, gentlemen."

Brewer just chuckled, as if he had already realized that there was no point in arguing with Eileen. They all moved to a long table hewn from thick planks. The aroma of roast beef was in the air, and it reminded Longarm that it had been a while since he'd eaten.

The agency building was simply but comfortably furnished, with some heavy chairs, bearskin and buffalo rugs on the floor, and several sets of moose and antelope antlers mounted on the wall above a big fireplace. There was one large main room, part of which was set aside as Brewer's office. That area was dominated by a massive rolltop desk that must have been a chore to haul out here by wagon.

Eileen must have made herself right at home in the kitchen. She had prepared an excellent meal of roast beef cooked with potatoes and wild onions, along with biscuits and gravy. Falls from the Sky seemed a little uncomfortable sitting at a white man's table and eating from real plates, but his son Samuel might as well have been sitting down to Yorkshire pudding. He was completely at ease.

"We raise the beef here on the agency," Allen said. "The army delivered a small herd of cattle to us when the agency was established. They're pastured up in the hills. Falls from the Sky and his people take care of them."

Longarm had heard of efforts similar to the one Allen Brewer described, attempts to turn Indians into cowboys. The hope was that that would work out better than past efforts to get them to embrace farming. A lot of the tribes down in New Mexico Territory were already farmers before the white man ever came, but it didn't sit right with the plains tribes. They were hunters, pure and simple. But in isolated instances, Indian agents now were persuading them to raise cattle rather than hunt buffalo. Whether it would work in the long run, nobody knew, but so far the idea seemed to be worth a try.

Longarm turned to Falls from the Sky. "Have any of those cows gone missing?"

"Rustlers, you mean?" The question came from Brewer. "No, we haven't been losing stock. Anyway, the herd's not big enough to attract thieves. It's just there to provide meat for the chief and his people."

Falls from the Sky nodded in agreement with the agent's assessment.

When the meal was over, Eileen shooed the men out of the building onto the porch. "I'll clean up. I swear, Allen, I don't know how you ever got along up here without me."

Brewer grinned. "Neither do I. Amazing, isn't it?"

Eileen was about to put on an apron. She laughed and playfully swatted him with it instead, then went back inside.

Longarm took out some cheroots and offered one to Brewer, who shook his head, as did Samuel. Falls from the Sky accepted one, though, and puffed on it as Longarm lit a lucifer and held the flame to the tip. The chief nodded solemnly when the cheroot was burning good. Longarm set fire to a gasper of his own.

It was a nice evening, or so Longarm thought until he looked to the west, where Happy Valley lay. The sun had set, but a deep red glow remained in the sky. As it washed over those big, oddly shaped rocks at the mouth of the valley, they looked for all the world like a pair of red skulls sitting there. They were even more grotesque now than they had been earlier in the day.

"My people have always called it the Valley of Skulls, you know." Samuel nodded toward the valley mouth. "We didn't always live in this area when I was a child, but we stayed here sometimes and passed through quite often. We all knew about the Valley of Skulls and knew it was a place to be avoided."

"Valley of Skulls is cursed." Falls from the Sky shook his head. "An evil place. White men should not have built their town there."

Longarm blew out a smoke ring. "It doesn't look like good farming land either."

"Not good for anything. Maybe trapping. The old one takes some pelts."

Longarm frowned. "The old one?"

Allen Brewer explained. "The chief is talking about some old codger who lives in the mountains at the far end of the valley. Like he said, the old-timer does some trapping. He takes the pelts to Casper to sell them once or twice a year."

"Has he been around these parts long?"

"I have no idea."

Falls from the Sky appeared to know the answer to Longarm's question, though. "Long time the old one lives in the mountains. Maybe longer than we have lived here."

"And he's a white man?"

Falls from the Sky nodded.

An old mountain man, more than likely, thought Longarm.

135

Some fella who had come west as a youngster and never gone home. But since it had been nearly forty years since the height of the fur trade, the hombre had to be getting pretty far along in years by now. Might even be half-crazy.

But Longarm wanted to talk to him anyway. Somebody who had been in these parts for so long might have some information that Longarm would find useful.

"This fella have a name?"

"They call him Old John." Brewer shrugged. "I have no idea whether John is his real name or not."

That was pretty common, too. A man might go through several names during a lifetime spent on the frontier, depending on what sort of trouble he got into.

Longarm nodded. "I might take a ride up there in a day or two and see if he'll talk to me. Could be he's seen something that might help me track down those owlhoots."

"I don't know what it could be. He never leaves the valley except to sell those pelts of his."

"Maybe not, but there's got to be something about the place that's attracted that gang. Maybe this Old John can give me an idea what it is."

Falls from the Sky shook his head. "Bad place. Smells bad. White men should leave."

"Some of them are thinking about it." Longarm turned to Brewer. "You've been around the settlement some. You must have heard the talk."

The agent nodded. "Yes, more and more of the settlers are getting discouraged. There's not enough business for the settlement to thrive, and the farmers are having a tough time making a go of it. I'm afraid their efforts are doomed to failure, but don't tell Mayor Decker I said that. He's a stubborn man. He's determined that Happy Valley is going to succeed. I think he was the one who sort of persuaded a lot of the people to move out here, so he feels responsible for what happens to them."

"I'd like to get my hands on the fellas who sold them that bill of goods about the valley being such fine farmland."

"So would I, Marshal. Those men were outright thieves."

They stood on the porch, smoking and talking, for a while longer until Eileen rejoined them. After a few more minutes, Falls from the Sky and Samuel Otter started back toward the Indian village, and Allen Brewer said good night and went inside.

That left Longarm and Eileen alone on the porch.

"I'm glad you came over here this evening, Custis." She placed a hand on his arm. "It was my first meal here, my first evening in my new home, and you helped to make it special." She sighed and moved closer to him, lowering her voice to a whisper. "I wish we could make it even more special, but . . ."

The way she tilted her head toward the door was eloquent. With her brother right inside, she and Longarm couldn't get up to any fancy carrying-on.

But that didn't mean he couldn't kiss her good night. He drew her into his arms and she tilted her head back, eagerly accepting his kiss. Longarm held her tightly for a moment before letting her go.

"Reckon I'd better be getting back to the settlement."

"Can you find your way in the dark?"

"I expect so. Once I've been over a trail, I don't usually have any trouble following it again."

"Well, then . . . good night, Custis. I'll see you again soon?"

He smiled. "Reckon you can count on it."

He didn't know for sure when he would be back here at the Indian agency, though. That would all depend on how his investigation played out. He had already decided that first thing in the morning he would ride to the other end of the valley and hunt up that trapper called Old John.

Even though it had been a nice, peaceful evening, as Longarm mounted up and rode back toward the settlement, his brain was still working on the problem that had brought him here. Given everything that he had been told about the outlaws, they didn't seem to be after anything in particular.

They just enjoyed scaring folks and making their lives miserable. On top of the poor conditions in Happy Valley, that was enough to make many of the settlers ready to give up and go somewhere else. The conclusion to be drawn from that was an easy one.

Those hooded varmints wanted the valley itself.

But for what? It seemed like one of the most worthless places Longarm had ever come across. You couldn't farm it. There might be enough graze to support some cattle, but it was far from prime ranch land, too. Not even the Indians wanted it. Everybody should have just left it to Old John.

Longarm frowned in the darkness as the bay jogged along toward town, heading between those big, ugly rocks. Maybe Old John was the unfriendly sort. Unfriendly enough to want everybody gone from the valley? That made sense only if he had enough money to hire a bunch of hard cases to throw a scare into the settlers, and from what Longarm had been told, that seemed unlikely.

Unless there was a lot more to Old John than met the eye.

Now *that* possibility, thought Longarm, was something worth pondering.

He might have pondered it longer if muzzle flame hadn't stabbed out of the darkness just then and sent a bullet racketing past his head.

Chapter 17

Longarm had been shot at often enough during his adventurous career that he knew to let his instincts take over. In this case, that meant leaning forward over the horse's neck to make himself a smaller target and jabbing his boot heels into the animal's flanks. The horse leaped ahead into a gallop, its hooves drumming against the road.

Several more shots blasted out, coming from both sides of the trail now. The riflemen were concealed in the smaller boulders clustered at the bases of those big, skull-like formations.

Even though quite a bit of light spilled down from the moon and stars, accurate shooting at night was a tricky proposition at best. Longarm didn't know where the bushwhackers' bullets went, but they didn't hit him or his mount, and that was all that mattered. As he left the big rocks behind, he pulled the Winchester from its sheath, slipped his feet out of the stirrups, and left the saddle in a rolling dive that carried him several yards across the ground.

In a continuation of that motion, he came up on his feet and ran into some brush a short distance off the road. As he dropped to a knee, he heard the hoofbeats of his horse as the bay continued running toward the settlement. Most horses, once they get going, will head for home, and that's just what the bay was doing.

Longarm knelt there in the brush and waited, and his patience was rewarded a few minutes later as two men emerged from the rocks and trotted along the road on foot for a short distance. They stopped not too far from the brush where Longarm was hidden and spoke to each other in low voices. Even this close, Longarm couldn't make out the words, only that the men were talking.

He didn't have to hear them clearly to know what they were talking about. The disgusted tone of their voices meant they were discussing the fact that he had gotten away, even though they'd had him trapped in a cross fire.

Longarm stepped out of the brush, leveled the rifle at the bushwhackers, and called out to them in a loud, clear voice. "Hold it right there, boys! Drop your guns and get your hands in the air!"

He didn't really expect them to do as he said, and he was right. Both men whirled toward him, bringing around the rifles they carried. They opened fire as Longarm went to one knee again and snapped the butt of the Winchester to his shoulder.

He sprayed lead toward them as fast as he could work the rifle's lever. At the same time, he felt as much as heard the wind-rip of several bullets as they passed close beside his ears.

Longarm aimed low, because he didn't want to kill the two men who had tried to ambush him. He would much prefer to knock their legs out from under them and take them prisoner so he could question them.

One of the men cried out, spun around, and dropped to the road. The other one broke to his right, firing on the run. Coolly, Longarm tracked him with the barrel of the Winchester, and was about to press the trigger when a slug suddenly hit the ground right in front of him and threw a spray of dirt and gravel into his face. Some of it went in his eyes, blinding him. He fell over backward and blinked in pain. That just made the fire in his eyes worse until tears started to flow and wash out some of the grit.

Another bullet hit close by. This one struck rock and whined off into the darkness, but not before sending some shards of stone into Longarm's face, too. They stung his cheek like pinpricks, but thankfully missed his already streaming eyes. Knowing that he had to move, he rolled back toward the brush where he had hidden a few minutes earlier. At least, he *hoped* he was rolling toward the brush and not farther out into the open, where he would be an easy target.

A third man had joined the fray. Before he was temporarily blinded, Longarm had caught sight of a muzzle flash from the corner of his eye, coming from the road between the skull-like rocks at the mouth of the valley. Either there had been a third bushwhacker, or this hombre had come along to check on the other two.

Longarm felt branches claw at his brown tweed suit, and forced himself among them, crawling on his belly until he was sure he was several yards deep in the brush. Then he stopped and listened intently.

The shooting had stopped, probably because the two would-be killers who were still on their feet had lost sight of him. He heard a low-voiced debate, but again couldn't make out the words. They were probably trying to decide whether to venture into the thicket and try to root him out of the brush. That would be a dangerous chore, and they didn't know that he couldn't see much of anything at the moment.

Longarm lay there, his heart hammering as he tried to catch his breath. He resisted the strong urge to paw at his eyes because he knew that would only make things worse. Tears continued to roll down his cheeks as he blinked furiously.

Just as his eyesight finally began to clear, he heard hoofbeats from the road. Sounded like three horses, he decided, and the noise dwindled as the men rode away. The two un-injured bushwhackers must have picked up the one he had wounded, put the man on his horse, and then all three of them had lit a shuck out of here. Their ambush had failed, so they were cutting their losses.

Longarm lay there for at least a quarter of an hour to make sure they were really gone and not trying to trick him. He didn't hear any horses or men moving around, and finally decided that it would be safe to emerge from the brush. He could see fairly well by now, although his sight was still a little blurry. In this light, it was hard to tell for sure how impaired his vision still was.

He walked to the road and saw no sign of his attackers. The wounded man was gone, just as Longarm expected. With a sigh, he looked toward the settlement and spotted the faint glow of a few lights. At least he had something to steer by, he told himself as he began trudging along the road.

As he walked, he thought about what had just happened. Had this been a random attempt on his life, a would-be robbery maybe, or had it been directed specifically at him because he was a lawman?

If it was the latter, then who knew that he carried a badge? Eileen and Allen Brewer, of course, along with Falls from the Sky and his son Samuel Otter, because all of them had just been discussing the case with him a short time earlier. But Mayor Richard Decker knew as well, and Longarm hadn't asked the mayor to keep that information to himself, so there was no way of knowing just yet who Decker might have told. It was even possible that Blind Pete or Jack Boggs might have overheard him talking to Eileen during the trip up here and guessed that he was a lawman.

What it boiled down to was at this point, Longarm didn't know who might have tried to ambush him, or even whether it was related to the assignment that had brought him to Happy Valley. It was still possible the riflemen could have been road agents trying to waylay a lone traveler. They might even be part of the gang he was after and still not know who he really was.

As he drew closer to the town, Longarm realized that something about the bushwhackers had struck him as odd, something about the way their dimly seen shapes had looked in the faint light. The problem was, he had never really gotten a good look at them before the shooting started again, and he couldn't figure out now what it was about their appearance that bothered him. His brain worried at the question for a while, like a dog stubbornly chewing on a bone, but he didn't come up with an answer, and finally put it out of his mind as he reached the settlement and went to the livery stable.

Vernon was waiting for him. "There you are. I was startin' to wonder if I ought to get up a search party and go lookin' for you, after that horse I rented you came back in by itself that way."

"The horse made it back here all right then?"

"Sure did. I got the rig off it, didn't see any sign of blood on the saddle, and figured I ought to wait a little while before I went over and told the mayor about it." The red-faced liveryman chuckled. "Get throwed, did you?"

"Something like that." Longarm knew that Vernon might spread that story and make him sound like some kind of tenderfoot, but he didn't care. He knew what had really happened.

And so did the men who had ambushed him.

Longarm walked to the hotel, noting as he did so that the town of Happy Valley practically rolled up the boardwalks at night. Most of the buildings were dark, and only one of the saloons was still open, with the faint, tinny music of a player piano drifting out into the night past the batwings. Longarm supposed that there just wasn't enough business for the other saloons to stay open this late. That was another sign that the settlement was dying on the vine.

When he reached the hotel, he found the lobby deserted. A single lamp was burning behind the desk, and it was turned down low. He went upstairs to his room, thinking that it was a damned shame he wasn't going to find Eileen waiting in his bed for him.

The match was still jammed right between the door and the jamb, low down where he had left it, telling him that no one had been in the room since he left. He unlocked the door, went in, and lit the lamp only briefly while he undressed and crawled into bed. He had hung his gun belt over the back of the room's lone chair and positioned it close beside the bed where he could reach the Colt easily in a hurry. The Winchester lay on the floor beside the bed, also in easy reach. Longarm didn't expect anybody else to try to kill him tonight, but in his line of work a fella always had to be ready for something like that.

He dozed off quickly, but his sleep was restless, haunted by dreams of giant red skulls . . .

Given the fact that there had already been one attempt on his life since his arrival in Happy Valley, Longarm wouldn't have been surprised if some no-good galoot had kicked his door in during the night and tried to blast him with a shotgun, the way Bob Caldwell had back in Cheyenne.

So it came as almost more of a shock when the rest of the night passed peacefully. He was still a mite tired when he got up the next morning, but a hearty breakfast and a couple of cups of strong black coffee at the nearby—and aptly named—Sunrise Café took care of that. The hotel didn't have a dining room, but the food at the café was good and the place was run by a nice-looking woman with just a touch of gray in her brown hair. She had a nice, friendly smile, too, and under different circumstances Longarm wouldn't have minded getting to know her better.

When he was done eating and had passed a few pleasantries with the comely proprietor, he walked along the street to the stage station, which evidently doubled as the mayor's office and town hall. Decker was there, along with four other men he introduced to Longarm as members of the unofficial town council.

"This is Roger Slidell, postmaster and owner of the general store. Ed Brady's our blacksmith, Ben Poston runs the Oasis Saloon, and Grant Vernon has the livery stable."

Longarm nodded to Vernon. "We've met already."

"We sure have." Vernon looked at Decker. "Say, Rich, this ain't the marshal you were just tellin' us about, is it?"

Decker nodded. "That's right."

Vernon grunted. Clearly, he didn't think much of a lawman who would let himself get thrown from a horse the way he believed Longarm had.

Under the circumstances, Longarm figured he'd best clear up that misconception. "The reason that horse came back by itself last night is because three rannies took some potshots at me up by those skull rocks."

Decker stared at him. "What are you talking about, Marshal?" The other men seemed equally surprised.

Longarm filled them in on what had happened the previous evening, including his visit to the Indian agency. He concluded by asking one of the questions that had cropped up the night before.

"Who did you tell that I'm a federal lawman, Mayor?"

Decker frowned at him in confusion for a moment, and then the man's round, friendly face turned darker as an angry frown creased his forehead. "What are you accusing me of, Marshal?"

"Nothing. I just want to know who you talked to about the fact that I'm here to run those owlhoots to ground."

Decker's answer was decisive. "No one. I didn't tell a soul that you're a deputy marshal until just now, when I was explaining it to these men. That's the truth, whether you believe it or not."

"Take it easy, old son. I believe you. And I'm more convinced than ever now that those three varmints were just bandits who thought they'd found some easy pickin's in one man riding alone at night."

145

That seemed to mollify Decker to a certain extent. "Well, from the sound of it, they were wrong. You said one of them was wounded?"

Longarm nodded. "I'm sure I winged one of them in the leg."

"We'll be on the lookout for a man who has an injured leg, won't we, fellas?" Decker looked around at the other men and received nods of agreement.

Slidell, the postmaster, spoke up. "I hope you can find that gang, Marshal. If we lose very many more mail pouches to stage holdups, postal officials back in Washington are liable to suspend the route. If Happy Valley loses mail delivery . . ." His voice trailed off and he shook his head in despair.

Longarm knew what Slidell meant. Losing the mail would be one more nail in the coffin of their efforts to establish a successful settlement here. Whether or not it would be the final nail, Longarm couldn't predict, but it sure wouldn't help the situation.

He looked at Decker. "Stage already pulled out this morning?"

The mayor nodded. "Yes, just a little while ago."

"Have the outlaws ever stopped the stage when it was on its way to Casper?"

"No, all the holdups took place on the return trip."

Longarm nodded. "We've got a few days then. Maybe I can get a line on those owlhoots before they have a chance to stop the stage again."

"That would be mighty fast work, Marshal."

A grin tugged at Longarm's mouth under the sweeping mustaches. "No point in wasting time, as the actress said to the bishop. Can any of you gents tell me how to find Old John's place?"

"Old John?" The question obviously took Decker by surprise, and the other men, too. "What do you want with him?"

"He's a crazy old coot!" The bluntly voiced opinion came from Grant Vernon, the liveryman.

Longarm explained. "Falls from the Sky told me about

146

him. From the sound of it, John's been around this valley longer than anyone else, maybe even the Indians. He might know something important. He might even be tied in somehow with those outlaws."

Decker shook his head. "That just doesn't seem possible to me, Marshal. He's just an eccentric old hermit who doesn't want much of anything to do with people. I think he's only been here to the settlement once since it was founded, and he didn't stay long then. In fact, he acted like he couldn't leave fast enough."

"Maybe he wants all of you out of the valley. Ever think about that?"

The townsmen traded puzzled, thoughtful glances. Obviously, that possibility hadn't ever occurred to them. Finally, Decker asked the question that all of them seemed to be thinking.

"Do you believe he could be responsible for our troubles, Marshal?"

Longarm took a cheroot from his pocket and clamped it between his teeth, leaving it unlit. "Could be. He'd have to have a good motive besides just wanting to be left alone, though. Those gun wolves wouldn't be working for him unless they thought there was a chance of a big payoff."

"I don't know what it could be . . . but I suppose anything is possible." Decker looked around at the others. "Any of you boys know how to find Old John's place?"

Ed Brady, the burly, taciturn blacksmith, spoke up for the first time. "I do. When he was here in town that one time, he had me take a look at one of his horse's shoes. He didn't talk much, but he did say that he's got a cabin all the way at the far end of the valley, just below the pass that leads out."

Longarm thought that if John was more closemouthed than the blacksmith, he must be a man of few words indeed.

"What's on the other side of that pass?"

Brady shook his head. "Don't know. Never been up that way."

Neither had any of the other men. But everything Long-arm had heard so far just increased his curiosity about the old-timer and his determination to investigate the man.

"I think I'll take a ride up there and see if I can get him to talk to me."

Decker looked concerned. "I'd be mighty careful if I was you, Marshal. Old John strikes me as a pretty unfriendly fel-low, and I've heard rumors that people who venture too close to the other end of the canyon get shot at sometimes."

"Sounds like an hombre who really values his privacy."

Decker nodded. "Maybe you're right. Maybe he values it so much that he's willing to kill to keep this valley to himself."

The same thought had crossed Longarm's mind the night before. Now, before this day was over, maybe he would find out.

Chapter 18

Matt Kincaid wasn't surprised that Blue Horse and the rest of the Cheyenne war party didn't double back to attack the wagon train again that first night. The renegades had taken a pretty good spanking, and they would probably want to lick their wounds for a while before making another try. They might not come back at all, but just continue on their bloody wandering to the northwest.

Matt had a hunch that wouldn't be the case, though. Being driven off like that would have been a blow to Blue Horse's pride. The war chief would want revenge.

During the night, the bruises Matt had suffered during his fight with Dave Lashley had darkened, and his sore muscles had stiffened up a mite. Those kinks would work themselves out, and the bruises would fade. Lashley, on the other hand, had a swollen nose and a couple of shiners that looked like they would last for a while. Matt took a certain pride in that when he caught a glimpse of the man the next morning, even though he knew he shouldn't.

He had spent a good portion of the night in Becky Hanover's wagon, making slow, sweet love to the beautiful widow several times before he slipped out of the vehicle in the hour before the sky began to turn gray with the approach of dawn. There was no way of knowing whether they would have a chance to be together again, and Matt wanted to make as much of this night as he could, for Becky's sake as well as his own.

Just before he left, she had clutched him tightly to her. "Thank you, Matt." Her voice was a soft, warm whisper in his ear. "You don't know what this night means to me."

Maybe he didn't know, but he thought he had a pretty good idea. And he hoped that it wouldn't be the last night they shared.

The cocaptains of the train, Nathaniel Peabody and Edgar Wilson, saw to it that everyone was ready to roll fairly early that morning. The sun had been up less than an hour when the wagons lurched into motion. Matt placed his men in flanking positions again, with him and Windy riding out ahead and a couple of men bringing up the rear.

Max Malone was surprised that he hadn't been assigned to ride drag again. Instead two men from Sergeant Olsen's squad, Livingston and Shaddock, were back there eating dust today. Malone was actually riding near the front of the line for a change, with the bugler, Reb McBride, beside him.

The two of them were riding near the wagon driven by the lovely blond widow, Mrs. Hanover. Malone nodded toward the vehicle and gave a lecherous chuckle. "I'll bet the lieutenant got more'n supper from her last night."

"What are you talkin' about, Malone?"

"That widow woman." Malone jerked his head toward the wagon again. "The blonde. She's the one Lieutenant Kincaid had supper with last night. I heard her invite him, after the tussle he had with that fella Lashley."

McBride didn't seem impressed. "So? She probably just wanted to thank him for stickin' up for her."

Malone cackled. "Oh, I bet he was stickin' up for her, all right. And I bet she thanked him two or three times, too."

McBride rolled his eyes and shook his head. "If the army gave a medal for bein' crude, Malone, I reckon you'd have a chestful of 'em."

"I'd rather pin somethin' on that widow woman's chest, if you know what I mean."

Malone was joking, but he felt a little resentful at the same time. Officers always got the best gals. Malone knew that a woman like Mrs. Hanover wouldn't even look at him twice, because he didn't have even a single stripe on his arm.

But there was nothing he could do about that. He wasn't cut out to be an officer. Just the thought of it made him want to shudder.

As usual, Windy Mandalian spent a lot of the day riding far out ahead of the wagon train, scouting not only for trouble but also for the best route for the heavy vehicles to follow. Dave Lashley had been guiding the train until now, but today he hung back and rode with the wagons, a sullen glare on his battered face.

Matt dropped back so that he was riding alongside Nathaniel Peabody's lead wagon. "How'd you happen to get mixed up with Lashley?"

Peabody didn't answer Matt's question directly. "I know the two of you don't get along after last night, Lieutenant, but Dave's been a big help to us. Edgar and I made his acquaintance in St. Louis, and it's a lucky thing we did. Tom Wilbanks, our wagon master, was experienced and had led several wagon trains to California, but he'd never been over this particular trail before. He accepted right away when Dave said he knew this country and offered to come with us. After Mr. Wilbanks died, I don't know what we would have done if Dave Lashley hadn't been with us."

"Uh-huh." Matt still sounded skeptical; he couldn't help it. "But you still haven't told me exactly how you met."

Peabody's tone was crisp and a little irritated. "If you must know, Edgar and I were in a tavern in St. Louis when Dave came up and started talking to us. He was just being friendly, and it was a coincidence that we had similar interests. He told us that he'd been thinking about coming west again, but he didn't want to travel alone."

"Well, that sounds like a stroke of luck for you folks, all right."

Matt didn't believe it for a second. He and Windy had discussed the situation at length, and both of them harbored suspicions about Lashley. They were convinced the so-called "government agents" who had organized this journey to Happy Valley were swindlers. Now, after hearing how conveniently Lashley had fallen in with the immigrants, Matt wondered if the man was somehow connected to those crooks. If he hadn't already been planning to keep a close eye on Lashley, he sure as hell would do it now after talking to Peabody.

By the middle of the afternoon, the rounded peaks of the Owl Creek Mountains were visible on the horizon. Excitement spread along the line of wagons, because the immigrants knew that their destination lay among those mountains.

During a brief stop to rest the oxen and mules pulling the wagons, Becky Hanover sought out Matt. "I saw the mountains up ahead." Excitement lit up her blue eyes. "Will we reach Happy Valley today?"

Matt hated to disappoint her, but he shook his head. "No, I'm afraid not. Appearances are mighty deceptive out here. Those mountains are still at least a day's travel from here."

"Oh. I was hoping we'd get there today . . ." She lowered her voice so that only he could hear. "So that we could spend tonight in a real bed."

Matt had to grin. "That'd be mighty nice, all right, but it'll just have to wait."

"Oh, well." She touched his arm lightly. "I suppose the pallet in my wagon is better than nothing. Much better actually."

Matt just smiled and nodded. He hoped that circumstances would permit him to pay another visit to Becky's wagon tonight, but he didn't want to promise anything he might not be able to deliver.

The air of excitement still permeated the camp that night. These pilgrims knew that their long journey was just about over. They built the fire inside the circle of wagons higher than usual, and several men broke out fiddles and guitars and started to play. Men and women who looked tired and careworn began to dance, and suddenly they seemed younger and livelier. Some of the immigrants sang along with the music rather than dance.

Windy Mandalian had returned to the train late in the afternoon and reported no signs of trouble ahead. He'd brought them to this spot, a nice level stretch next to a small creek, an almost perfect campground. Now the scout stood with Matt Kincaid and shook his head as he looked at the big campfire and watched and listened to the festivities.

"All this hullabaloo goin' on is enough to wake up every hostile in a hundred miles. And that fire's big enough to lead 'em right to us."

"I wouldn't worry too much about it, Windy. Blue Horse already knows the wagon train is here, and he and his men may be the only hostiles in these parts. Anyway, these folks are excited. Their journey's almost over, and it hasn't been an easy one. You can't blame them for wanting to let off a little steam."

"I reckon not." The scout didn't sound too convinced, though. "You'd better post plenty of sentries tonight anyway."

Matt nodded. "I plan to."

"And I think I'll circulate a mite."

Matt knew what Windy meant. The hawk-faced civilian would slip off in the darkness and spend the night watching over the wagons and their occupants.

"You'd better try to get a little rest, too," Matt said.

Windy grunted. "You know the old sayin' . . . plenty of time to sleep when you're dead."

The scout disappeared into the shadows, like little more than a shadow himself, and a short time later Becky sought out Matt and took hold of his hand.

"Come with me."

Matt hesitated. "The way that fire's burning, I'm not sure we can climb in your wagon without folks seeing what we're doing."

She laughed. "Are you worried about your reputation, Lieutenant?"

"Not as much as I am about yours."

She grew more serious as she moved closer to him. "I know that, and it's very sweet of you, Matt. But I wasn't intending to go to my wagon. I thought we might take a stroll down by the creek instead."

Now that sounded interesting, Matt had to admit. "Give me a few minutes. I have to speak to Sergeant Olsen and Corporal Wojensky about posting some guards tonight."

"I'll wait for you about fifty yards downstream."

He nodded. "All right. But be careful. Could be danger lurking out there."

"Then don't leave me alone for long."

Matt didn't intend to.

In fact, he was able to find Olsen and Wojensky and quickly make arrangement for guard details, so that less than five minutes had passed before Matt was moving quietly along the creek, in the shadows of the scrubby cottonwoods that lined the banks.

Worry started to gnaw at him as he looked for Becky and didn't see her. He shouldn't have let her come out here alone like this. As he had told her, dangers could lurk in the darkness—too damned many of them! Indians, wild animals, even Dave Lashley, who might have seen Becky leaving the camp and followed her along the creek . . .

He had unbuttoned the flap of his holster before setting out, and now his hand closed around the butt of the Schofield revolver as something rustled in the brush nearby. But before he could draw the gun, a figure stepped out and warm arms went around his neck. Becky laughed softly. Instinctively, Matt brought up his left arm to embrace her and felt only bare flesh.

"Good Lord! You're naked."

"That's right." She pulled his face down to hers, and their mouths found each other in the darkness.

As Matt hugged her, he realized that there was something incredibly arousing about holding a completely nude woman in his arms and kissing her while he was still fully dressed. On the other hand, his uniform suddenly seemed awfully constricting, especially the trousers . . .

Becky must have felt the same way, because she began tugging urgently at his buttons. Matt helped her, shedding his clothes as quickly as he could. They wound up lying on the creek bank, under the trees. A scanty carpet of grass grew here, and while it wasn't much, it was better than bare dirt and rocks.

Becky urged him onto his back and knelt beside him, stroking her hands up and down his erection. She leaned closer and closer to it.

"I've always wanted to try this."

He didn't have to ask her what she was talking about, because without hesitating, she opened her lips wide and took the head of his hard cock in her mouth.

Matt sighed and closed his eyes as he lay back. There wasn't much else he could do at the moment, since all the blood in his body seemed to be rushing to the long, thick organ that jutted out stiffly from his groin. Becky ran her tongue around the head and nibbled on it delicately with her teeth. Her words had seemed to indicate that she had never performed this particular act before, but if that was the case, she sure as hell had a natural-born talent for it.

He felt his sap rising. As it did, the thought crossed his mind that Windy Mandalian was out here somewhere in the darkness and might be watching them at this very moment. Maybe he should have said something to Becky about that. But on the other hand, what she didn't know wasn't going to hurt her, at least in this case, and Matt trusted Windy's discretion. Matt happened to know that the scout lived with two and sometimes three Indian women back at the village near Outpost Number Nine, and he doubted if there was any sort of mischief betwixt man and woman that Windy hadn't gotten up to at one time or another. Windy wasn't going to be shocked by anything he happened to see tonight.

If Becky truly was a novice at this, she might not realize what was about to happen. Knowing that he couldn't hold back for much longer, Matt rested a hand on her bare shoulder and forced himself to speak.

"You better be careful. It won't be much longer before I have to—"

She lifted her head and tossed it to get some of her hair that had fallen forward out of her eyes. "I know. I want to taste you, Matt Kincaid."

With that, she took him back in her mouth, swallowing even more of his length than she had before, and started sucking harder.

Matt gave a mental shrug and let himself go. His climax blasted out of him and into the hot cavern of her mouth. She swallowed as the scalding jets slid down her throat.

For a few seconds as he peaked, Matt didn't know where he was or what was going on. To him the entire world consisted of Becky's hungry mouth. But after he had emptied himself inside her, his senses came rushing back, seemingly more keen and heightened than ever.

That was when he heard the faint rustling in the brush nearby. Windy?

No. A figure moved across Matt's field of vision, momentarily blotting out the few stars he could see through the trees. He caught only a glimpse of the man, but that was enough to tell him that it wasn't Windy or one of the sentries.

This hombre wore feathers.

Shit! Blue Horse was back.

And Matt Kincaid was going to have a devil of a time defending the wagon train, naked and with his cock still in Becky Hanover's mouth!

Chapter 19

Matt sat up and put a hand on Becky's naked shoulder. He squeezed hard, causing her to lift her head in surprise from his groin. At the same time, he reached out with his other hand and clamped it over her mouth so that she couldn't make any outcry.

Not understanding the situation, she began to struggle. He leaned down and put his head next to her so that he could whisper into her ear.

"Don't make a sound. The Indians are back."

His words were nothing but a faint breath in her ear, inaudible more than a foot or two away. But she must have heard them clearly enough, because she suddenly stiffened as if in sheer terror.

Matt saw several more figures moving in the shadows about twenty yards upstream. That meant the renegades were between the wagon train and him and Becky. He hoped that either Windy or one of the sentries posted by Sergeant Olsen would detect the skulking savages and raise the alarm, but if that didn't happen, Blue Horse was going to surprise the immigrants. The musicians were still playing, the raucous strains of their tunes dancing through the night air. Those pilgrims were caught up in their celebration and weren't expecting any trouble, despite everything that had happened so far.

The fact that he and Becky were still alive told Matt that the renegades had no idea they were there on the creek bank, not far from where the war party was crossing the stream. He put his mouth next to her ear again.

"Stay here. Lie down flat on the ground and stay as still as possible."

"What are you—"

She barely started asking the question before he laid a finger on her lips to stop her. After a second she nodded, acknowledging that she would do as he'd told her.

As quietly and carefully as possible, he slid toward his clothes, which he had piled on the bank as he had been taking them off with Becky's help. He knew he didn't have time to pull all of his uniform back on, which might cause some damage to Becky's reputation, but in the long run the lives of all those settlers were more important. He slipped into the bottom half of his long underwear and, working by feel in the dark, unfastened the flap on his holster.

He drew the Schofield and stood up. Barefooted, he darted from trunk to trunk of the cottonwoods, working his way toward the Indians. His eyes were fully adjusted to the darkness, so he avoided looking at the leaping flames of the campfire inside the circle of wagons. He held his breath as he came within a few yards of a Cheyenne warrior crouched behind a tree.

Matt was confident that he hadn't made a sound that would give his presence away, but the renegade suddenly whirled toward him anyway, bringing up a rifle. The Indian must have *smelled* him.

As swift as the man's reaction was, Matt's was faster. The Schofield blasted, flame leaping from its muzzle as Matt fired. The bullet smashed into the renegade's chest and drove him backward against the tree trunk. He bounced off and pitched forward on his face without firing his weapon.

The sudden whip-crack of a rifle shot came from behind Matt, though, and splinters stung his cheek as the bullet chewed a hunk of bark from the cottonwood next to him. He was about to spin around and try to draw a bead on the man who had shot at him, when not far away a dull boom sounded. Matt recognized it as the sound of a Sharps Big Fifty.

Windy!

Knowing that the scout had taken care of the hostile who was behind him, Matt raised his voice in a shout. "Indians! Indians!" If the gunfire hadn't already alerted the immigrants and the rest of the patrol from Outpost Number Nine, that certainly did the trick. Matt dived to the ground as shots began erupting all around the circle of wagons. Inside the circle, people scrambled for cover and some of the men began returning the fire.

From his vantage point, Matt saw the sentries on this side of the wagon train withdrawing behind the vehicles. That was a smart move, because that way they could be confident that everyone *outside* the circle was an enemy . . . well, except for Matt and Becky and Windy, of course, but nobody knew they were out here.

Keeping his head low as bullets whipped through the trees above him, Matt crawled toward the creek. He wanted to make sure Becky was still all right, and reclaim his uniform if possible.

Just before he reached the place where he had left her, he heard a short, frightened cry come from her, followed by some thrashing and grunts of effort as a fight of some sort broke out. Matt lunged to his feet, heedless of the danger from stray bullets, and rammed through the brush toward Becky.

He spotted the figures swaying back and forth on the bank, locked together in a desperate struggle. One of the renegades must have started to retreat when the shooting broke out, and literally tripped over her as he fled. With that unexpected opportunity dropped in his lap, though, he was determined to take a captive with him. The fact that it was a naked white woman made the prospect that much more appealing.

With the two of them so close together like that, Matt knew he couldn't risk a shot. He dived forward instead, tackling them both and driving them off their feet. He hoped that the collision would knock Becky loose from the Indian's grip, and that was what happened as they all crashed to the ground. From the corner of his eye, he saw her roll free.

"Becky! Get out of here! Stay low!" Bullets were still flying in the darkness, so the very real danger of being struck by a wild shot remained.

Matt had a more immediate danger to worry about right now, though, in the form of a furious, bloodthirsty renegade. The sharp stench of bear grease and unwashed flesh filled Matt's nostrils as the man leaped on top of him. Acting blindly and instinctively, Matt flung his hands up, and sure enough, he caught hold of the warrior's wrist. A stray beam of moonlight winked off the blade of the knife that the renegade had just tried to plunge into Matt's throat.

Matt heaved himself up from the ground and hauled hard on his opponent's arm. The Indian toppled off to the side, and when Matt rolled, too, he wound up on top. Using both hands, he banged the renegade's knife hand against the ground in an attempt to knock the weapon out of the man's fingers.

That worked. The knife went skittering away across the ground. But at the same time Matt's head was left defenseless. The Indian's other hand balled into a fist and slammed into the side of Matt's head. The blow landed with stunning force, and for several long seconds it was all the lieutenant could do to hang on to consciousness—and to the Indian, who was struggling to get loose.

As Matt slumped forward, the renegade brought a leg

up and hooked it in front of his neck. When he straightened his leg, the wrestling move drove Matt backward. As he sprawled on the ground, Matt was thinking clearly enough to roll away, knowing that he needed to put some distance between himself and his kill-crazy enemy.

Both men scrambled to their feet at the same moment. The renegade lashed out, aiming another blow at Matt's head. Matt ducked under it, though, stepping inside and hooking a hard left into the Indian's belly. As the man started to double over, Matt threw a right cross that landed solidly on his jaw. Matt was a lot more experienced at this sort of fighting than the Cheyenne warrior was. He had been in plenty of behind-the-barracks brawls during his army career, stretching back to West Point.

The renegade stumbled backward as Matt jabbed a fist in his face. He was almost at the edge of the bank. Matt tackled him again, knocking him backward into the creek. The water rose up in a big splash around them as they landed.

The fall from the bank was about six feet. The Indian landed on the bottom, and the impact must have been enough to drive the air out of his lungs. Matt knew this was his best chance to end the fight. He reached into the water and his hands clamped around the renegade's neck, holding his head under the surface.

The next minute or so seemed to last an hour or more as the Indian bucked and heaved and fought for breath. But he couldn't dislodge Matt, whose fingers were locked in a death grip. Finally, after that seeming eternity, the man who was pinned underneath him relaxed and stopped fighting. Matt hung on for another minute just to make sure that the renegade was really dead.

When he let go and staggered to his feet, the Indian still didn't move, but just lay there submerged in the creek, which was no more than two feet deep. That was deep enough, thought Matt. Deep enough to have ended the renegade's bloodstained career of plundering and killing.

Rapid footsteps on the bank made Matt whirl around. He was unarmed, half-naked, and exhausted. But he would fight again if he had to.

"Matt?"

Relief washed through him. "Down here, Windy."

The scout appeared on the bank and looked down at him. "You all right?"

"Yeah." Matt dragged the back of a hand across his mouth. "I reckon."

Windy reached down toward him. "I'll help you climb out of there. You'd better get your uniform back on. Folks will be looking for you in a minute."

There was a note of dry amusement in the scout's voice. As Matt had thought, Windy probably knew what had been going on out here before the battle with the renegades broke out.

Matt gripped Windy's wrist and climbed up the bank from the creek. He was aware now that the shooting had stopped, but he could hear loud voices from the wagon train. "Where's Mrs. Hanover?"

"Back at the wagons. With all the commotion goin' on, she was probably able to slip back in without anybody noticin' she was gone."

Matt hoped that was the case. "Blue Horse and his men are gone?"

"Yeah, they put up a little bit of a fight, but then lit a shuck out of here when they realized their sneak attack wasn't going to work." Windy nodded toward the creek and the dead man lying there. "Unless that's Blue Horse his own self down there."

Matt grunted. "I wish we could be that lucky."

They weren't. Once they had hauled the dead renegade out of the creek and gotten a look at his face in the light of a lantern, it was obvious that he wasn't Blue Horse. The war chief's long, equinelike countenance was unmistakable to anyone who had ever gotten a good look at him.

Matt Kincaid hated to think about how Blue Horse's face had been the last thing that many unfortunate settlers had seen before they met a screaming, agonizing death.

One of the immigrants had been killed in tonight's attack on the wagon train, and a couple more had been wounded. Really, they had gotten off lightly in Matt's opinion. If the war party had managed to get closer before the alarm was given, the impromptu celebration those pilgrims had been putting on could have easily turned into a massacre.

Matt managed to catch a moment alone with Becky Hanover. "I'm sorry we got interrupted when we did."

She smiled at him and kept her voice pitched equally low. "So am I. It could have been worse, though. Those Indians could have come along a minute or two earlier."

"Yeah, but I feel like I kind of, uh, owe you something . . ."

She laughed and put a hand on his arm. "I suppose you could look at it that way. Let's say that you *do* owe me a certain favor, Matt. Why don't I collect on that debt when we get to Happy Valley?"

"That's a deal."

And it was something to look forward to as well.

Sergeant Olsen doubled the guard that night without even being told to, but the men didn't have anything to do other than be watchful. The Indians didn't come back. Matt had a feeling that they weren't through with Blue Horse, though. Having attacked the wagon train twice and having been driven away both times, the war chief was probably seething with hatred for them by now.

Blue Horse wouldn't have many more chances to strike before the wagons reached Happy Valley. The immigrants' destination was less than a day away now.

They got an early start the next morning, and Nathaniel Peabody and Edgar Wilson kept the train moving at a brisk pace. They might not be experienced Westerners, but Matt had come to realize that both of them were competent men. If their lack of seasoning didn't wind up getting them killed, they might even turn out to be good solid pioneers.

After scouting ahead of the wagon train, Windy Mandalian reported that Blue Horse's war party was still headed northwest, into the Owl Creek Mountains. "Could be they're headed for Happy Valley, too. You reckon I ought to ride ahead and warn the settlers who're already living there, Matt?"

The lieutenant thought it over and then nodded. "That might not be a bad idea. They need to be ready in case Blue Horse decides to raid them, too . . . I've been wondering about something, Windy."

"What's that?"

"You've been all over these parts, haven't you?"

The scout rubbed his grizzled jaw. "Yeah. It's been a while, though."

"You ever heard of a place called Happy Valley?"

Windy didn't hesitate. He shook his head. "I sure haven't."

"Neither have I. I don't know this part of the territory nearly as well as you do, though."

"Could be that Happy Valley is just some name those so-called government agents came up with to help rook these folks out of their money."

Matt grunted. "Those swindlers, you mean."

"Yeah." Windy frowned. "You know, there's a place up in the Owl Creeks that the Indians call the Valley of Skulls." He explained about the giant rock formations at the entrance to the valley and their bizarre appearance. "I remember seeing them once. Damned spookiest thing I ever saw. Surely *that's* not what those crooks were calling Happy Valley."

"Why not?"

"Because if it is, these pilgrims are not gonna be very happy when they get there. The place stinks."

Matt's eyebrows lifted. "It's that bad?"

"No, I mean it really stinks. Sort of like hellfire and brimstone." Windy shook his head. "And the ground's not good for farming at all. Those pilgrims will be mighty disappointed if it turns out that's where they're going."

"Well, maybe it won't be. After all the trouble they've had, they deserve to wind up in a place that ought to be called Happy Valley."

"Well, you know what they say . . . the only thing worse than not getting what you deserve in life . . . is *getting* what you deserve in life."

With that cynical comment, Windy lifted a hand in farewell and rode off ahead of the train, vanishing in the distance as he left the slow-moving vehicles behind.

Matt hoped Windy was wrong. For the sake of Becky Hanover and Nathaniel Peabody and Edgar Wilson and all the rest of the immigrants, he hoped that the place they were headed truly would turn out to be a happy valley.

And not a valley of skulls . . .

Chapter 20

After the informal meeting with the town's leaders at the stage station, Longarm walked back to the livery stable with Grant Vernon. The big lawman saddled the blaze-faced bay himself, although Vernon offered to handle the chore. The liveryman had a repeat of the warning that Decker had given Longarm, too.

"You be careful up there, Marshal. Old John ain't very friendly. He's liable to take a shot at you if he sees you coming."

Longarm smiled. "Maybe I'll see him first." He swung up into the saddle, heeled the bay into motion, and rode out of the stable.

The valley was at least five miles long. He figured it would take him about half a day to reach the other end, which would put him back in the settlement a little after dark, allowing for some time spent talking to the old-timer he was looking for.

The ride gave Longarm a chance to take a good look at the rest of the valley. He hadn't really seen any of it except the settlement so far. It didn't take him long to realize that everything he had heard about Happy Valley was true.

The stink in the air was ever-present. At some places it was worse than others, especially around hollows where black, greasy-looking mud had gathered. He had seen similar mud pits in the Yellowstone country, but these were even uglier and fouler in the stench they gave off.

The sparse grass and scrubby vegetation gave testimony to the poorness of the soil, too. The stagecoach road that led to the settlement turned into a rough trail west of there, and as Longarm followed it he passed numerous farms. The immigrants who had started those farms were working hard in the fields, but Longarm didn't see any crops that he would consider any better than pitiful. Those poor folks were doing a lot of work for not much reward. Several of the farmers stopped and leaned on their plow handles to watch him as he rode past, but not one of them raised a hand to wave. They all looked too beaten down for that.

Farther west in the valley, as the terrain grew more rugged, the farms disappeared and Longarm saw cattle grazing instead. This was the area where a few hardy souls were trying to establish ranches.

Those cows were pretty unimpressive-looking, though. Most were thin; some were gaunt and sickly.

Longarm reined in and studied one bunch of cows grazing not far off the trail. He frowned as he tugged his earlobe, then ran his thumbnail along his jawline. Those were Texas longhorns, bred to thrive on the poor graze down in the Nueces country and in West Texas. Happy Valley must really be a piss-poor place for raising cattle if those longhorns were doing this badly here, he thought.

He was still sitting his saddle, looking over the stock grazing nearby, when three men on horseback emerged from some trees and rode toward him. Longarm stayed where he was, waiting to see what was going to happen. He tensed as the men increased their pace and drew rifles from sheaths strapped to their saddles.

He didn't try to flee, though. That would just draw their fire, and besides, he hadn't done a damned thing wrong and wasn't the sort to run away from trouble anyway. He was still sitting there calmly on the bay when the three men spread out and half-surrounded him.

"What the hell are you doing here, mister?"

The harsh challenge came from the man who seemed to be the leader, a tall, sinewy cowboy with a lantern jaw and a shock of black hair under a pushed-back Stetson. He didn't aim his Winchester directly at Longarm, but he had it pointing in the lawman's general direction.

Longarm nodded toward the cattle. "Just looking over those cows, old son. They don't appear to be doing so good."

"Those cows are none of your business, unless maybe you're planning to steal them."

Longarm shook his head. "I'm no rustler."

One of the other men spoke up. "Don't take his word for it, Boss. He looks like an owlhoot to me."

Longarm thought he looked perfectly respectable in his brown tweed suit, vest, string tie, and snuff brown Stetson. He didn't take offense at the cowboy's words, though. Obviously, these fellas were a mite jumpy, and he didn't want them getting trigger-happy.

He addressed the lantern-jawed man again. "I reckon these are your cows?"

"What if they are? You still haven't told me who you are or what you're doing here."

Longarm kept his voice steady. "Well, if you'll let me reach inside my coat without blasting me out of the saddle, I'll show you."

The man thought it over, then jerked his head in a curt nod. "Don't try anything funny, though." Now his rifle *was* pointing directly at Longarm, as were the weapons carried by the other two men.

"Funny's the farthest thing from my mind right now, old son." Carefully, Longarm reached inside his coat to the pocket that held the leather folder with his badge pinned to it. His identification papers were in there, too. He took out the folder and handed it to the leader of the trio, who opened it and studied Longarm's bona fides.

After a moment, the man glanced up in surprise. "You're a deputy U.S. marshal?"

"That's what it says there." Longarm nodded toward the folder. "Mayor Decker in the settlement will vouch for me, too, and so will Allen Brewer, the Indian agent."

"Hell, boys, he's not a rustler. He's a lawman." The man lowered his rifle and handed the folder back to Longarm, who stowed it away in its usual place. "Sorry, Marshal. I reckon we're a little proddy these days."

Longarm made a guess. "Been losing stock lately?"

"Yeah. Nothing big, just a steady drain on the herd." The man's voice caught a little in frustration. "Like it wasn't gonna be hard enough already to make a go of it here in this damned valley . . ."

"Two days ago the bastards killed Ben Dooley." The harsh words came from one of the other men.

Longarm lifted his eyebrows. "One of the hands from this spread?"

"Yeah, Ben was one of my boys. I'm Dice Hargett, by the way."

Longarm shook hands with the cattleman. "What happened to Dooley?"

"He was riding the south pasture, checking on the stock there." Hargett nodded toward the southern reaches of the valley. "When he didn't come back, we went to look for him. We found him facedown with a bullet in his back, and about half as many cows down there as there was supposed to be. Reckon he must've ridden up just as the wideloopers were about to make off with another bunch."

Hargett's voice was thick with anger as he spoke, and Longarm understood how the man felt. Longarm had cowboyed enough in his younger days to know that the loyalty of men who rode for the brand usually ran both ways. Hargett was a good owner who hated to see his riders come to any harm.

"Were you able to trail the cows that disappeared?"

Hargett shook his head. "For a ways, but then the trail petered out in the mountains. The country's bad, but not so bad that you can't drive cattle over it if you're careful. There are too many stretches of rock that won't take tracks."

Longarm rubbed his jaw in thought before he went on. "No offense, Hargett, but these ain't prime beeves. Looks like if somebody wanted to set up a widelooping operation, he could find a better place for it than Happy Valley."

Hargett shrugged. "I'm an honest man. I don't know how rustlers think. And even if those cows aren't much, they're all I've got."

"You know if the other fellas who have spreads in this end of the valley have been losing stock, too?"

One of the other men answered. "The other day I saw a pard o' mine who rides for one of the other spreads. He said they'd lost fifty head in the past couple of weeks."

"Anybody killed over there?"

The cowboy shook his head. "Not that I know of, but I reckon it's just a matter of time until somebody else stumbles over those varmints and gets a bullet for his trouble, like poor Ben did."

Longarm thought that was pretty likely, too, if the rustling was as widespread as it appeared to be. He put another question to Dice Hargett.

"How come you didn't report Dooley's murder?"

"Report it to who?" Hargett shook his head. "It's not like there's any law in the settlement, just some fellas who call themselves the mayor and the town council. You're the first star packer Happy Valley's seen in, well, likely forever, Marshal."

"You gonna put a stop to the rustlin', Marshal?" The anxious question came from one of the other men.

"That's why I'm here. Is there anything else you can

tell me? Has anybody actually seen any of those cow thieves?"

Hargett shook his head. "Nobody that I know of. Ben might've seen 'em before they gunned him down, but there's no way of knowing even that. Shot from behind like that, he might not've ever known what hit him."

Longarm thought that was probably the case. He had one more question for Hargett and his men.

"You know an hombre called Old John?"

Hargett grunted. "That crazy old coot? We know enough to steer well clear of his place. He'd as soon shoot at you as look at you."

"Has he ever taken a shot at you or your men?"

Hargett hesitated while he glanced at his two companions. "Well . . . no, not that I know of. But we've heard that he's trigger-happy."

Longarm had started to wonder about Old John and whether or not the rumors concerning his dangerous nature had any basis in fact. He wished he had thought to ask Decker and the other men in town if they knew for certain of anyone who had been shot at by the old-timer.

He would soon be finding out for himself, though, so he supposed it didn't really matter.

"Can you tell me where to find his cabin?"

"Follow the trail." Hargett indicated the rough path that ran toward the end of the valley. "When it starts to climb toward the pass, you can see his cabin in the trees to the left of the trail, if you know where to look."

Longarm nodded. "I'm obliged."

"You're really going up there?"

"Thought I would. I want to have a talk with the old fella."

"Well . . . if I don't see you again . . . it was good to meet you, Marshal. Good luck."

Hargett didn't add, *You'll need it,* but Longarm heard it plain as day anyway.

* * *

As he continued riding toward the western end of the valley, Longarm thought about everything he had learned so far, trying to rearrange the facts in his head into a pattern that made sense.

He started with the stagecoach robberies. The outlaws had gotten the mail pouches and had stolen some money and valuables from the passengers, but the total take from those holdups couldn't have amounted to much. Split that loot up among a gang that numbered two dozen or so members, and each man's share would be paltry indeed.

Then there was the rustling Dice Hargett had told him about. He supposed the cow thieves would be able to sell the stolen stock—there were always shady cattle buyers to be found who didn't care all that much about brands and bills of sale and suchlike—but again, the profit would be small because the cattle were of such poor quality.

Of course, Longarm had no evidence that the rustlers were the same bunch that had pulled the stagecoach robberies, but his instincts told him they were. The explosions of lawlessness centered around Happy Valley all had to be tied together.

That brought him to the raid on the Indian village. The hooded riders hadn't stolen anything there. Falls from the Sky and his people didn't have anything worth stealing.

So what Longarm was left with was a well-organized, efficient gang of outlaws going to a lot of trouble to accomplish . . . well, nothing much to speak of. They certainly weren't getting rich off their efforts in and around Happy Valley. As far as Longarm could see, they'd just been wasting their time.

Maybe Old John would tell a different story. He probably knew more about the valley than anyone else, and Longarm wasn't discounting the possibility that the hermit was actually responsible for the trouble, for some still unknown reason.

Longarm knew he was getting close, though. He could see the rocky slopes at the end of the valley rising toward the jagged notch of the pass. The trail was visible as it meandered its way up there. Longarm reined the bay to a halt and studied the landscape in front of him.

The trees were thicker here, although they played out up above, before the trail reached the pass, which was surrounded by bare rock. Down here were clumps of aspen and juniper. More grass grew, too, and a breeze swept down from the pass that cleared some of the stink from the valley out of the air. This was actually the only halfway decent place to live in Happy Valley, Longarm decided . . . and Old John, whoever he was, had claimed the spot for himself.

Longarm had to study the trees for several minutes before he was able to make out the log cabin situated in a stand of juniper a couple of hundred yards off the trail. The structure really blended into its surroundings, and Longarm figured that was just what its owner had in mind when he built it. Longarm clucked to the bay, tugged on the reins, and rode slowly toward the cabin.

The place was small but solidly built. Longarm was willing to bet that the walls were thick. There were no windows, but he spotted some narrow openings that had to be rifle slits. The roof had sod covering it, so flaming arrows couldn't set it on fire. The closer Longarm came to the place, the more he realized that it had been built with defense in mind, too. Old John had been expecting trouble. Question was, did he have specific enemies that he feared, or was he just spooked in general?

Longarm didn't see a corral. If there was one, it had to be around back of the cabin, so he couldn't tell if there was a horse in it. Nor did he see any smoke coming from the cabin's chimney. The old hermit might not even be here, in which case the long ride up here had been for nothing.

Well, not really nothing, Longarm amended. He had run into Dice Hargett and learned about the rustling going on in Happy Valley . . . but all that had done was deepen the mystery surrounding what was going on here.

Longarm felt his muscles tensing involuntarily as he drew closer to the cabin. He was well within rifle range now. If Old John wanted to take a potshot at him, there wasn't much he could do about it except hope that the man's aim wasn't too good.

The cabin still sat silent and apparently empty when Longarm reined the bay to a halt about fifty yards from the door. He lifted his voice in a shout that echoed back from the slopes above.

"Hello, the cabin! Anybody home?"

For a second, he didn't think there was going to be any response.

Then he saw a dark cylinder shoved through one of the chinks in the wall near the door, and recognized it as the barrel of a rifle. A Sharps, from the look of it. The big bore looked like the mouth of a cannon, and Longarm figured it threw at least a .50-caliber slug.

At this range, all that would do was blow a hole as big around as a fist right through him.

It was enough to make a man proceed mighty careful-like.

"I see that Big Fifty you're pointing at me, old son. No need for that. I'm not looking for any trouble. Just want to talk to you, if you're the hombre they call Old John."

Longarm paused, weighing his options. If he announced that he was a deputy U.S. marshal and Old John really was tied in with the outlaws, maybe even their boss, that would be just asking for a bullet.

On the other hand, if the hermit was honest and had nothing to do with the owlhoots, he might be more likely to talk if he knew Longarm was a lawman.

Well, just getting out of bed in the morning was fraught with risks, Longarm told himself. He wasn't going to accomplish anything by just sitting here. He raised his voice again.

"Name's Custis Long. I'm a deputy United States marshal out of Denver, but I'm not looking to arrest anybody. I just want to talk to Old John."

The barrel of that Sharps stayed where it was, rock steady, for a long moment as the echoes of Longarm's words gradually died away.

Then it was pulled back through the rifle slit, vanishing into the cabin.

That was progress of a sort, Longarm told himself. It was usually better *not* to have guns pointing at you.

The cabin door swung open, revealing that it was thick enough to stop bullets, too. The inside of the cabin was dark. Longarm couldn't see the man who lived there, but he heard the deep, powerful voice that called out.

"Come on in, but take it slow."

The voice didn't sound like the cracked, querulous tones of the crotchety old-timer Longarm had been expecting. He rode to within about twenty feet of the opening before Old John spoke again.

"That's far enough, Marshal."

The man stepped out of the cabin then, and if his voice had been something of a surprise, his appearance was an even bigger one. Instead of the scrawny, white-bearded old pelican Longarm thought he would see, this man was tall, straight, and broad-shouldered, with a rugged, clean-shaven face. He had plenty of years on him, true enough, but he carried them well.

He carried that Sharps, too, along with a big Colt holstered on his right hip. The bone handle of what was probably a bowie knife jutted up from a fringed sheath on his left hip. He wore fringed buckskin trousers that were tucked into high-topped black boots, and a faded blue shirt. A flat-crowned black Stetson rode on iron gray hair. His piercing eyes were a bluish gray, like chips of flint or ice.

The realization that he knew who this man was hit Longarm in the gut like a fist.

Longarm wasn't the only one who'd had a moment of recognition. Old John studied him keenly for a moment, and then nodded as if making up his mind about something.

"You're the one they call Longarm, aren't you, Marshal?"

"That's right." Longarm's mind was still reeling a little from discovering who "Old John" really was. "And you . . . Good Lord, mister! You're John Fury."

Chapter 21

Windy Mandalian spotted the two big rocks when they were still a couple of miles away from him. As soon as he saw them, memories came flooding back to him. Once seen, those grotesque formations would never be truly forgotten.

He reined in his horse and sat there staring at the skull-like rocks. They lay directly in a line with the route the wagon train had been taking. The uneasy suspicions Windy had harbored earlier now appeared to be confirmed.

Unless he was missing something, that so-called "Happy Valley" those pilgrims were headed for was really the Valley of Skulls, a place so misbegotten and godforsaken that even the Indians didn't want anything to do with it.

Thinking about Indians made Windy recall that the Cheyenne renegades led by Blue Horse had swung off to the north about a mile back. At least that was what the tracks indicated. Windy had thought about following the war party, but then he'd decided to come in on this direction for a ways, just to see where the wagon train was liable to end up. Now that he knew, he was faced with a dilemma.

Should he ride back and warn them, or let them come on and discover for themselves just how badly they'd been swindled?

Windy postponed the decision by choosing to investigate a little more before he followed either of those courses of action. He heeled his mount into motion again and rode toward the giant rock formations that so eerily resembled human skulls.

When he came within sight of the Indian village, he didn't hesitate. He swung his horse in that direction.

The dogs started raising a ruckus, as dogs always did whenever any strangers approached a village. Windy rode toward the lodges deliberately, not rushing in. That gave enough time for the people who lived here to form a reception committee. Half a dozen men came out to meet him.

Windy was surprised to see that one of them was white, a man a little below medium height with a mild face, very fair skin, and brushy red hair. With him was an older man whose calm expression and dignified bearing told Windy that he was probably the chief of this band. The others were all young warriors, one of whom stepped out in front with the chief and the redheaded white man.

Windy reined in and lifted a hand in greeting. These people were Cheyenne, too, although they appeared to be much more peaceful than Blue Horse's renegades. Windy spoke in that tongue, telling them his name and that he had come in peace.

The chief surprised him a little by replying in English. "I have heard of you, Windy Mandalian. It is said that you are a friend to my people."

"As long as they're friendly toward me and my friends."

"You work for the bluecoats."

Windy inclined his head in acknowledgment of that fact.

"We have no quarrel with the bluecoats, or any other white men," said the chief. "We have made the decision to live in peace. I am Falls from the Sky." The chief nodded

179

toward the young warrior who stood next to him. "My son, Otter That Glides."

"I say, old man, it's a pleasure."

Windy's eyebrows arched in surprise at the young man's British accent. That brought a chuckle from both Otter That Glides and the redheaded man.

"I've told him he shouldn't do that, but he loves the expressions of surprise on people's faces." The redhead stepped forward and held a hand up to Windy. "I'm Allen Brewer, the Indian agent for the Happy Valley agency."

Windy reached down and shook hands with Brewer, then with Otter That Glides, who had picked up that white man's mannerism in England along with the accent.

"My apologies, Mr. Mandalian. I was educated at Oxford, you see, and when I speak English, I can't help sounding this way."

Windy grunted. "That's all right. I've run across more'n a few Britishers out here." He waved a hand toward the rock formations at the mouth of the valley. "So that's Happy Valley, eh? I was afraid of that."

Falls from the Sky looked disdainful. "My people know it as the Valley of Skulls."

"Yeah, that's the name I know it by, too. But there's a wagon train full of immigrants headed this way who are expecting to find the closest thing to paradise on earth."

Brewer frowned. "What's that? Another wagon train?"

"Yeah. It'll be here later today." Windy scratched at his chin. "There are other settlers already here?"

"A townful! Good Lord, how many victims did those swindlers rack up anyway?"

"Mind if I dismount? I want to hear about this."

Falls from the Sky gestured for Windy to get down from his horse. "You are welcome in our village, Mandalian. Come. We will smoke a pipe."

Windy felt a surge of impatience, but he suppressed it. When you needed information from Indians, the best way to get it was to go along with their customs and let them reveal things at their own speed.

Windy spent the next half hour in the lodge of Falls from the Sky, smoking a pipe and talking with the chief; Samuel Otter, as the young man wanted to be called; and the Indian agent, Allen Brewer. Nothing he heard boded well for the wagon train that Matt Kincaid and the men of Easy Company were bringing in. Quite a few immigrants had already settled down in the misnamed Happy Valley, which hadn't improved any since Windy had been in these parts some years earlier. Not only were the people from the wagon train coming to a place that wasn't anywhere nearly as good as they'd been promised, but they were also getting here late, after the best claims—or at least the ones that weren't as bad as the others—had already been taken.

There was nothing Windy could do about that, but he supposed he really should go back and warn them.

That wasn't the end of the bad news, though. His hosts also told him about the hooded outlaws who had been wreaking havoc in the area of late.

Brewer shook his head solemnly. "If I were you, I think I would advise those people to turn around and go back where they came from. They may think they're going to make their homes here, but they're going to be bitterly disappointed."

Samuel Otter nodded in agreement. "It really would be better. The Valley of Skulls is no place for decent people."

"Can't argue with that, but it's not my place to tell those folks what to do." Windy got to his feet. "Anyway, they'll be here later on today. No point in them turning back when they've come this far. They can at least take a look around."

Brewer got to his feet and brushed off the seat of his pants after sitting on the buffalo robe spread on the floor of the chief's lodge. "Of course. And if there's anything I can do to help, Mr. Mandalian, please let me know."

Windy grunted and shook his head. "Unless you can make the valley bigger and figure out some way to improve the soil, I don't know of a thing you can do." He started to leave the lodge, then thought of something and turned back. "I need to pass along a warning to you folks. A band of renegades led by a war chief called Blue Horse is in these parts. We've had trouble with them a few times already, and I don't know if they plan to stay around and get up to any mischief, or if they're still moving toward the northwest."

Falls from the Sky made a face. "Blue Horse! I have heard of him. He is said to be crazy with hatred for the white man."

Windy nodded. "That pretty much sums it up, all right, from what I've seen of him and his bunch."

"They will not bother us. We are of the same blood."

Falls from the Sky was probably right about that, but Windy couldn't be certain. It was hard to know what a kill-crazy varmint like Blue Horse would do. He was certainly capable of turning on his own people if the impulse to do so struck him.

Allen Brewer looked worried. "I'd better get back over to the agency. My sister is alone there. Just because this Blue Horse might not attack the village doesn't mean he would leave a white woman unmolested."

Windy nodded. "Yeah, I reckon that would be a good idea. Want me to come with you?"

"No, that's all right, Mr. Mandalian." Brewer smiled humorlessly. "You need to get back to that wagon train and tell those poor people what they're getting into. I don't envy you that job."

Windy sighed. "Nope. I'm not looking forward to it very much myself."

By the time Matt Kincaid spotted the scout riding back toward the wagon train, the heavy, canvas-covered vehicles had drawn within sight of what appeared to be a pair of gigantic human skulls perched on either side of an opening in a long ridge. At first, only a few of the immigrants had taken note of the eerie sight, but they had pointed it out to others, and soon the entire train was buzzing with worried talk.

Matt rode a short distance ahead of the wagons and then reined in. He took out his field glasses and lifted them to his eyes, focusing them on the skull-like formations. After a few minutes of study, he turned and trotted his horse back to Nathaniel Peabody's lead wagon.

"I reckon you've seen what's up ahead of us, Mr. Peabody."

The cocaptain of the wagon train wore a strained expression on his lean face. "Indeed I have. So has everyone else by now."

"Well, it's nothing to worry about. It's just a couple of big rocks. They've been eroded by wind and weather until they look like that."

Peabody stared at Matt. "You're saying those are *natural* formations, Lieutenant?"

"That's what they look like to me. I reckon we'll have to get closer to tell for sure."

"I was thinking we'd try to swing around them." Peabody shook his head. "I don't want to get too close to them, and I doubt if anyone else does either."

Matt frowned in thought. "You've been heading northwest, and they lay right in your route . . ."

Peabody shook his head again.

"Well, Windy ought to be back soon. Maybe he's found out something, like the trail swings one way or the other before it reaches that ridge."

Even as Matt spoke, he had his doubts. For the past mile or so, the trail followed by the wagon train had merged with another trail that showed wheel ruts, as if it had been traveled recently and fairly often. That trail pointed straight as an arrow toward the big rocks, and to Matt's experienced eyes, it looked like a stage road.

Things were getting odder and odder.

It was a few minutes later when Matt saw the rider coming toward the wagons and recognized the man as Windy Mandalian. He rode ahead to meet the scout.

Windy lifted a hand in greeting as he reined in a couple of hundred yards ahead of the wagon train. Matt kept going until he reached the spot.

Windy got right to the point. "I figured we'd better have a talk just between the two of us, Matt. I have bad news for those folks."

"They're headed for those two big rocks that look like giant skulls?"

A short bark of laughter came from the scout. "Yeah, but that's not the worst of it. Those rocks mark the entrance to Happy Valley, all right, although the Indians who live around here call it the Valley of Skulls."

Matt grimaced. "Not a very appealing name."

"It's not a very appealing place. Fact is, those pilgrims couldn't have picked a much worse place to settle."

"Damn it!" Matt smacked his right fist into his left palm. "We knew they'd gotten rooked."

Windy nodded. "Yeah, and that's still not all."

"Good Lord. What else is there?"

"Those so-called government agents who swindled these folks worked the same trick in other places back East. There are already settlers in the valley. They even have themselves a town."

Matt's eyes widened in surprise and anger. "Is there any room left for these folks?"

"Yeah, there's room." Windy shrugged. "It's a good-sized valley, a couple miles wide and five or more long. But the best places are already taken . . . not that they were any too good." The scout nodded toward the approaching wagons. "These folks will be getting the leavings, in a valley where the best places weren't much good to start with."

Matt's heart sank. "Somebody has to tell them. They deserve to know what they're getting into."

"Yeah, I feel the same way. It'll be fine with me if you're the one to do it, though."

"I suppose it's my responsibility."

Of course, it really wasn't. Matt hadn't been given any orders regarding these immigrants. He had appointed himself and his men their protectors. But even knowing that didn't make him feel like he could shirk the unpleasant task that now faced him.

"One more thing you ought to know . . ."

Matt raised his eyebrows. "Don't tell me there's something *else* wrong with Happy Valley?"

"Well . . . just a gang of masked outlaws that's been robbing and killing lately."

Matt digested that unwelcome news, then heaved a sigh. "We'll tell Peabody and Wilson and put it to them to figure out what they want to do."

He wheeled his horse and rode back to the wagons along with Windy. It didn't take long, because the wagon train had drawn closer while he and the scout were talking. As he rode up to Nathaniel Peabody's wagon, Matt held up a hand in a signal for him to stop.

Peabody hauled back on his reins, bringing his team of oxen to a halt. Behind him, everyone else in the train stopped, too. Matt sent Windy back to fetch Edgar Wilson.

Peabody looked more worried than ever. "What's wrong, Lieutenant? Is there a problem?"

"Let's wait until Windy gets back with Mr. Wilson. That way I'll only have to tell it once."

That answer didn't do anything to reassure Peabody. "See here, Lieutenant, I demand to know—"

"Here they come."

Wilson had climbed down from his wagon and was now hurrying forward, his short legs carrying his rotund figure with surprising speed. Windy followed, on foot now and leading his horse.

Wilson was a little out of breath by the time he got there. "Mr. Mandalian says . . . there's a problem, Lieutenant."

185

Matt turned in the saddle and pointed. "That's where you're headed. The Indians don't call it Happy Valley, though. They know it as the Valley of Skulls. They consider it a cursed, evil place."

Peabody looked like he was about to explode. "I don't care what a bunch of ignorant savages call it. That doesn't have anything to do with us."

"Maybe not, but the other things Windy found out have something to do with you folks." Quickly, Matt summed up Windy's discoveries. As he spoke, the expressions of disbelief on the faces of the wagon train's cocaptains turned into looks of despair and dismay.

"But . . . but that's impossible!" Wilson could barely get out the words when Matt was finished. "Those government men assured us that Happy Valley was prime land and that we would be the first settlers there!"

"They lied to you. They weren't government men, Mr. Wilson. They were thieves."

"Same thing sometimes." Windy muttered the words under his breath, but Matt heard them.

Peabody and Wilson were too upset to pay any attention to the scout's cynical comment. Peabody looked like he was torn between being sick and wanting to hit somebody. "What are we going to do?"

"The Indian agent for this area suggested that you might want to turn your wagons around and go back where you came from."

Peabody jerked his head from side to side. "Impossible! We don't have enough supplies to do that, and even if we did . . . even if . . ." The words seemed to choke him; he couldn't get any more of them out.

Wilson finished the thought for him. "Even if we did, we have no place to go back to. We sold our homes, our businesses . . . everything!" He waved a pudgy hand at the wagons. "Everything we have in the world is right here, Lieutenant. We have to go on and make the best of it."

Matt nodded. That was just about what he had expected them to say.

"All right. At least you know what the situation is now. You can tell the other folks or let them find out when they get there. That decision is up to you."

The cocaptains looked at each other for a long moment. Wilson finally broke the strained silence. "They have a right to know, Nate."

Peabody answered in a reluctant growl. "I suppose you're right. Pass the word for everybody to assemble, and we'll tell them what's going on."

Matt lifted his reins. "I'll take care of that for you. That'll give you two a chance to figure out exactly what you want to say."

He and Windy rode along the wagon train, telling all the immigrants to gather around Peabody's wagon. The puzzled pilgrims climbed down from their vehicles and began streaming forward to the head of the train.

Becky Hanover looked as worried and confused as everyone else. "What is it, Matt? Is something wrong?"

"Mr. Peabody and Mr. Wilson have something to tell everybody." Matt didn't like keeping the truth from her, but it wasn't his place to interfere.

Several members of the patrol rode up, and Private Malone put a blunt question to Matt. "What's wrong, Lieutenant?"

Matt waved toward the front of the train. "Go on up there and put a ring around those pilgrims, just in case Blue Horse comes along again. You can listen to Peabody and Wilson while you're up there."

The soldiers did as he told them. Within minutes, all the immigrants and all the men from Easy Company were gathered within earshot of Peabody's wagon. The soldiers remained mounted.

Peabody stood up on the wagon seat, lifted his arms, and called for quiet. When the puzzled hubbub of the crowd died down, he began telling them what Windy had found out about their destination. A surprised, unhappy clamor rose immediately, and it didn't subside no matter how loudly Peabody and Wilson shouted for the immigrants to settle down.

Matt finally had to raise his voice in a tone of command that cut through the commotion. He rode forward, the crowd parting to let him through. When he reached the wagon, he turned his mount so that he was facing the immigrants.

"Mr. Peabody and Mr. Wilson have told you what you're facing! What you have to decide now is whether you're going ahead or turning back!"

"We *can't* turn back!" The cry from one of the men was almost a wail. "I got nothin' to go back to!"

Shouts of agreement came from just about everybody in the crowd.

Peabody waved his arms for quiet. "We'll put it to a vote, just like we have with everything else! Who wants to turn back?"

No one responded.

"Then you all want to go ahead?"

"It ain't that we want to, Nate." That comment came from one of the other men. "We *got* to."

More shouts of agreement with that sentiment sounded.

"I reckon it's settled." Peabody turned to Matt. "We're going to Happy Valley, Lieutenant."

Matt nodded. "Let's get the wagons rolling then. You'll be there in another hour or two."

Chapter 22

Longarm had never met the man called John Fury, but Fury had been pointed out to him once in a Santa Fe saloon some years earlier. Fury had already been old at the time, but then, as now, he carried himself like a younger man.

Twenty-five years earlier, there had been no better known frontiersman than John Fury. He had guided wagon trains across the plains, rescued captives from Indians down in Texas, helped steamboats navigate the Missouri River, and mined for gold in California. He had a reputation as a gunman, yet he had never been known to go out of his way to look for trouble. It seemed to find him naturally.

After being badly wounded in a shoot-out in a ghost town in Nevada, Fury had dropped out of sight for a while. There were rumors that he'd died, but more than likely he'd just been holed up somewhere his enemies couldn't find him, recuperating from his injuries.

When he turned up again, he had two companions with him, a cantankerous old pelican who called himself Cougar Jack, and an Arapaho shaman named Snow Eagle. They had traveled together for a while, not surprisingly getting into a few scrapes here and there, but Fury was a loner at heart and eventually, after a visit to a settlement down in Colorado that was named after him by the pilgrims he'd led there some years earlier, John Fury had ridden on by himself. Not long after, Longarm had seen him in Santa Fe, Fury vanished again, and most folks seemed to think that the odds had finally caught up to him, that he had met a violent end at last . . .

Clearly that wasn't the case, because the man himself stood there right in front of Longarm, glaring at him.

"What is it you want with me, Marshal? I'm not wanted anywhere as far as I know."

Longarm shook his head. "That ain't it." Any thought that "Old John" might be mixed up with the outlaws who'd been raising hell around here had vanished from Longarm's brain. John Fury had always been on the side of law and order. He had even worn a sheriff's badge a time or two, although he'd never made a career out of being a lawman.

"Well, what is it then?" Fury didn't bother to keep a tone of impatience from edging into his voice.

"I've been sent up here to corral a bunch of varmints who've been holding up stagecoaches, rustling cattle, and terrorizing the Indians who live just outside the valley. I was told that a fella called Old John lived up here, and that he'd been in these parts maybe longer than even the Indians."

"So you came here thinking that I might give you a hand tracking down those outlaws?" A shrewd expression appeared on Fury's weathered face. "Or did you think I might be in cahoots with them, Marshal?"

Longarm shrugged. "No offense, but the thought crossed my mind. Didn't know who you were then."

"But you don't think so now, is that it?"

"I never heard any talk about John Fury siding with owlhoots."

Fury tucked the Sharps under his left arm. "I reckon that's true." He chuckled, but didn't sound particularly amused. "The folks in that settlement call me Old John, do they?"

"They're mostly pilgrims from back East. They don't have the faintest notion who you really are."

"That's the way I want it."

"You think there are still some fellas who might be holding a grudge against you? Might want to look you up and try to settle some old scores?"

"I know I'm getting a mite long in the tooth, but I'm not so ancient that everybody I ever knew has gone under, Marshal."

Longarm shook his head. "That ain't what I'm saying. I can understand why, if you found a nice peaceful place like this, you'd want to keep quiet about who you really are. I've made a few enemies myself."

Fury grunted. "I'll just bet you have. I've heard stories about *you*, too, Marshal."

Longarm was beginning to get impatient. "I didn't come up here to stand around jawing about the past. What can you tell me about those masked owlhoots I'm trying to track down?"

"Not a damned thing."

"I know you don't have anything to do with them, but you might have seen something—"

"Sorry. I never laid eyes on them. I can't help you, Marshal."

Longarm frowned. "Hear me out. Even if you haven't ever seen that bunch, you must know this valley as well or better than anybody else. Maybe you can tell me where they might be hiding out."

"Not in the Valley of Skulls." Fury sounded a hundred percent certain of that. "Those damn fool settlers have spread out all over the valley. If that gang you're talking about had a hideout anywhere around here, somebody would have stumbled across it by now."

Longarm glanced up the trail at the pass above them. "What about on the other side of that pass?"

"You ever been over there?"

Longarm shook his head. "Nope."

"I didn't think so. That's mighty rugged country on the other side of that pass. Rocky breaks with no water or grass for miles. There's no fitting place for a gang to hole up, and even if there was, they couldn't get into the valley, or out the other end, without coming by here. I'd have seen them if they were doing that—and I haven't."

"Maybe you just missed them."

Even as he said it, Longarm didn't believe it. John Fury would have had to be dead to miss two or three dozen owlhoots riding past his place.

Fury didn't dignify the suggestion with a direct answer. "I've told you all I can tell you, Marshal, which is nothing. Anything else I can do for you?"

Longarm turned to indicate the valley with a sweeping gesture. "Tell me about this place."

"What's to tell? The air stinks, the water doesn't taste very good, and the ground's not good for raising crops or cattle. Those people who came here thinking they were going someplace worth living in made the worst mistake of their lives."

"But *you're* here."

"This is the only place in the valley that's halfway decent. When I found it, I knew I'd be left alone here. The Indians avoid it because those big ugly rocks at the other end of the valley and the stink make them think it's cursed and full of evil spirits. I never dreamed anybody would be crazy enough to try to settle here and even start a blasted town."

"Those folks got swindled. Some fellas who claimed to be government men convinced them to homestead here . . . for a fee."

Fury shook his head. "Like I said, damn fools."

That angered Longarm, even though he had thought the same thing about the inhabitants of Happy Valley. "They just wanted to make life better for themselves and their families.

You can't blame folks for that. The way I heard it, you guided more than a few wagon trains out to the frontier yourself."

After a moment, Fury nodded. "That's true enough. I reckon Decker and the others aren't really to blame for the fix they find themselves in . . . but there's nothing I can do to help them either, and whether they make it or not is their own lookout."

"They'll stand a lot better chance if I can run those outlaws to ground. And you can help me with that, Fury."

Without hesitation, the old frontiersman shook his head. "Sorry, Marshal. These days, I mind my own business and don't stick my nose in where it isn't wanted. And any time I forget about that, I've got a heap of scars to remind me of the times when I didn't follow my own advice."

"That don't sound like the John Fury I've heard all those stories about."

Fury's expression hardened, and he shifted the Sharps so that he was holding it in both hands again. "It's not my problem what stories people tell or don't tell about me. And it's not my problem what happens to those settlers either. I was doing just fine here in this valley by myself before they showed up."

"I can't change your mind?"

Fury shook his head. "Sorry, Long."

"Yeah, so am I. But this won't stop me from going after those owlhoots on my own."

"And I wish you luck with that."

Inhospitable cuss, thought Longarm as he mounted up and rode back to the trail. Fury hadn't even invited him in for a cup of coffee or something to eat. Out here in the West, folks almost always did, even if they were your worst enemy.

The biggest disappointment, though, was Fury's refusal to help him run those masked varmints to ground. The trip up here had been almost for nothing. The only thing Longarm had gotten out of it was that he could eliminate "Old John" as an associate of the outlaws—or even their leader.

When he reached the trail, he turned left toward the pass, rather than right toward the rest of the valley and the settlement. It wasn't that he didn't believe Fury about the country on the other side of the pass; he just wanted to see it for himself.

Fury was right, Longarm admitted when he rode through the pass and reined in to look out over miles and miles of rugged badlands. Everything was gray and brown and tan as far as the eye could see, without even a single spot of color to mark any vegetation. A hideout had to have water and grass. Obviously, neither of those things were to be found anywhere close in this direction.

Longarm saw no need to venture into the breaks. He was convinced that wherever the outlaws were hiding between jobs, it wasn't here. He turned the bay and rode back down the trail into the valley, past John Fury's cabin, and on toward the settlement.

He cast a glance in the direction of the cabin as he passed by. John Fury sure hadn't lived up to the stories Longarm had heard about him. But he supposed anybody could get old and tired and just want to be left alone . . .

This time he didn't see any punchers from the cattle spreads in this end of the valley as he followed the trail. It was late afternoon, and the sun was lowering toward the mountains behind him. But in its slanting rays he saw something else that caught his eye.

Dust was rising in the distance, coming from the direction of the settlement. At first, Longarm thought it was smoke and worry shot through him, worry that the town might be on fire, but then he realized that the cloud wasn't dark enough for that. It was dust, all right, thin and hazy, but enough to tell him that it came from quite a few hooves.

The bay was tired, but Longarm had no choice but to push the horse to a faster pace. A sense of urgency was growing inside him. He wanted to get back to the settlement and find out what was going on.

By the time Longarm reached the western edge of town,

the sun was almost down and the dust that had been hanging in the air was gone, dispersed by the foul-smelling breeze. He saw right away what had been causing it earlier, though.

More than a dozen canvas-covered immigrant wagons were parked in the street. Teams of oxen or mules were still hitched to the wagons, so they hadn't been here long. The area around the wagons was crowded with people, including a bunch of men wearing the blue uniforms and black campaign caps of the United States Army.

Longarm could tell by the uniforms that the soldiers were mounted infantry, not cavalry. Some folks didn't think there was any difference, but he had worked with the army enough to know that there was. These men might ride to a battle, but they would get off their horses to fight it. Such outfits lacked the dash and glamour of the cavalry, but they were in large part responsible for extending civilization as far westward across the country as it had reached.

The townspeople of Happy Valley had turned out to welcome the newcomers, probably with mixed emotions. They would be glad to see new faces and grateful for the break in the monotony of day-to-day frontier life, but they wouldn't be happy to see even more victims of those land swindlers showing up to make the valley that much more crowded.

Longarm knew without even thinking about it that these folks must have fallen prey to the same crooks who had lured Decker and all the other settlers out here after taking their hard-earned money. That was the only reason for a whole wagon train full of pilgrims showing up this way.

Longarm brought his horse to a stop near a group of the soldiers and hailed them. "Where's your commanding officer?"

A couple of the men came over to him. One was extremely tall and gangling; the other was a muscular Irishman with the look of a brawler about him. He was the one who responded to Longarm's question.

"What business is it o' yours, mister?"

Longarm felt a surge of irritation but reined in his temper. "I need to talk to him, Private, and the badge and bona fides of a deputy United States marshal that I carry make it my business."

The soldier looked a little abashed, but not much. He jerked a thumb toward the stage station. "The lieutenant's in there talkin' to some fella who claims he's the mayor."

"Who's in charge of this wagon train?"

"There are a couple of captains, name of Peabody and Wilson. They're in there, too."

Longarm nodded. "I'm obliged." He gave in to a moment of curiosity. "Where are you fellas from? What post, I mean?"

The tall drink of water answered this time. "Outpost Number Nine, south of here a good ways."

Longarm had heard of the place. He dredged the name of its commanding officer out of his memory. "Captain Conway still running things there?"

"That's right, sir." The towering soldier grinned. "You know the captain, sir?"

Longarm shook his head. "Never had the pleasure. But I traded telegrams with him once on some matter, I think. Been so long, I sort of disremember. What's your lieutenant's name?"

"Kincaid, sir. Lieutenant Matt Kincaid."

The Irishman made a disgusted sound in his throat. "Don't go tellin' this lawdog anything else, Dobbsy. We don't have to answer to him."

Longarm fixed the man with a hard stare. "You got something against lawmen, Private?"

"No, but I've been thrown in the hoosegow enough times I don't have any special fondness for star packers neither." The man turned away. "Come on, Dobbs."

The tall soldier lifted a hand in farewell. "So long, Marshal."

Longarm rode over to the stage station. Along the way,

he passed a wagon with a very pretty young blond woman still sitting on the driver's seat. She looked tired and worn— all the immigrants did, so he knew they must have been on the trail for quite a while—but she summoned up a polite smile as Longarm nodded to her and tugged on the brim of his flat-crowned hat. The smile made her even prettier.

Then he forgot about the blonde, because he had reached the stage station and heard loud, angry voices coming from inside it as he reined in and swung down from the saddle. He looped the bay's reins around the hitch rack and started inside, anxious to talk to Lieutenant Matt Kincaid and find out if his hunch about what this wagon train full of immigrants was doing in Happy Valley was right.

Chapter 23

The main room of the stage station was crowded. There were Mayor Decker and several members of the informal town council, including the stable man, Grant Vernon. The blue-uniformed Lieutenant Kincaid was there along with a couple of men from the wagon train and a stocky, buckskin-clad man with a hawklike face and skin weathered to the same shade as Longarm's, which was the color of old saddle leather.

The two men from the wagon train—Peabody and Wilson, Longarm recalled—were trading harsh words with Decker, Vernon, and the other townsmen. Kincaid looked frustrated and irritated, but he was keeping his mouth shut for the moment. The hombre in buckskins just stood there watching the fracas with a tolerant, faintly amused smile on his lips.

"Why didn't you let us know you were coming?" Decker put the question to Peabody and Wilson. "We would have told you that the valley has already been settled."

The taller of the two men from the wagon train looked like he was about to explode. "How could we tell you anything? We didn't know you were here! Those government agents told us we'd be the first settlers in Happy Valley!"

"Those so-called government agents were thieves! They swindled you just like they swindled us!"

Lieutenant Kincaid held up his hands and stepped between the men. "Take it easy, Mr. Peabody." He turned his head to look at Decker. "You, too, mister. Shouting at each other isn't going to solve anything."

Decker got even huffier. "You don't have any authority here, Lieutenant."

"Actually, I do, sir." Kincaid's voice hardened. "I have the authority of the United States Army behind me."

"But . . . but we're civilians!"

"Not if I place this valley under martial law."

Longarm thought things had gone far enough down that trail. He stepped forward. "Hold on a minute, Lieutenant. The governor of the territory can declare martial law. I ain't sure you got the right to do that."

Kincaid swung around to face him. "Who're you?"

"Custis Long. Deputy U.S. marshal out of Denver."

The name must have struck a chord of memory in the buckskin-clad man. "You're the one they call Longarm. I've heard of you."

Longarm shrugged. He couldn't control what people had heard about him.

Kincaid looked at Longarm and nodded. "I've heard of you, too, Long. You're supposed to be quite a lawman. Are you taking the side of these people?" He jerked his head toward Decker and the other townsmen.

"I'm not taking anybody's side. I'm just saying that if you try to run roughshod over these folks, you'll be stepping over the line, Lieutenant. And I'll have to stop you."

Kincaid frowned. "I've got two squads of mounted infantry out there."

"Don't make any difference. My job is still my job."

The man in buckskins moved forward. "Take it easy, Matt. You and Long here just got off on the wrong foot, that's all."

He held out a hand to Longarm. "I'm Windy Mandalian, head scout for Easy Company. We're up here chasing a war party of renegade Cheyenne led by Blue Horse."

"Hostiles?" The half-groan came from Decker. "What other problems are going to descend on us?"

Longarm hesitated for a second, then shook Mandalian's hand. He could tell by looking at him that the scout was an experienced frontiersman, much like John Fury. Longarm figured he might be able to talk to Mandalian easier than he could to that stiff-necked first lieutenant.

The scout wasn't finished. "Maybe we should all sit down and talk about this calmly."

Decker shook his head. "There's nothing to talk about. We were here first. The valley is ours."

"It's big enough for everybody!" That angry claim came from Peabody.

"Have you seen how poor the soil is? Have you smelled the air?"

Peabody was insistent. "We can make a go of it. We have to."

Decker stared across the desk at him. "That's what we thought, too . . ." With a sigh, he sat down and settled back in his chair. "That's what we thought."

The look of defeat that washed over Decker helped to defuse some of Peabody's anger. The tall, lean immigrant frowned. "You're saying that it's been hard here for you?"

Decker nodded. "You can see for yourself what the valley is like. The smart thing to do would have been to turn around and go home. But we didn't have homes to go to anymore."

"Neither do we." That bleak statement came from Wilson.

Some of the tension had gone out of the air as each group realized the problems that the other faced. Longarm jerked a thumb over his shoulder and made a suggestion to Kincaid. "Why don't we go outside and talk this over, Lieutenant? That way these folks can get to know each other better."

"Well . . ." Kincaid finally nodded. "All right."

The two of them stepped out onto the boardwalk in front of the stage station, followed by Windy Mandalian. The street was still crowded with a mixture of newly arrived immigrants, the settlers who already lived in Happy Valley, and the soldiers who had come into town with the wagon train. Longarm spotted a sergeant and a corporal who were trying to keep the men in blue grouped together, but the noncoms weren't having an easy time of it. The soldiers had been on the trail for a while, and the lure of the saloons was strong.

Mandalian had taken note of the same thing. "You'll have to let the men blow off some steam, Matt, or you're liable to have a riot on your hands."

Kincaid wore a grim expression on his face as he nodded. "You're right." He raised his voice. "Olsen! Wojensky!"

The two noncoms came over.

"Split the squads up into smaller groups and let a few of them at a time go over to the saloon." Kincaid indicated the Oasis. "I don't want them getting drunk or going off whoring, though."

The sergeant nodded, but the corporal looked dubious. "That's liable to be a tall order, Lieutenant, especially where some of the men are concerned."

"Then impress it even more strongly on Malone, Wojensky." Kincaid obviously knew where trouble was likely to crop up among his men.

Corporal Wojensky nodded glumly and went to carry out Kincaid's orders.

The lieutenant turned to Longarm again. "I take it you're here on an assignment, Marshal?"

Longarm nodded. "There's a gang of owlhoots that's been making life miserable for these folks lately. I've been sent to put a stop to it."

Mandalian spoke up again. "I told you about that, Matt. The Indian agent explained all of it to me when I was at the agency earlier."

That interested Longarm. "You've met Brewer?"

"Yeah, and Falls from the Sky and that son of his who talks like an Englishman, too." Mandalian rubbed his heavy jaw. "I don't know everything that's been goin' on around here, Marshal, but I don't see why a bunch of outlaws would come after these folks. They don't hardly have anything worth stealing as far as I can see."

Mandalian had quickly grasped the same thing that had been troubling Longarm. He sensed a kindred spirit in the rough-hewn scout.

"Why don't we go over to the Oasis ourselves and have a palaver about the things that brung us here? Maybe we can help each other out."

Kincaid looked like he doubted that, but after a moment he nodded. "All right, Marshal. We'll leave these people to try to work things out among themselves." He managed to summon up a chuckle. "I suppose such things aren't really our business anyway. We each have other concerns."

The three of them walked across the street to the saloon. Several of the soldiers were there already, having practically stampeded to the Oasis as soon as Kincaid's orders were carried out. The Irishman and his tall friend were among them, standing at the bar with a burly blond soldier who didn't seem to speak much English. When Longarm heard the man's Prussian accent, he was reminded of Wilhelm Schott, the scientist who had shared the stagecoach with him and Eileen. He hadn't seen anything of Schott for a while and wondered what had happened to the man.

There were more pressing matters to be dealt with, though. Longarm signaled for the bartender to send beers over to the table where he, Kincaid, and Mandalian sat down.

Once a nice-looking gal in a tight green dress had delivered the drinks, Longarm took a sip of his beer and sighed. "I don't suppose you fellas spotted any sign of those owlhoots I've been looking for, while you were escorting that wagon train?"

202

Kincaid shook his head. "No, we didn't encounter any outlaws. You haven't seen Blue Horse and his renegades?"

"Nary a sign of hostiles."

"They're out there." Windy Mandalian took a drink from his mug and nodded. "We've tangled with them several times, and I followed the war party's trail to within a couple of miles of the valley before it swung off to the north."

"Maybe they kept going."

"Yeah, we thought about that. I'll have a look tomorrow, see if I can follow the tracks. Blue Horse hasn't been trying to hide them so far." Mandalian frowned. "Sooner or later, though, he's gonna try something tricky, and I've got a hunch that's just about due."

Longarm shook his head. "The last thing these folks need here in Happy Valley is Indian trouble. Don't seem likely it'll happen, though, since the whole valley is considered cursed. Falls from the Sky and his people won't set foot in it."

"That whole Valley of Skulls business, eh?" The scout nodded. "I've heard about it, too. No offense, Marshal, but Blue Horse and his bunch of killers are different from some tame Indians who are trying to keep the peace. If there's something in here Blue Horse wants, he'll go after it."

"I've heard of the varmint, but I reckon you know him better than I do."

Kincaid grunted. "We know him all too well. We've buried three men because of him since we left Outpost Number Nine."

"If I see or hear anything about him, Lieutenant, I'll let you know as soon as I can."

Kincaid nodded his thanks. "And we'll do likewise if we run across any information about those outlaws you're after."

With their initial friction put behind them and a truce declared, Longarm enjoyed talking to Kincaid and Mandalian. The lieutenant was still a mite stiff-necked for Longarm's taste, but overall he wasn't a bad sort, the big lawman decided. And Mandalian was a tough, savvy veteran of the frontier, the sort of hombre that Longarm would ride the river with any day.

He was about to bring up John Fury and ask the scout if he'd ever crossed trails with Fury, when a loud commotion broke out at the bar. The Irishman Longarm had spoken to earlier had gotten into some sort of argument with one of the locals, and it looked like punches were about to be thrown at any moment.

Kincaid uttered a frustrated curse. "Malone . . . !" Clearly, the Irishman had a history of getting into ruckuses like this. Kincaid came to his feet and raised his voice. "Private Malone!"

At the bar, Malone turned a belligerent glare toward the lieutenant. "What?"

Kincaid stalked toward him. "I'm going to ignore your insubordinate tone of voice *this* time, Private, but get on out of here right now." Kincaid jerked a thumb at the batwinged entrance. "Dobbs, Holzer, you go with him and make sure he stays out of trouble."

"Aw, Lieutenant." The protest came from the towering Dobbs. "That ain't fair. We barely had a chance to wet our whistle—"

"You've had at least three beers just since I've been in here, Private. That'll have to be enough."

Still glowering, Malone allowed Dobbs and the big German to escort him out of the saloon. When Kincaid returned to the table, Mandalian chuckled. "What was the argument about?"

"I didn't even ask. With Malone, does it really matter?"

Longarm smiled. "Fella's got a habit of getting into trouble, does he?"

"If there's a record in the army for being promoted to corporal and then busted back down to private, Max Malone must hold it. I'm sure he would have been thrown out completely by now if it wasn't for one thing."

"What's that?"

Kincaid laughed. "He's a damned good man in a fight. But if you tell him that, Windy, I'll deny I ever said it."

Mandalian shook his head. "Malone and I ain't what you'd call close friends, Matt."

The three men spent a few more minutes talking, but Longarm didn't think to bring up his visit to John Fury. Kincaid made it clear that he expected the citizens of Happy Valley to give the new immigrants a fair shake.

"They were victimized just like the original settlers were. And they can't go back any more than Decker and his friends could. They deserve a chance to make new lives for themselves."

Longarm was equally adamant. "Not at the expense of crowding out the folks who are already here."

This time Kincaid didn't argue. "You're right, of course. Peabody and Wilson and their people will have to take whatever land is left, no matter how good or bad it is."

"It's bad." Mandalian's voice was flat and hard as he interjected that comment.

Longarm agreed. "The odds are against everybody in the valley. But I want to see to it that they have a fighting chance. That's what I was sent here to do by busting up that gang of owlhoots."

"That's a mighty big job for one man."

Longarm shrugged. "Not the first time I've had the odds against me."

"If there's anything we can do to help while we're here, Marshal, don't hesitate to call on us. But our mission is to track down Blue Horse, so we may not be around for very long."

"Well, good luck in that, old son." Longarm stood up and stretched. "Been a long day. I'm gonna tend to my horse and then see about getting on the outside of a hot meal. See you fellas later maybe."

He strolled out of the saloon, picked up the bay from the hitch rack where he'd left it, and headed for the livery stable.

He felt a little guilty for not seeing to the horse's needs earlier. The unexpected arrival of the wagon train and the soldiers had thrown him for a loop.

Vernon was back at the stable when Longarm led the bay in. "Did Mayor Decker get anything worked out with those pilgrims?" Longarm asked.

The liveryman's heavy shoulders rose and fell in a shrug. "They're going to camp right outside of town for the time being, while they look over the valley and see if they can find some empty land for farms. Even if they do, they're not gonna be able to grow much." Vernon shook his head. "Poor bastards. Poor dumb bastards." He laughed humorlessly. "Same as us."

When the bay had been unsaddled, rubbed down, grained, and watered, Longarm left the horse in its stall and headed for the hotel. He was tempted to go straight to the café and get something to eat, but after all the riding he had done today he was covered with trail dust. He decided to wash up a mite before he ate.

The tiny piece of matchstick lay on the floor in front of the door to his room. It had fallen from its place between the door and the jamb. As soon as Longarm spotted that, his hand moved to the butt of the Colt in the cross-draw rig on his left hip.

But before he could draw the gun, the door swung open and a familiar voice greeted him. "I thought I heard someone out here, and I was hoping it was you, Custis."

He was looking into the smiling face of Eileen Brewer.

Chapter 24

Longarm was glad to see her, but he was also surprised. "How'd you get in here?"

Eileen laughed. "The clerk downstairs was willing to let me in when I told him that you and I were old friends. Also, I told him that Allen is my brother, so I guess he thought I was trustworthy." She moved back from the doorway. "Aren't you coming in?"

Longarm stepped into the room, and Eileen closed the door behind him. The next second, as soon as he turned toward her, she was in his arms, her mouth desperately seeking his.

They stood there kissing for a long moment. Her body was molded to his, and he felt the soft mounds of her breasts flattened against his chest. He felt the hard buds of her nipples as well.

When Eileen finally broke the hot, searching kiss, she was breathless. "Oh, Custis, I . . . I've been wanting that so bad. Wanting you. Needing you. I was beginning to wonder if I was ever going to have a chance to be alone with you again."

Longarm chuckled. "That's always good to hear, but it hasn't been *that* awful long, has it?"

"Long enough so I thought I'd die!" She started tugging at his clothes. "Come on. Let's get to bed."

"Well, I haven't had supper yet, and I'm a mite dirty from riding around the valley today . . ."

She stared at him as if she couldn't believe he was reluctant to make love to her. Then her expression cleared and she laughed.

"You're just having a little fun at the expense of a poor, lovelorn woman, aren't you?"

"Oh, now, I wouldn't say—"

She didn't let him go on. "Fine. If that's the way you want it, come over here to the table. I'll wash you."

She grabbed his hand and tugged him over to a small table that had a basin of water on it along with a cloth. Longarm played along with her, allowing her to strip off his coat, vest, and shirt. He wasn't wearing any long underwear on top, so his chest was bare. Eileen dipped the cloth in the water and then swabbed it across his broad, muscular chest, which was matted with dark brown hair. She paid particular attention to his nipples.

After a moment, she set the cloth aside. Her hands went to the buckle of his gun belt and unfastened it. She coiled the belt around the holster and placed it on the table next to the basin, then reached for the buttons of his trousers.

"Going to get you nice and clean."

The softly murmured words gave Longarm a pretty good idea what she intended to do. She lowered his trousers and then pulled his long underwear down after them. That freed his manhood, which by now was hard enough to spring up and jut outward from his groin as soon as it escaped from the tight confines of the garments.

Eileen picked up the washcloth again and stroked Longarm's hard cock with it. The soft, teasing touch sent a throb through his long, thick shaft. Eileen knelt in front of him and continued washing him. She wrapped the cloth all the way around his organ and used both hands to slide it up and down.

Longarm closed his eyes and clenched his jaw as waves of pleasure coursed through him. His cock was like a bar of iron by now. His heart slugged in his chest and a pulse pounded inside his skull as he felt the warmth of Eileen's breath on the highly sensitive flesh.

"Now I have to make sure you're really clean." Her tongue circled the head in a searing oral caress.

Longarm fought down the impulse to thrust forward with his hips as her lips closed around him. As she began to suck him, she moved the damp cloth to his balls and used it to cup and massage the heavy sacs and stroke between his legs. Her mouth opened wider so that she could engulf more and more of him.

Just when she had brought him to the verge of eruption, she pulled back, letting go of him. As she stood up, he saw that her face was flushed and her breasts were rising and falling rapidly under her dress. She was clearly as aroused as he was. She yanked up her dress and petticoats and spread her legs wide as she fell back onto the bed, revealing that she had already removed her other undergarments before he reached the hotel room.

"Oh, God, Custis, put it in me! Put it in me now!"

Normally, Longarm liked to oblige a lady in everything she asked of him. But in this particular instance, he figured he might feel guilty, considering what she had just done for him, if he didn't return the favor. So he moved to the edge of the bed, knelt beside it, and lowered his head between her open thighs.

Eileen's hips jerked and a muffled cry came from her lips as Longarm used his thumbs to spread the folds of her sex and speared his tongue between them. She was already wet, but she grew even more so as he ran his tongue from one end of her opening to the other. He lingered at the top of it, teasing the little nubbin of flesh he found there. Eileen trembled as he skillfully worked her passion higher and higher, all the way to a fever pitch.

Then and only then did he move so that he was poised over her with the head of his shaft at her drenched gateway. With a powerful surge of his hips, he sheathed his cock inside her. She wrapped her arms and legs around him as he buried its full length in her heated depths. Her lips found his and she whispered an urgent entreaty against them.

"Fuck me, Custis, please fuck me."

Longarm did, driving in and out of her in a pounding rhythm that had both of them gasping. It was a hard ride, a passionate gallop that never left the bed, but took them from one end of the earth to the other. And in the end, the earth moved as Longarm exploded inside her and Eileen bucked and spasmed underneath him. His juices flooded out in a seemingly never-ending stream that filled her to overflowing before the inevitable lassitude came crashing down on both of them.

Longarm rolled off her and hoped that they hadn't raised enough of a ruckus so that the whole hotel had heard what they were doing. At the moment, though, he didn't really care all that much. He would have almost shouted from the rooftops that he and Eileen Brewer had just fucked their brains out.

But he was too much of a gentleman to do that, of course, so he slid an arm around Eileen and pulled her closer against him, nestling her to his side.

"I guess you're not . . . clean anymore." She was out of breath and having trouble talking.

So was Longarm. "Well, I don't reckon it'd be a good idea . . . for you to start washing me again . . . considering how carried away we got that time. How about we . . . get dressed and go get something to eat . . . instead?"

She laughed. "That sounds good to me, Custis. Just let me . . . Goodness! Just let me catch my breath first."

The way Longarm felt right now, he didn't know if his

heart was ever going to stop thundering along like a whole herd of stampeding longhorns.

It was well after sundown and full night had fallen. Longarm and Eileen walked up the street to the Sunrise Café. The woman who ran it looked a little disappointed when Longarm came in with the auburn-haired beauty on his arm, but that didn't stop her from dishing up an excellent supper for the two of them.

While they were sipping coffee after finishing the meal, Eileen brought up the subject of the newcomers to Happy Valley. "I've never seen a wagon train like that before. And there are soldiers all over the place. Allen says having them here is liable to cause trouble."

Longarm nodded. "It's already come close to starting a ruckus. The settlers who were already here felt like they had it bad enough to start with, what with being swindled out of their money and stuck with a place like this instead of the good land they were promised."

"The people from the wagon train are just as bad off, though, aren't they?"

"Worse." Longarm gave a sympathetic shake of his head. "I don't know what'll become of them once the soldiers leave. Lieutenant Kincaid's sort of appointed himself their protector while he and his men are here, but soldiers have got their own chore to do—chasing down that bunch of renegade Cheyenne they followed up here."

"Do you think we're in any danger from the Indians?"

Longarm took another sip of coffee before he answered. "It's hard to say. They don't like this place. They think it's cursed. But Blue Horse, the leader of the war party, is plumb loco when it comes to killing whites. He's liable to see the settling of the valley as a chance for him to wipe out a bunch of his enemies at once."

A little shiver went through Eileen. "Allen says that the Indians aren't dangerous, and I suppose that's true of Falls from the Sky and his people. But I don't see how he can be sure that none of the others represent a threat."

"There's an old hymn that says further along we'll know more about it. I reckon that means we'll just have to wait and see."

"What about those outlaws you're after? Have you had any luck getting a line on them?"

"Not really. I had hopes today that I'd find something out when I rode up to the far end of the valley to see an old hermit who lives up there. He's been around here longer than maybe anybody else, even the Indians, so I thought he might know something."

"Did he?"

Longarm shook his head. "Claimed he didn't. And I reckon I believe him, since he turned out to be John Fury."

Interest lit up Eileen's green eyes. "Who's John Fury? I don't think I've ever heard of him."

"I'm not surprised, since you grew up back in St. Louis. If you'd lived out here for very long, you'd have heard stories about Fury."

He filled her in on the famous frontiersman's adventurous life. Eileen leaned forward and listened raptly until Longarm was finished.

"He sounds like he'd be just the man to help you track down those outlaws, Custis!"

Longarm shook his head ruefully. "I thought so, too, but he turned me down flat. Said it was none of his business. Some fellas are like that, especially when they get older. They go off by themselves somewhere and just want to be left alone."

"That's a shame. Are you sure he wouldn't reconsider?"

"Well, I don't know . . . Fury's always been on the side of the law, even wore a badge a time or two himself. I've got a hunch that having a bunch of owlhoots raising hell in *his* valley might gnaw at him enough to get him interested after a while."

Eileen smiled. "I hope that turns out to be the case. Not

that you can't handle those outlaws on your own, of course."

Longarm chuckled. "Don't worry about hurting my feelings. I'd take John Fury's help in a minute, and be glad to get it, if he ever decides to take a hand in this game."

He had enjoyed Eileen's visit, from their romp in the hotel room to this meal he had shared with her, but it was getting late now and he'd had a long day. He asked her how she had gotten to the settlement.

"I brought the wagon from the agency. I can handle a team fairly well."

"Even so, I reckon I ought to ride back out there with you, since it's dark now, just to make sure you get home all right."

"Do you think there really are evil spirits abroad in the night, Custis?" Her green eyes twinkled as she asked the question.

"Well . . . I don't know about evil spirits. But there are masked owlhoots and Cheyenne renegades around, no doubt about that. I wouldn't feel right, letting you drive back out to the agency by yourself."

She reached across the table and clasped his hand. "That's very sweet of you, but there's one thing you're not considering."

"What's that?"

She smiled. "Who says I'm going back to the agency tonight? I told Allen I wouldn't return from the settlement until tomorrow. He thinks I came into town to buy some things to make our quarters at the agency less barren, and I fully intend to do that . . . after I spend the rest of the night with you."

That sounded pretty promising to Longarm. He might not get as much sleep this way, but he was willing to bet that he would feel fairly rested come morning.

They were about to leave the café when shouts sounded outside in the street. Longarm could tell from the timbre of them that something was wrong. He got to his feet.

"I'd better go see about that. Stay here in case there's trouble."

Eileen shook her head and stood up, too. "I'm going with you, Custis. I live here, too, now, you know. I have a stake in what happens in Happy Valley."

Longarm supposed she was right about that. Along with the other people in the café, they hurried outside to see what was going on.

A crowd was gathering around a buckboard that was stopped at an angle in the street. A woman sat on the seat with her arm around a man huddled beside her, holding him up. In the lamplight that spilled from nearby buildings, a ragged crimson flower was visible on the breast of his shirt. Longarm had seen enough bloodstains to recognize this one. The hombre appeared to have been shot.

The woman was babbling. "We barely got away! They shot Hiram! They were burning down the Braddock place! It was awful!"

Longarm shouldered through the crowd with Eileen following him. When he reached the side of the buckboard where the terrified woman and the wounded man sat, he saw Mayor Decker and Lieutenant Matt Kincaid, along with Windy Mandalian, converging on the vehicle, too. Decker knew the woman and spoke urgently to her.

"Mary Lou, what happened? You say the Braddock place was on fire?"

The woman jerked her head in a nod. She seemed to be on the verge of hysteria, but she made a visible effort to control herself.

"Hiram and I were driving over there to see Joe and Caroline Braddock. Caroline's in a family way, you know, and due to deliver any day now. But we saw the flames and then heard the shots . . . then some of those devils saw us and . . . Oh! They shot Hiram! I thought they were going to kill us both! But Hiram got us away from them, and then . . . and then I brought the buckboard on into town . . . I didn't know what else to do . . ."

A shudder went through her. She tightened her grip on her wounded husband.

Longarm looked closer and saw that the man was more than wounded. His eyes were open and glassy and lifeless. Hiram was dead, but at least he had gotten his wife out of danger before he died.

"Ma'am." Longarm grasped the rail at the edge of the buckboard seat. "Ma'am, I'm a deputy U.S. marshal. Did you get a good look at those outlaws who were attacking the Braddock farm?"

"Outlaws?" The woman stared at him as she repeated the word. "Who said anything about outlaws?"

Decker spoke up again. "It wasn't the same bunch that's caused all the trouble around here, Mary Lou? The ones who wear the long coats and the hoods?"

"No! Hiram will tell you—" She turned then to look at her husband, and a wail of grief and despair came from her as she realized that he was dead. "Hiram! Oh, God!" She turned her tear-streaked face toward Longarm, Decker, and the soldiers again. "It was Indians who killed him! Indians!"

Chapter 25

Malone tilted the bottle to his lips and took a long swig of whiskey from it. The raw, fiery liquor burned all the way down his gullet, but only added to the pleasant warmth already in his belly. He didn't like the way he'd been ordered out of the saloon by the lieutenant, just because of an argument with some dumb townie, but Dobbs had managed to get a bottle somewhere and so Malone was happy again.

He sat with his back resting against a wagon wheel. Dobbs was on one side of him, Holzer on the other. They had been passing the bottle back and forth for a while now.

"Here you go, Wolfie." Malone pressed the rotgut into Holzer's hands. "Don't drink it all."

"*Ja.*"

Malone didn't know if Holzer understood him or not. Holzer was drunk enough that he wasn't even attempting to speak his rudimentary version of English anymore. When he muttered something, it was in German. Holzer lifted the bottle and some of the whiskey *glug-glugged* down his throat.

Dobbs reached across Malone. "Gimme that, you big Dutchman."

"Nein!"

"Ten!"

Malone thought Dobbs's response to Holzer's protest was incredibly funny, and leaned over to pound his fist against the ground as he laughed. He managed to choke out a number of his own. "Eleven!" That was even more hilarious.

Dobbs wrestled the bottle away from Holzer, who either muttered something in German or cleared his throat, Malone couldn't tell which. Then Holzer stood up and stumbled to the rear of the wagon. He groaned and leaned over like he was going to be sick.

Something must have distracted him, though, because he straightened and walked toward the mouth of a nearby alley. Malone called after him.

"Hey, Wolfie, don't wander off."

Holzer turned and pointed into the alley, jabbering something in his native tongue. Malone didn't understand a word of it, of course. He waved Holzer back over to the wagon.

"Come on, there's still some whiskey left. Have 'nother drink."

Holzer was still muttering to himself as he rejoined Malone and Dobbs. He seemed to have sobered up a little. *"Ölbrunnen? Was ist ölbrunnen?"*

Malone took the bottle from Dobbs, swallowed another nip himself, and then extended it toward Holzer. "What're you goin' on about? Have a drink!"

Before Holzer could answer the question or take the bottle, people started shouting in alarm down the street. The three soldiers looked in that direction and saw a crowd gathering around a buckboard. Dobbs nudged Malone in the ribs. "Reckon we better go see what it's all about?"

Since Malone still had the bottle in his hand, he took another drink, then shook his head. "Nah. Whatever it is, it ain't any of our business."

217

Only a few minutes had gone by, though, before shouts of "Indians! Indians!" rose in the street, and Malone let out a groan. Whenever civilians started yelling about Indians, one thing was certain . . .

The army—which meant him and his pards—was about to be up Shit Creek again.

Eileen Brewer had followed Longarm into the crowd. He turned to look at her as the woman on the buckboard collapsed into wracking sobs as she held her husband's body against her.

"Could Falls from the Sky and his people be the ones who did this?"

Wide-eyed with horror, Eileen shook her head. "No! It's not possible. I know I haven't been out here for very long, Custis, but I can tell that they're truly peaceful. And Allen says that they don't want trouble of any sort. I can't imagine them attacking the settlers, especially without any provocation!"

Matt Kincaid had been listening to Eileen's answer, too. "You're sure about that, Miss Brewer?"

Eileen nodded. "I'm certain."

"Then it has to be Blue Horse who's responsible. He and the rest of his renegades slipped into the valley." Kincaid drove his right fist into his left palm. "Blast it! I was afraid something like this would happen."

Windy Mandalian spoke up. "Like I said, Blue Horse doesn't care about curses or evil spirits as long as there are enemies to kill."

Decker motioned several of the townsmen forward. "Help me get Hiram down from there. We'll take him into the stage station. And some of you ladies, see what you can do for poor Mary Lou."

Kincaid turned away from the buckboard and raised his voice. "Olsen! Wojensky! Get the men ready to ride!"

"You're going after those renegades tonight?"

The lieutenant looked at Longarm and nodded. "That's right. We'll ride out to the farm they attacked anyway, and see if there are any survivors. That's where we'll pick up the trail, even if we have to wait until morning." Kincaid paused. "Would you like to come with us, Marshal?"

Longarm frowned as he considered the invitation. This attack by the Cheyenne war party had nothing to do with the assignment that had brought him here. On the other hand, Billy Vail had given him the job of making Happy Valley safe for the settlers again, and as long as Blue Horse and his renegades were on the loose, folks in these parts would be in danger.

Besides, if he gave Kincaid a hand, then maybe the lieutenant would be willing to help him run that outlaw gang to earth.

Longarm nodded as he reached his decision. "Sure, I'll go with you, Kincaid."

Eileen's voice was low and urgent as she clutched his arm. "But Custis . . ."

"I'm sorry, Eileen. You stay here in town, and I'll be back as soon as I can. Maybe tomorrow."

"But if you go with the soldiers, it could be dangerous."

"I expect it will be. But then, so's my regular job."

She clearly didn't like it, but after a moment she nodded. "All right. I'll be here waiting for you. Just don't be gone too long."

"I'll try not to be." He grinned as he said it, but he knew that there was really no way of knowing how long it would take the soldiers to catch up with Blue Horse.

Kincaid said that the men of Easy Company would be riding in fifteen minutes. Longarm hurried to the hotel and changed into range clothes that were more suitable for a long ride than his brown tweed suit. Carrying his rifle and saddle, he went to the livery stable to get a horse. The bay was worn out after the trip up the valley and back, so Grant Vernon told Longarm he could take a long-legged dun.

"Since you're going after those savages with the army,

Marshal, I won't even charge you any extra for switchin' horses."

"I appreciate that, old son." Vernon didn't appear to catch the sarcasm in Longarm's words.

By the time he rode out of the livery barn into the street, most of the soldiers were mounted and ready to ride. At Windy Mandalian's suggestion, Kincaid had picked out eight men to leave behind in the settlement, just in case Blue Horse's attack on the farm was a feint designed to draw the patrol off so that he could then raid the town.

Kincaid was standing on the porch of the stage station talking to Mayor Decker when Longarm rode up. Longarm could tell that Decker was giving the lieutenant directions for reaching the Braddock farm. Kincaid nodded, shook hands briefly with Decker, and then strode over to his horse and swung up into the saddle.

With a wave of his gauntleted hand, Kincaid led the patrol—along with Windy Mandalian and Longarm—out of the settlement.

The Braddock place was about two miles west of the settlement and a quarter of a mile north of the main trail, according to Decker. Matt Kincaid didn't think that he and his men would have any trouble finding it.

He and his men and Marshal Long, Matt reminded himself. He hoped that he wouldn't have occasion to regret his impulsive decision to ask the big lawman to ride along with them as they pursued Blue Horse.

Matt had known Long for only a few hours, but he generally prided himself on his ability to size a fella up in a hurry. As an officer, he often had to make decisions quickly and then stand by them. He hadn't liked Custis Long very much at first; the man's self-assured, almost arrogant attitude rubbed Matt the wrong way.

But Matt knew he sometimes came across to people the same way, so he was willing to give Long the benefit of the doubt, and by the time he and Windy had talked to the lawman for a while, Matt was willing to concede that Long might not be such a bad sort after all. He certainly had an air of easygoing competence about him that suggested he would be a good man to have on your side in a fight.

In fact, it was Long who first spotted the flames in the distance and pointed them out. "Looks like the cabin is still burning."

Matt swung his mount toward the fire. "Bugler! Sound the charge!"

Reb McBride followed the shouted order, the notes pealing out from his bugle. The renegades were probably long gone by now, but if they weren't, they would know that the soldiers were coming. But they would have known anyway, Matt told himself, because it was impossible for that many riders to approach without being heard.

As they came closer to what was left of the log cabin where the Braddock family had lived, Matt saw that most of the damage had already been done. The flames were dying down now because the roof had already fallen in and three out of the four walls had collapsed. Only part of the last wall was still standing as the dancing orange flames licked at it.

Off to one side, a shed was still standing, but a dark lump nearby was the milk cow that had lived there, lying on its side riddled with bullets and arrows.

There was no sign of the marauders who had carried out this destruction. Blue Horse was gone, just as Matt expected. As the members of the patrol reined their horses to a halt, he called out orders.

"Dismount and spread out! Search the brush around the cabin for survivors!"

"There won't be any." Windy Mandalian leaned over in his saddle and spat on the ground. "You'll likely find the lady inside. There's the man."

He raised his rifle and used the barrel to point to something that Matt hadn't noticed before. A man was strung up

221

at the side of the shed, hands tied over his head to one of the roof beams. Matt dismounted and walked toward the grisly figure, leading his horse. Windy and Long came with him.

The fading glow from the flames was still bright enough for Matt to be able to see the rictus of agony that stretched across the dead settler's face. The man's eyes were gone, gouged out, and his tongue appeared to have been hacked from his mouth. His clothes had been ripped off, and the renegades had taken their knives to his body, slashing it and carving off hunks of skin and flesh. Where his genitals had been was just a gaping, bloody wound.

Matt had witnessed the results of such savagery many times before in his military career, but it never got any easier to see things like this. Sickened, he turned his head.

He felt even worse a second later when a choked moan came from the tortured figure strung up against the shed wall.

"Good Lord!" Matt couldn't believe it. "He must have heard us ride up. He's still alive."

"He don't want to be." Longarm's face looked like it had been whittled out of a piece of wood. He glanced at the scout. "You or me, Mandalian?"

"I'll take care of it." Windy lifted his Sharps and eared back the hammer. Matt knew what Windy was about to do and had time to stop him . . . but he didn't.

The heavy rifle roared. The dying man's head exploded in a spray of crimson. Matt's jaw tightened, but he didn't look away. He wanted to remember this atrocity, and the man who was responsible for it—Blue Horse.

Windy turned out to be wrong, which was unusual. There *was* one survivor of the renegades' attack on the Braddock farm. Malone came out of the brush cradling a good-sized yellow dog in his arms. The animal had an arrow buried in its right hip.

"Found him layin' out there, Lieutenant. The Indians must've thought they killed him, but I don't think he's hurt too awful bad."

As if to confirm Malone's words, the dog twisted his head and licked the brawny Irishman's cheek. That brought laughter from some of the other soldiers. They shut up in a hurry, though, when Malone glared at them. Nobody wanted to get too far on Malone's bad side.

Matt had to smile a little. "All right, Malone, see if you can get that arrow out and bandage the wound. The rest of you, keep searching in case anybody else—anybody human—hid in the brush after being wounded."

That wasn't the case, though. The area was deserted. Once Matt was sure of that, he called the men in and told them to make camp. Then he turned to Windy.

"Unless you think we can follow their trail tonight?"

The scout shook his head. "Be better to wait until morning. I know that'll give Blue Horse a lead on us, but I don't know these parts well enough to risk reading sign in the dark."

"All right. Let's pull back a ways from the cabin and establish a camp." Matt turned to Long. "You're not under my orders, Marshal. You can do whatever you want."

"I'll stick with you fellas, at least for now."

Matt posted plenty of guards, even though he thought the chances of Blue Horse returning to this place tonight were mighty slim. As it turned out, he was right. The rest of the night passed peacefully, the only sounds, other than the usual cry of night birds and rustle of small animals, being the occasional loud pop from the cooling embers of the burned cabin.

By dawn, those ruins had cooled enough for Matt and a couple of the men to poke among them until they found the charred body of the woman who had lived here. She and the baby she would have soon given birth to if not for Blue Horse were both dead. The bodies were so burned that it was hard to tell, but Matt thought the child had probably been hacked out of the woman's womb while they were both still alive.

He'd had men digging a couple of graves even before

dawn. The luckless, mutilated homesteader went in one, mother and child in the other. After the holes were filled in, the men gathered around them and an awkward silence fell as everyone waited for Matt.

"I haven't . . . said words over the graves of that many civilians . . ."

Matt was glad when Marshal Long spoke up. "I have." The lawman held his snuff brown Stetson over his heart as he bowed his head. "Lord, these poor folks had a hard life and an even harder death. But if You've welcomed 'em into Your home, as I reckon You have, they're well past all that now. Show them Your mercy and give rest and peace to their souls, because they've got it coming. Amen."

The hard-bitten soldiers echoed that "Amen," then put their caps and hats on and turned to their horses.

They were ready to find the renegades who had committed this evil and put a stop to such things once and for all. Within minutes, the sound of hoofbeats rolled through the dawn as the men of Easy Company—plus one deputy U.S. marshal—took up Blue Horse's trail.

Chapter 26

Mornings were the best. The breeze was stronger then, sweeping down from the pass to carry the smell away from John Fury's cabin. Fury could step out his front door and take a deep breath of air that smelled almost as clean as any he had ever experienced in more than sixty years of living. It was enough to make a fella forget for a while the inevitable aches and pains that came with age.

Not enough to make all the memories fade, of course.

Nothing could do that.

There were better places than this isolated corner of the Valley of Skulls. Fury had visited many of them during his life. But this place had one advantage that the others didn't, and that was why he had chosen to settle here.

As long as he stayed here, folks would leave him alone, because of the stink and because there was no real reason for anybody to come here. Even the Indians avoided the valley. The first time he had seen it, Fury had known that here he would find the solitude he craved.

He stepped outside this morning and picked up the ax that leaned against the wall near the door. Even though the

225

season was mild, the nights were chilly and he liked to have a fire in the morning to chase away the stiffness in his bones. He went to the stack of cordwood piled against the wall and picked up a piece, setting it on the stump he used for splitting wood. He spat in the palms of his hands and rubbed them together, then took a good grip on the handle as he swung the ax above his head.

It wasn't that he was an unfriendly man. He'd had plenty of friends in his life . . . Joe Brackett, the fastest man with a gun Fury had ever seen; Reese Driscoll, his old trapping partner, a flawed man but a decent one; even the girl called Loney, who'd been like a daughter to him for a while . . . and after that, Cougar Jack and Snow Eagle, and Boone Cantrell, who'd worn the sheriff's badge in that town down in Colorado those immigrants had insisted on naming after Fury . . . good folks all, and Fury had been proud to call them friend, each and every one.

But there were the others, the friends and relatives of men he'd been forced to kill who wanted to settle those scores with him, and even worse, the men who had never even met him but wanted to kill him anyway. Wanted him dead so they could *brag* about it. In the end, that was why Fury had come to the Valley of Skulls, and why he avoided human contact as much as he could these days.

He didn't want to have to kill anybody else. He'd had his fill of it.

He brought the ax sweeping down toward the chunk of firewood.

And in that exact moment, something clanged off the head of the ax, striking it so hard that the handle was ripped right out of Fury's hands. Pain leaped up his arms and numbed his hands. He heard a high-pitched whine, and recognized it as the sound of a ricocheting bullet.

Somebody had just taken a shot at him, and only pure luck had put the ax head between him and the bullet.

Instinct sent him diving to the ground and rolling behind the stack of firewood. It gave him a little cover, but he had to stay pressed up against the outer wall of the cabin or risk exposing himself to more shots. He glanced along his body toward the door. He'd been carrying his Sharps when he came outside, but he'd set it down, leaning it against the wall where the ax had been until he picked it up.

Now the ax was lying out there where it had fallen, well out of his reach. Not that it would have helped him against a bushwhacker's rifle anyway. He needed the Sharps for that, and it was out of reach, too. Fury frowned as he tried to figure out his next move.

The bushwhacker was somewhere along the wooded slope, over toward the trail leading up to the pass. A little above him maybe. Fury knew he couldn't stay where he was, because if he did, the bastard would just work his way around toward the front of the cabin and have an easy shot at the man who lay beside the stack of firewood. He was probably on the move already.

Fury's hat had stayed on when he lunged to the ground. He snatched it off now, already moving to carry out the plan even as it formed in his mind. With a flick of his wrist, he sent the hat sailing out across the clearing in front of the cabin.

Fury surged to his feet as another shot rang out. He had to hope that the bushwhacker's instincts had taken over and made him jerk the rifle toward the hat, firing at any motion. Fury moved with all the speed he could summon, making a try for the door before the gunman had time to swing the rifle back toward him again.

A third shot blasted as Fury flung himself headlong through the open door. The slug chewed splinters from the jamb. His hand slapped the barrel of the Sharps as he went past, and he dragged the heavy rifle with him as he sprawled on the puncheon floor.

Fury kicked the door closed and felt his heart leap in his chest. *Let's see the son of a bitch get me now!* it seemed to be saying.

Fury leaped to his feet and went to one of the rifle slits.

He pressed his eye to it in time to see the puff of smoke from the trees about two hundred yards away as the bushwhacker fired again. The bullet thudded against the door, but didn't even come close to penetrating it. Fury's mouth stretched in a savage grin. The damn fool wasn't accomplishing anything except to tell Fury where he was.

Fury thrust the barrel of the Sharps through the slit, drew a quick bead on the place where he had seen the smoke, and fired.

Two hundred yards was practically point-blank range for a big old Sharps like the one he carried. The rifle kicked heavily against his shoulder. Fury withdrew the barrel from the slit and began reloading. The fact that only a few minutes earlier he had been thinking about how he had come to the Valley of Skulls because he didn't want any more trouble, because he didn't want to have to kill anybody else, didn't even occur to him.

All of that was forgotten now that somebody had tried to blow a hole in him.

No matter how philosophical the bear may look, you still don't want to poke him with a stick.

Fury looked out the rifle slit again, searching for something else to shoot at. Instead, he heard drumming hoofbeats, and then a second later saw a man on horseback burst out of the trees and race toward the trail. Fury just caught a glimpse of him, not enough to see anything except a man bent low over the neck of a galloping horse. He tried to swing the Sharps enough to the right to take a shot, but the rifle slit didn't give him enough of an angle to do that. He bit back a curse, pulled the rifle back, and ran to the door.

Even as he threw it open, he realized this might be a trick. There could be *two* bushwhackers out there. He pressed his back against the wall next to the door and waited.

No shots came screaming in through the open door. Fury let several minutes go by before he left the cabin in a crouching run. The bushwhacker was out of sight now, but that didn't matter. Fury had seen the direction the man was going and was confident that he could trail him. Still alert for a possible trick, he ran around back to the shed and corral where he kept his horse.

This end of the valley was quiet again. No more shots rang out. With no wasted motion, Fury threw his saddle on his horse and cinched it in place. He opened the corral gate, swung up into the saddle, and rode out, carrying the Sharps in front of him.

All he'd wanted was to be left alone. Now whoever had fired that shot at him was going to find out what a mistake they had made.

The war party's tracks led toward the pass at the far end of the valley. Since Longarm had been up there, he described the terrain on the other side to Lieutenant Matt Kincaid and Windy Mandalian.

"It's mighty rough country. If Blue Horse is holed up over there, you'll have a hard time rooting him out."

Kincaid shook his head. "We won't have much choice in the matter. We have our orders. Anyway, if we don't deal with him, he and his men will lurk around this valley, hitting and running until they've wiped out half the settlers— or more. I won't have that."

"I was just saying that it's gonna be a pretty prickly job."

"Easy Company is used to that."

Longarm hoped that Kincaid was right. One thing they had on their side was that Windy Mandalian was a fine tracker. If anybody had a chance of finding where Blue Horse was hiding, it was Mandalian.

Or John Fury, Longarm suddenly thought as he glanced toward the area where Fury's cabin was located. He wondered if it would be worth making a slight detour to see if the old frontiersman wanted to join their party. Fury had refused to help him go after those outlaws, but he might feel differently about the threat of a bloodthirsty bunch of renegade Cheyenne warriors.

Before Longarm could suggest it or even bring up the subject, he noticed a man riding along the trail toward them.

Surprise went through him as he recognized the lean, muscular figure and the flat-crowned black hat. He'd just been thinking about John Fury, and now here came the man, his own self.

Longarm wasn't the only one who had spotted Fury. Windy Mandalian's keen eyes had seen him, too. "Who's that?"

"An old hermit who lives up close to the pass. Folks around here call him Old John." Longarm didn't reveal Fury's real identity; he wanted to respect the man's desire for privacy if he could. A thought occurred to him. "If those renegades went through the pass last night, this fella might've heard 'em."

A moment later, as Fury continued to approach the patrol, Longarm's attempt at discretion proved not to have been needed, as a sharp exclamation came from Windy Mandalian.

"Old hermit, hell! That's John Fury!"

The scout galloped his horse ahead to meet Fury. Longarm and Kincaid exchanged a glance, then rode after him. The rest of the soldiers followed at a somewhat slower pace.

"Fury, you old horse thief!"

"Windy? Is that you?"

Longarm heard the two men exchange greetings as he and Kincaid rode up to join them. Fury and Mandalian both dismounted and slapped each other on the back, putting enough strength into the exuberant blows that some men would have been knocked flat on their faces by them.

"I reckon you two know each other." That wry observation came from Kincaid. He and Longarm had reined in to watch the reunion.

Mandalian grinned. "Just for the past twenty-five years or so. It's been a good ten years since I've seen this old varmint, though. You haven't changed much, John."

"We both just got older, that's all."

"Yeah. A few more scars here and there."

Fury looked with interest at Longarm and at the soldiers who had come up behind the lieutenant and the big lawman. "What's going on here? Did you convince the army to help you look for those outlaws you're after, Marshal?"

Longarm shook his head. "Nope, today we're looking for Mister Lo. Bunch of renegades led by a war chief called Blue Horse. They raided a farm back up the valley last night. Killed the man and woman who lived there and set fire to the place."

Fury's face hardened. "I thought I heard a few shots in the distance last night, but I wasn't sure. Didn't see the flames. I turned in early. Time I heard the shots, it would've been too late to help those pilgrims anyway." He gestured toward the tracks that the others had been following. "I reckon this is the war party's trail?"

"That's right." Kincaid didn't waste any time getting to the point. "We think they fled through the pass into the badlands on the other side. Did you hear a group of riders go by during the night?"

Fury shook his head as his jaw tightened even more. "No, I didn't. Like I said, though, I was asleep. Could be I just missed hearing them."

Mandalian put a hand on the shoulder of his fellow frontiersman. "Come with us, John. Help us track down those hostiles so they don't have a chance to kill any other innocent settlers."

Longarm saw the indecision on Fury's face. He half-expected Fury to turn down the invitation, but he wasn't all that surprised when the man nodded in acceptance.

"I was tracking somebody else, but I reckon this is more important. I'd lost the trail I was following anyway. The fella gave me the slip."

Longarm wondered who Fury might have been following, but he didn't press the issue. He was just glad that Fury had agreed to come along with them. That made their chances of finding Blue Horse that much better.

Fury and Mandalian mounted up again, and now with Fury as part of the group, they resumed following the rene-gades' tracks. As they rode toward the pass, Longarm moved his horse alongside Fury's and asked the question that had begun to nag at him.

"You said you were following somebody else. Mind if I ask who?"

Fury's reply was curt. "Son of a bitch who took a shot at me this morning."

Longarm looked over at the frontiersman and frowned. "Somebody tried to bushwhack you?"

"Yeah, while I was out splitting some firewood in front of my cabin. He missed, though, and I was able to get back inside my cabin. He took off for the tall and uncut when he saw that he wasn't going to be able to kill me."

"You get a look at him?"

Fury shook his head. "Just a glimpse, not enough to ever recognize him again."

Windy Mandalian and Lieutenant Kincaid had been lis-tening to the conversation. Mandalian spoke up. "A man like you is bound to have a lot of enemies, John. It sort of goes with the territory."

Fury nodded. "Yeah, I reckon. But I didn't think anybody in this valley knew who I really am. That's why I've stayed here all this time, having as little to do with folks as I can. I got tired of hombres with a grudge coming after me."

"Still, somebody could have seen you and recognized you. The word could've gotten around."

"Yeah, I guess."

Longarm reached up to tug as his earlobe as he thought about what Fury had just said. Somebody *had* seen Fury and recognized him—Longarm. But he'd tried to keep quiet about it for the very reason that Fury had just mentioned. Fury didn't want to be found, and Longarm was going to honor that wish.

Except . . .

He had told Eileen Brewer who Fury really was.

And less than twelve hours later, somebody had tried to kill the old frontiersman.

That had to be a coincidence. Longarm hoped that it was. But as his jaw tightened and his forehead creased in a frown, he knew that when he got back to the settlement, he was going to have to have a talk with Eileen.

He hoped that she had the right answers.

Chapter 27

As before, the renegades seemed unconcerned about hiding their trail. Windy could tell that struck Matt Kincaid as the height of foolish arrogance on Blue Horse's part, but the scout wasn't really surprised.

Blue Horse was mad, as in plumb loco. And the young warriors who followed him had worked themselves up into such a frenzy of hatred for the white man that they didn't care whether they were caught or not. Anything that gave them a chance to kill more of the enemy was all right with them.

As the patrol rode up the slope at the end of the valley toward the pass, John Fury pointed out the cabin where he had spent the past few years. "That's my place, Windy." His voice was low, intended only for his old friend's ears. "Bothers the hell out of me that those varmints rode right past without me ever knowing. They could've murdered me in my bed, and I couldn't have done a blasted thing about it."

"Chances are they were moving pretty quietlike, John.

There's a reason people came up with that old saying 'Quiet as an Indian,' you know."

Fury shook his head. "I'll bet my horse smelled 'em and moved around some in the corral. There was a time when something like that would have roused me from sleep. There's no gettin' around it . . . I'm getting old, Windy. Loo ing my edge."

"Hell, no! That's just not possible." Windy grinned. "Because if it's true, then *I'm* getting old, too, and we both know that's not the case."

That drew a chuckle from Fury, but he still gave a rueful shake of his head. "I just hope that having me along with you boys doesn't turn out to be a liability."

"Huh! That'll be the day."

As the patrol approached the pass, Matt decided that someone should ride ahead and have a look, just to make sure that Blue Horse and his men hadn't set up some kind of ambush. Windy had been waiting for that, and nodded at the young lieutenant after he asked for a volunteer.

"I'll go." Windy heeled his horse into a trot. Not surprisingly, Fury fell in beside him.

"We'll both go."

Windy grinned. "I wouldn't have it any other way."

When they reached the pass without seeing any signs of a trap, they reined in and looked out at the rugged landscape beyond. Fury shook his head. "Not going to be easy to find them in that. The ground's so hard the trail will peter out pretty soon." He suddenly leaned forward in the saddle, frowning as he peered intently at the ground. "Windy, take a look at those tracks."

The hoofprints weren't more than faint marks in the dust, vague and ill-defined because the Indian ponies were unshod. But it took Windy only a moment to understand what Fury had noticed.

"They rode out through the pass . . . but then they rode *back*—"

Both men whirled their horses around to race back to the patrol with a warning. It was too late, though. Gunshots had begun to blast, shattering the midday quiet. And from above the two veteran frontiersmen came a distinct rumble.

Fury jerked his head back to look up. "Avalanche!"

Rocks had begun to tumble down from both rims above them. That didn't happen by accident. The whole thing was suddenly plain as day in Windy's mind. The renegades had ridden through the pass, then, knowing the soldiers would probably come after them, had doubled back. Most of the war party had probably hidden in the trees and let the patrol move on past them, climbing higher and higher.

A few of the Cheyenne, though, had climbed to the rims above the pass and waited for the right moment to start rock slides that would block the passage. At the same time, the rest of the renegades attacked the soldiers from behind—and the men of Easy Company had no place to run because the pass was closed off. They would be trapped against the rubble.

Yeah, thought Windy as he and John Fury rode as hard as they could in an attempt to escape the double-barreled avalanche, Blue Horse was loco . . . but that didn't mean he wasn't smart!

Longarm and Matt Kincaid watched Mandalian and Fury ride on ahead to the pass leading out of Happy Valley, which was still about five hundred yards away. Longarm nodded in the direction of the two frontiersmen. "It don't surprise me that those two know each other. I reckon they were both out here when the West was still mighty wild."

Kincaid laughed. "It's not all that tame now, Marshal. We're chasing renegade Cheyenne, after all, and you came up here to start with because of a gang of outlaws."

"Yeah, but it ain't really the same." Longarm took a cheroot from his shirt pocket and put it in his mouth, clamping his teeth on the gasper but leaving it unlit. "The

Indian wars ain't over, but more and more of the chiefs are getting the same idea as Falls from the Sky, that it's better for their people to be alive than to be wiped out. And law enforcement's getting organized to the point that it's not gonna be near as easy to be an outlaw as it used to be. Now a sheriff can communicate with lawmen all over the country by telegraph. Whenever an owlhoot rides into a new town, he can't be sure that the local badge toter ain't already on the lookout for him."

"You know what will happen, don't you, Marshal?"

"What's that?"

"If the law gets too organized for the criminals . . . then the criminals will organize, too."

Longarm frowned. "Organized crime? You mean more than just a gang with a dozen or two hard cases in it?" He shook his head. "Maybe. Hard to believe that something like that could happen, though, at least not out here. I recollect a case that took me to New York City a few years back. They got some big gangs there. And of course, there're the tongs, the Chinese gangs in San Francisco. I've run into them, too. Come to think of it, there's this cartel run by a German gal . . . Shit, Kincaid, you're right! Organized crime is what it's gonna come to, and probably sooner instead of later."

"And what will you do then?"

Longarm's teeth bit down harder on the cheroot. "Same thing I always have. Do whatever it takes to see that they get what's coming to them."

"Well, good luck with—" Kincaid stopped short and rose a little in his stirrups. "Windy and Fury are turning back, and they look like they're in a hurry. Something must be—"

The sound of a shot kept him from finishing the sentence. Hard on the heels of that blast, more shots erupted, and Longarm heard a rumble and saw dust begin to rise from the pass. "Son of a bitch!" He wheeled his horse and pulled his Winchester from its sheath in the same motion.

Spurts of muzzle flame showed orange in the shadows under the trees on both sides of the trail.

They had ridden into a trap, all right, and it was closing around them by the second!

Malone, Dobbs, Holzer, and Rafferty were riding together as usual when the shooting started. Malone heard a bullet whip past his head and let out a yell. He lifted his Springfield and twisted around in the saddle, trying to see where the shot had come from.

The next second, there were a lot more shots, and it wasn't hard to tell where they originated. The damned renegades were in the trees on both sides of the trail. The lieutenant and Windy Mandalian had led them into an ambush. Malone bit back a curse as he lifted his rifle and tried to draw a bead on one of the Indians now charging out of the trees on those nimble little ponies.

"Hold your fire! Hold your fire! Fall back!"

Malone thought about ignoring the shouted orders from Lieutenant Kincaid, but in the end he was just enough of a soldier that he couldn't do it. He snarled and lowered his Springfield. Jabbing his heels into his horse's flank, he sent the animal lunging up the trail along with the others.

Running away from a fight went against Malone's nature, but the lieutenant was probably right. If they made a stand up at the pass, they would have the high ground.

They couldn't go *through* the pass, that was for sure, because a bunch of rocks were tumbling down on both sides of it, creating an impassable stone barrier and throwing up a big cloud of dust. The renegades had the patrol between the proverbial rock and a hard place.

But the odds were roughly even, and Malone wasn't going to ask for any more than that. Just a fighting chance.

Malone saw Windy Mandalian and that old hombre who'd joined up with them come shooting out of the pass just ahead of the avalanche. Within seconds, the two riders had rejoined the rest of the patrol and waved the men of Easy Company on toward the fallen rocks. The rumble was starting to die away now, although echoes from it rolled off down the valley.

Some of the boulders that had fallen to block the pass had rolled out away from it a short distance. Kincaid led the men into those scattered rocks. He shouted more orders. "Dismount and find cover! Return the hostiles' fire at will!"

With practiced swiftness, the soldiers swung down from their saddles, taking rifles and ammunition pouches with them. A couple of men from each squad had been designated to take charge of the horses during a battle. They did so, freeing the other men to find shelter and begin putting up a fight. The men holding the horses retreated into some trees in an attempt to protect the animals from stray bullets.

Malone, Dobbs, Holzer, and Rafferty each found a rock and hunkered behind it. That was a little hard for Dobbs to do, since he was so tall, and within moments a slug had snatched the cap off his head.

"Damn it! Now what am I gonna do?"

"Don't worry about the sun beatin' down on your head, Dobbsy. Just think about how close the bullet came to that noggin of yours."

Dobbs paled at the wry comment Malone called over to him. Meanwhile, still chuckling, Malone edged the barrel of his Springfield over the top of his rock and drew a bead on one of the renegades. He fired, but just as he pressed the trigger the Indian swerved his pony a little, so that Malone's shot struck him in the right elbow, rather than in the chest as the Irishman intended.

Of course, in the long run it didn't really matter, since the .45-70 slug shattered bone and practically tore the renegade's arm off at the elbow. The hand and forearm swung wildly in the air, still attached to the rest of the arm only by a few strands of muscle and skin. The Indian toppled off his pony, stunned senseless by the wound. He lay in a heap on the ground, where he would probably bleed to death before he ever regained consciousness.

And that was just dandy with Private Max Malone, who was already reloading, not even looking at his Springfield as he did so. He was busy looking for somebody else to kill.

Longarm knelt behind one of the boulders and braced the barrel of his Winchester against the rock. He began squeezing off rounds in a swift, efficient manner. Only a couple of heartbeats passed between each shot, just enough time for him to work the rifle's loading lever and find another target.

A few yards away, Lieutenant Kincaid was crouched behind another rock, firing his Schofield toward the attackers. Beyond him were Windy Mandalian and John Fury. The two frontiersmen were using one of the larger boulders as cover for both of them, and they fired from opposite sides of the big rock. Both men carried Sharps carbines, and the big guns boomed almost like cannon.

Several members of the patrol had fallen in the first moments of the ambush, and as Longarm glanced over at Kincaid, he saw bitter anger on the lieutenant's face. Kincaid didn't like having his men killed or wounded. That was the sign of a good officer . . . although, of course, a good officer would be willing to sacrifice his men—and himself—if that was what it took to accomplish the objective he had been given.

Longarm didn't think that was going to be necessary here. Blue Horse was canny, but he was also a mite crazy. When the ambush had failed to wipe out all of the patrol at once, he should have fallen back. True, the soldiers had retreated, but into a position of strength. Now, as Blue Horse threw his warriors against the enemy, all he was doing was getting the poor bastards slaughtered.

One after another, the renegades fell victim to the deadly,

accurate fire coming from the men of Easy Company. The Indians toppled off the backs of their ponies, or the mounts themselves went down in a welter of dust and slashing hooves. It was sheer, blood-soaked madness. Within minutes, the open ground just below the pass was littered with the bodies of men and horses. The renegades had probably worked themselves up into such a highly charged emotional state that they thought their "medicine" would protect them from being struck down by bullets. In these frenzied moments of violence they had learned just how tragically wrong they were.

Finally, only one member of the war party was left, and the buckskins he wore were dark with blood from the wounds he had already suffered. That didn't stop him, though. He continued to charge toward the rocks, waving a rifle over his head and shrieking a war cry.

"Hold your fire! Hold your fire!"

The guns fell silent at Kincaid's shout, and in the eerie hush that always followed the abrupt silencing of battle, the thin, warbling cry from the Indian sounded futile and lost.

"It's Blue Horse." That from Windy Mandalian. "He must be out of bullets."

Fury spoke from beside the scout. "He wants us to kill him. He wants to fall in battle."

"Hold your fire, men." Matt Kincaid's voice was cold. If a warrior's death was what Blue Horse wanted, then Kincaid wasn't going to give it to him.

Longarm felt a bitter, sour taste welling up under his tongue. He understood what Kincaid was doing—the fight, for all intents and purposes, was over after all—but that didn't mean he had to like it.

"Matt . . ." That was Mandalian again. "This isn't right."

Blue Horse's pony came to a halt. The war chief sat there, swaying back and forth a little, struggling to stay on as the pony danced around skittishly.

"Windy's right, Lieutenant." John Fury had his Sharps trained on Blue Horse. All it would take was the slightest pressure on the trigger, and Longarm could tell that Fury was struggling not to exert that pressure.

Kincaid, his face dark with anger, glanced over at Longarm. "What about you, Marshal? Do you think I'm wrong, too?"

Longarm just shrugged and shook his head. "That's your decision to make, old son. I'm no soldier."

"Damn it . . ." Kincaid looked down and checked the loads in his revolver. Then he stepped out from behind the rock, the Schofield hanging down at his side.

Blue Horse's head had begun to sag forward. Now it jerked up and a savage, triumphant grin appeared on his long face. He yelled and pumped the rifle in the air and kicked his pony in the sides, sending it leaping forward again.

"Matt, watch out!"

The cry of warning came from Windy Mandalian as Blue Horse suddenly snapped the butt of the rifle to his shoulder so he could draw a bead on Kincaid. The wily son of a bitch had one last trick left in him.

And one round left in his rifle.

A shot slammed out from Kincaid's Schofield a shaved heartbeat ahead of the crack from Blue Horse's rifle. The renegade's final bullet went harmlessly into the air as the barrel tilted up. Kincaid's slug had crashed into Blue Horse's chest just as the war chief pulled the trigger, driving him backward off the charging pony. Blue Horse's body thudded to the ground and didn't move again.

Looking just a little pale and shaken, Matt Kincaid glanced around at Longarm, Windy, and Fury. "You knew he was going to do that, didn't you?"

Windy shook his head. "Didn't occur to me until you stepped out in the open like that, Matt."

Longarm grinned. "Pretty good trick, though. Almost worked, too."

Kincaid continued looking at the three of them for a long moment, then sighed. He turned to the rest of the patrol. "Olsen, Wojensky, report! McBride, see to the wounded! Let's get this cleaned up. We're a long way from home, and I'm ready to get started back there."

Chapter 28

Three of the soldiers had been killed in the fighting, and eight more had suffered wounds, mostly minor. Only two of the Cheyenne renegades were left alive, and they were wounded, too. The injured were tended to, the captives' hands were bound, and the patrol got ready to ride back to the settlement. Windy Mandalian suggested that the bodies of Blue Horse and his men be left where they lay. Falls from the Sky and his people could come and claim them and send them on to the next world according to Cheyenne custom. It was a gesture of respect for fallen foes, although no one had any respect for Blue Horse himself. The man had been a mad dog.

Longarm had other things to worry about, so he put all thoughts of Blue Horse behind him now that the war chief was no longer a threat to the peace of Happy Valley. Instead, the big lawman was left with his suspicions of Eileen Brewer.

Longarm brought his horse alongside Fury's as the group rode back down the valley. "Mind if I ask you a little more about that bushwhack attempt on you?"

Fury shrugged. "Ask me whatever you want, Marshal, but I've already told you all I know about it. Somebody took a couple of shots at me, missed, and hightailed it when he saw that I was holed up in my cabin."

"Yeah, but are you sure nobody in Happy Valley knew who you really are?"

"The Valley of Skulls is a lot better name for the place . . . but to answer your question, I can't be sure. As far as I know, though, everybody in these parts just thought of me as Old John. That's the way I wanted it. I never told any of the settlers my full name, that I'm certain of." Fury's eyes narrowed in shrewd speculation. "You did, though, didn't you?"

Longarm grimaced. "Yeah. Somebody I trusted."

"Maybe you made a mistake."

"Maybe I did."

Longarm wasn't going to convict Eileen without talking to her first, though. And for the life of him, he couldn't see how she could be connected to the gang of outlaws who'd been harassing the folks in the valley. There was no escaping the conclusion that the owlhoots wouldn't want the famous John Fury helping Longarm. They could have decided to eliminate Fury, even though he had already turned down Longarm's request for aid, just to be sure that the frontiersman wouldn't change his mind.

The possibilities whirled through Longarm's brain, occupying his thoughts so that he almost didn't hear the words coming from a small group of soldiers riding nearby. It took him a few seconds to realize that one of the men was speaking German.

One word of it anyway. Longarm looked around and saw the big Prussian private, Wolfgang Holzer. Holzer was talking to Malone and the towering Dobbs and another private whose name Longarm hadn't heard.

"Ölbrunnen. Was ist ölbrunnen?"

Malone shook his head. "You're gonna have to talk English, Wolfie. You know I don't speak that Dutchie talk."

Neither did Longarm, but something about the word Holzer had just spoken seemed familiar to him, as if he had heard it before. The only person he'd been around lately who spoke German was the scientist who had come to Happy Valley on the stage with him and Eileen, Wilhelm Schott.

Holzer struggled to put his thoughts into English. "Wells . . . like water from which flows . . . only . . . wells from oil . . . oil wells! What are these . . . oil wells?"

Longarm's eyes widened as the implications of Holzer's question burst on his brain like an explosion. He jerked back on the dun's reins. "Son of a *bitch*!"

Fury looked over at him in surprise, as did Matt Kincaid and Windy Mandalian. The lieutenant asked the question that all of them were obviously thinking. "What's wrong, Marshal?"

"I know what it's all about. It all makes sense now." Longarm turned to Holzer. "Private, where did you hear about oil wells?"

Holzer looked confused and just a little scared, like he thought he had done something wrong. Longarm felt a surge of impatience and anger as the private failed to answer his question, but he reined it in and asked again, smiling to let Holzer know that he wasn't in any trouble. The soldier's expression finally cleared.

"In town, *ja?* Men in alley, they talk . . . with my words . . . *Deutsche, ja?*"

"You heard men in an alley talking German?"

Holzer smiled in relief and nodded.

"But you didn't see them?"

"Nein."

Longarm knew by now that meant "no" in German. He also knew the real reason Wilhelm Schott had come to Happy Valley, and he had a pretty good idea who Schott worked for.

Longarm turned to Kincaid. "We ought to get back to the settlement as fast as we can."

246

"I was just thinking the same thing." Kincaid pointed. "Look!"

Longarm bit back another curse as he saw the smoke rising in the air in the distance. It was coming from just about where the town of Happy Valley was located.

He didn't waste any time. With a yell, he kicked his horse into a hard run and headed for the settlement as fast as the animal would carry him. Kincaid, Mandalian, Fury, and the men of Easy Company were right behind him.

Longarm just hoped they would get there in time, before utter destruction came to Happy Valley.

They heard the shooting before they came in sight of the settlement itself. That was encouraging, thought Longarm, because it meant that the settlers were still putting up a fight. And the thick column of smoke, while black and menacing, hadn't spread as much as Longarm feared that it would. The fire certainly wasn't contained yet, but it wasn't blazing completely out of control and threatening to engulf the entire town either.

The patrol still had a chance to swing the odds of battle against the hooded outlaws. Even though Longarm hadn't seen them yet, he had no doubt that was who was responsible for this attack on the settlement. The men behind all the trouble were tired of waiting. They wanted to destroy the town and force all the settlers out of Happy Valley once and for all, before Longarm had a chance to put them out of business. Blue Horse's attack on the Braddock farm had been a fortuitous coincidence for the plotters, because it had drawn Longarm and the patrol from Outpost Number Nine out of town and given the masked riders the opportunity to strike a death blow.

They had been just a little late in doing so . . . or at least Longarm hoped that was the case.

As he and his companions pounded into sight of the town, he saw it was true. Several buildings clustered together were

247

on fire, but the flames hadn't spread to the rest of the structures. The outlaws were attacking in full force, though, galloping up and down the street and shooting into the buildings where the citizens had taken cover. Longarm spotted a few bodies lying in the street, and felt a surge of anger as he realized that the attack had already taken a deadly toll.

"Hit 'em hard!" Longarm didn't even think about the fact that he was shouting orders to men who weren't under his command. They were soldiers, not posse men. "They're all wearing dusters and masks!"

It was true; the raiders were all garbed in those concealing outfits, just as Longarm had heard them described. Matt Kincaid confirmed Longarm's orders with a shouted command of his own, and the patrol swept into the settlement, firing as they came.

The outlaws had been so caught up in their attack that they didn't see the men of Easy Company coming until it was too late. The two forces came together in the street in a dust-swirling, gun-blazing melee. It was bloody chaos as bullets flew and men and horses went down.

John Fury darted here and there, the heavy Colt in his hand thundering. He had been drawn back into this fight despite all his intentions, but now that he was in the thick of it, he didn't hold back. And the outlaws that fell before his gun proved that age had not slowed John Fury's hand nor dimmed his eye. He was as deadly as ever.

Not far away, Windy Mandalian's Sharps boomed, and a .50-caliber slug sent one of the outlaws cartwheeling off his horse with a fist-sized hole blown through his middle. Windy didn't take the time to reload, but swung the heavy Sharps instead, using its barrel to club another outlaw to the ground.

Matt Kincaid's Schofield barked rhythmically as he kept up a steady fire and coolly ignored the bullets whipping around his own head. He had been through enough battles with Easy Company so that this clash was nothing new to him. He was as human as any man and felt fear coursing through his veins, but he was able to control it and do what needed to be done, and try to look out for his men's safety at the same time.

From one bloody ruckus right into the middle of another, thought Malone as his Springfield kicked against his shoulder and one of the outlaws spun out of the saddle. Wasn't that always the way? And as a fighting grin spread across his rawboned face, he knew he wouldn't have it any other way.

Dobbs, Holzer, Rafferty, Reb McBride, Sergeant Olsen, Corporal Wojensky, and all the other men of Easy Company were acquitting themselves well, too. Within a few violent, action-filled moments, they had broken the back of the outlaws' attack and sent some of the hooded riders fleeing from the settlement. The ones who remained continued to put up a fight, but it didn't last long before they were driven from their saddles by U.S. Army lead.

Longarm had emptied his Colt and seen a couple of the raiders struck down by his bullets. He was thumbing fresh rounds into the revolver's cylinder when he spotted three of the masked owlhoots galloping out of town. Since Kincaid and the rest of his allies seemed to have things in hand here, Longarm jammed the now fully loaded Colt back in its holster and kicked his horse into a run after the fleeing outlaws.

He had a pretty good idea who might be under one of those hoods, but he wanted to find out who the other two were. He suspected that they were the ringleaders, taking off for the tall and uncut when they realized they weren't going to win.

The sounds of battle faded somewhat behind Longarm as he raced after the three fugitives. They were several hundred yards ahead of him, but he was able to keep them in sight as they pounded through the mouth of the valley, between the giant, grotesque-looking rocks that gave the place the name by which the Indians knew it. Longarm wasn't sure he believed in curses and evil spirits, but considering all the blood that had been spilled in recent days and the bodies that now lay scattered between here and the pass at the other end of the valley, the name sure as hell fit.

He saw smoke and flame geyser from a gun barrel up ahead. The outlaws had spotted him pursuing them and one of the men had hipped around in the saddle to fire at him. The range was much too long for a handgun, though, and Longarm wasn't worried about it. He pressed on, urging the dun to greater speed.

Up ahead, the trio of owlhoots reached the village of Falls from the Sky and his people and veered off the trail. They were headed for the Indian agency now. Longarm wasn't surprised by that, although he didn't see what sanctuary they would find there. Chances were they were just running blindly now, their scheme ruined and their heads full of thoughts of escape.

The Indians had heard the thundering hoofbeats and emerged from their lodges to see what was going on. As Longarm flashed past, he heard angry cries from some of the men. They had recognized the hooded, duster-clad figures, and no doubt wanted vengeance on the men who had raided their village. From the corner of his eye, Longarm saw some of them running after him, carrying bows and arrows.

Those warriors were on foot, though, and Longarm and his quarry swept past and left them behind in a cloud of dust. The agency building was visible up ahead now. Longarm caught a glimpse of fiery auburn hair on the porch as Eileen came outside to see what was going on. He didn't quite know what to hope for. If she was one of the plotters, then it was his job to bring her to justice, too. But if somehow she were innocent, then the fleeing outlaws might grab her and try to use her as a hostage. Either way, within moments her life would be in danger . . .

And Longarm didn't know if he would be called upon to save her—or bring the full force of the law to bear on her.

Back in the settlement, the shooting died away as the last of the outlaws was gunned down by John Fury. Matt Kincaid shouted for his men to hold their fire. As the guns fell silent, townspeople rushed from their hiding places and ran toward the burning buildings.

Matt raised his voice again. "Help folks get those fires put out! Move!"

The soldiers hurried to obey the order, dashing down the street to help the citizens form a bucket brigade stretching from the town's well to the site of the conflagration. While they were doing that, Matt, Windy, and Fury began checking the bodies of the fallen outlaws. Some of them might still be alive and needing medical attention.

Matt leaned over the first body he came to. The man's duster was sodden with blood in several places, so it was unlikely he was still alive. His hat had come off when he fell from his horse, but the hood was still in place over his head. Matt reached down, grasped it, and tugged it off.

He recoiled in surprise. Shock was actually more like it.

Because although the dead outlaw was dressed in white man's clothing, staring up lifelessly at Matt was the coppery-hued face of a young Indian warrior.

"What the hell!"

Matt's startled exclamation drew the attention of Windy and Fury. When Windy saw what Matt had discovered, he reached down to another body and removed the hood, too. He found the same thing, a young Indian clad in the garb of a white outlaw.

Windy was as baffled as Matt had been. "What in blazes is going on here?"

Another question had occurred to Matt. "Where's Marshal Long?"

John Fury supplied the answer. "I saw him take off after

three of these hombres who ran out when the fighting got too hot. I reckon we've got a pretty good idea now where they were headed."

"The Indian village!"

"Or the agency." Fury grabbed his horse's reins. "We'd better go see if Long needs a hand."

Matt and Windy agreed. Leaving Olsen and Wojensky to handle things here in the settlement, Matt, Windy, and Fury swung up in their saddles and raced toward the valley mouth, where those great skull-like rocks stood eternal guard.

Chapter 29

Longarm couldn't hear Eileen's surprised scream over the pounding of hooves, but he saw her gaping mouth as one of the hooded figures grabbed her after sliding his horse to a halt in front of the agency and flinging himself out of the saddle. The outlaw swung her around to use her as a human shield as he yanked his gun out and fired at Longarm, who was rapidly closing in.

One of the other two leaped off his horse as well and ran toward Eileen and her captor. The first man twisted toward him and triggered again. This time Longarm was able to hear Eileen's scream as the second hooded outlaw doubled over and crumpled to the ground.

That brutal falling-out among the hooded men gave Longarm enough time to reach the agency. He couldn't risk a shot as long as Eileen was in the way, but he did the next best thing.

He kicked his feet out of the stirrups and launched himself from the saddle.

The outlaw tried to swing his gun back toward Longarm, but didn't have enough time. He jerked the trigger anyway. The revolver blasted, but the bullet screamed off wildly, not coming anywhere close to Longarm.

The next second, the big lawman slammed into Eileen and the hooded man, and all three of them went crashing to the porch of the agency building.

As Longarm had hoped, the collision knocked Eileen free from the man's brutal grip. She rolled away, gasping for breath. At the same time, Longarm struggled to his knees and swung a punch at the man's head. Fist thudded against bone, although the hood the man wore kept the impact from being what it might have been. Snarling unintelligible words, the outlaw grabbed Longarm and heaved him to the side. Longarm crashed against the wall.

The outlaw leaped after him and landed on top of him, driving a knee into the lawman's stomach. He got his hands around Longarm's neck and started to squeeze.

Longarm was caught without much air in his lungs, and in only seconds his pulse was pounding inside his skull like a sledgehammer striking an anvil. A red mist floated in front of his eyes as he struggled to dislodge the man who was trying to choke the life out of him. One of Longarm's hands got hold of the hood and jerked it off the man's head, revealing the hate-twisted features of Wilhelm Schott.

Longarm wasn't surprised to see the Prussian scientist. He had already realized that the panting curses coming from his enemy were in German. Now, as Schott's hands bore down on Longarm's throat, he spoke in English.

"You have ruined everything, you *verdammt Amerikaner*, but at least this time the Empress will know that you paid with your life for your interference!"

Longarm felt rage welling up inside him. He wasn't going to give Katerina von Blöde the satisfaction of hearing about how Schott had killed him!

Instead, he arched his back and heaved upward with all his strength. At the same time, he hammered a fist against the side of Schott's head. The Prussian's fingers slipped, and Longarm hit him again, knocking Schott completely off him.

Unfortunately, where Schott landed was right next to the gun he had dropped when Longarm had tackled him a few moments earlier. With a cry of triumph, Schott snatched up the weapon and whirled around on his knees, jerking the trigger even as he turned.

Longarm rolled to the side as slugs from Schott's gun chewed up the porch planks next to him. He reached for his own gun, hoping that the Colt was still in its holster and hadn't fallen out during the struggle.

His fingers touched the well-worn walnut grips and the Colt practically leaped into his hand. As he came to a stop stretched out full-length on his belly, Longarm tipped up the barrel of the gun and fired twice. Both bullets ripped into Schott's chest and drove him backward. He dropped his gun again as he sprawled on the porch. His bloody chest rose and fell spasmodically a couple of times, then stopped as death claimed him.

Longarm didn't have time to catch his breath, though, because another shot roared somewhere close by and a bullet plowed into the porch in front of his face. He rolled again and twisted, bringing up his gun . . .

"Drop it, Marshal! Drop it or I'll kill her!"

The voice was familiar. Longarm saw that the third outlaw had stopped, too, and now sat on his horse with his gun pointed at Eileen, who was huddled on her knees next to the body of the man Schott had killed. She had pulled her hood off, and had his head pillowed on her lap as she sobbed, either unaware or uncaring about the danger she was in. Her tears fell on the lifeless face of her brother Allen.

Longarm's hunch about the identity of the third outlaw was confirmed as the man spoke again. "I mean it, old boy, I'll shoot her if you don't drop your gun."

Moving deliberately and never taking his eyes off the hooded man, Longarm climbed to his feet. "And then after

I drop my gun you'll kill me anyway, and her, too, to keep us from telling anybody what you've been up to, Otter That Glides."

"Don't call me that, damn your eyes!" The Colt in Otter's hand shook a little as he shouted at Longarm. "My name is Samuel Otter. I'm not one of those bloody red heathens."

His words had penetrated Eileen's grief and caused her to lift her head and twist her neck to look around at him in shock. Clearly, she hadn't known the identity of at least one of her brother's partners. She might not have known anything about anything, Longarm reminded himself.

Most of his attention was focused on Otter, though. Longarm wanted to keep him talking.

"Who noticed the oil first, you or Brewer? I imagine you're educated enough now to know that it might be worth something if you could get your hands on the land."

The sneer on Otter's face couldn't be seen because of the hood, but it was plain enough in his voice. "I'm better educated than you ever will be, you uncouth lout. I came back from England and realized that my father's people, and those dirt-grubbing settlers, were sitting on something more valuable than a gold mine! Oh, yes, the field stretches out of the valley and under the agency land, too. Schott confirmed it, but I was already convinced. That's why I'd already brought Brewer in on the arrangement with the Cartel."

"Now how in the world did a fella like you ever wind up doing business with the Empress?"

"I met her in London when she was on her way back to Germany a couple of years ago, after her first efforts to reorganize the Cartel ran into trouble."

The trouble the Outlaw Empress had run into had been none other than Longarm himself, along with Jessie Starbuck and Ki, but Longarm didn't see any need in pointing that out now. Anyway, Otter was still talking.

"She was quite taken with me, you know. Quite impressed with my intelligence . . . and my other skills. She

256

called me her noble savage and promised me a place in her organization. When I got in touch with her and told her what I'd found here, she sent Schott right away."

"So all you were trying to do was force the settlers out of Happy Valley, and then you figured with Brewer's help you'd connive your way into grabbing the agency land, too."

Otter jabbed the gun toward Longarm. "And it would have worked, too, if not for you! For God's sake, who ever dreamed that anyone would be foolish enough to try to settle in the Valley of Skulls?"

"Yeah, that was mighty inconsiderate of 'em, wasn't it, getting in the way of making you a rich man."

Otter laughed. "I'll still be rich. Maybe not here, but I'll find something else. Once you and the woman are dead, Long, I'll slip up into the hills, get rid of these clothes, and come back as Otter That Glides . . . the son of a filthy savage! I'll have to bide my time, but I'll be free of these dreadful primitives sooner or later."

Longarm shook his head. "You ever hear the phrase 'silent as an Indian,' old son?"

"What? What are you talking about?"

"Your father's standing right behind you, boy, and he's heard most of what you've been saying."

Otter stiffened in the saddle and started to turn his head, then stopped. "No! It's a trick! You're lying, Long, and now you're going to die!" He thrust the gun at Longarm, ready to pull the trigger.

But before his finger could tighten on it, a bowstring twanged and Otter cried out as he was driven forward by the arrow striking him in the back. He caught himself before he fell, and jerked his gun up again, struggling to get a shot off. Longarm fired first. His bullet hammered Otter out of the saddle. The young man fell heavily to the ground as his horse danced away, spooked by the gunfire.

Falls from the Sky cast his bow aside and ran forward, dropping to his knees beside his son. He pulled the hood off, revealing Otter's pain-wracked face. Otter looked up and managed to gasp only a couple of words before he died.

"F-filthy . . . savage . . . !"

Falls from the Sky closed his eyes and began rocking back and forth slightly as he keened a death chant for his son. While the Cheyenne chief was doing that, Longarm holstered his Colt and went over to Eileen, who was still quietly sobbing over her brother's corpse. He eased Brewer's head out of her lap, took hold of her, and gently lifted her to her feet. He led her over to the porch, out of the merciless sun.

"He . . . he tried to save me." She struggled to get the words out. "He told that man to leave me alone . . . said he would kill him if he hurt me . . ."

"I reckon your brother loved you, Eileen, no matter what else he'd done."

She covered her face with her hands.

Longarm left her there and went over to Falls from the Sky, who had finished his song and gotten to his feet. The chief's eyes were dry as he looked at Longarm, but the big lawman could see the terrible grief and loss in them.

"I have killed my son. My own flesh and blood."

Longarm shook his head. "No. Your arrow struck him in the shoulder. You fired it to keep him from killing me. It was my bullet that ended his life."

"You do not understand, Marshal. I killed my son when I allowed him to be taken far from home and taught the ways of those who were not his people. His death has only now caught up to him."

Longarm didn't know what to say to that, so he didn't say anything. Instead, he looked toward the sound of hoofbeats and saw Lieutenant Matt Kincaid, Windy Mandalian, and John Fury riding swiftly toward the agency. They must have come to see if he needed any help.

They were too late for that. As Longarm looked at the bodies of Allen Brewer and Otter That Glides, and the man and the woman who grieved for them, he reflected that it was too late for much of anything except explanations.

And explanations never changed a damned thing.

"So it was all about that . . . that black gunk?"

Longarm nodded in response to Matt Kincaid's question. "Yeah. Most folks call it oil, but its real name is petroleum. Folks back East in Pennsylvania and places like that have been drilling wells for it and refining it and selling it for more than twenty years."

Windy Mandalian reached for the mug of beer on the table in front of him in the Oasis. "So it's worth a lot of money, is it?"

"It can be, if there's enough of it and it ain't too much trouble to get to it. Fella name of Rockefeller is getting rich off it, from what I hear. He owns a company called Standard Oil."

"Foolishness." That muttered comment came from John Fury. "Folks keep this up, they're going to ruin the West."

Longarm took a sip of his beer and then nodded. "It'll be different, that's for damned sure."

The four men sat in the Oasis, going over everything that had happened. Down the street, the fires were out in the buildings that had been destroyed. They could be rebuilt, if that was what their owners wanted. Longarm was wondering, though, if anybody would want to stay in Happy Valley now that they knew the truth.

Kincaid leaned forward. "What's this Cartel you mentioned?"

"Remember when we were talking about owlhoots getting organized? Well, the Cartel is the biggest outlaw gang you'd ever want to see. They started out in Europe, but they used to operate all across the United States, too, until they got put out of business a few years back, mostly by a friend of mine named Jessica Starbuck."

259

Fury nodded. "I've heard of her."

"Anyway, a German gal named Katerina von Blöde, who's the daughter of the Cartel's original leader, has been trying to rebuild it the past couple of years. I've crossed trails with her once, and gotten mixed up in another scheme of hers since then. She calls herself the Empress, but I sort of think of her as the Outlaw Empress."

Kincaid was staring at him. "No offense, Marshal, but all this sounds rather . . . far-fetched, if you ask me."

"That's the Cartel for you. Everything they get involved with is usually a mite off the beaten path, you could say. I remember Jessie telling me about a mountain of gold down in Arizona somewhere, and this tribe of Indians that lived inside it that nobody had seen for hundreds of years . . ." Longarm shook his head, not wanting to delve too deeply into some of the bizarre yarns Jessie Starbuck had told him. "Anyway, she'd mentioned to me that the Cartel has gone after oil deposits before, and when that German private of yours said something about oil wells, everything sort of fell into place in my head. I knew why it stunk so bad here in the valley, and I figured Schott was working for the Cartel. More importantly, it gave me a reason why those hooded varmints wanted to run folks off when it didn't seem to make any sense otherwise."

Fury gave Longarm a hard look. "And you suspected that Brewer was involved, too, because you'd told his sister about me."

"That bushwhack attempt was too much to write off as a coincidence." Longarm sighed. "I suspected Brewer of being tied in with the outlaws, or Eileen, or both of them. Turned out she didn't know anything about what her brother was up to with Schott and Otter, but she did tell him who you really are, Fury. And when he told the other two, they decided to get rid of you just in case you changed your mind and started working with me. That's the way it looks to me anyway. Since all three of the ringleaders are dead, I don't reckon we'll ever know all the details."

Windy waved a hand to indicate their surroundings. "What are these folks going to do now? They won't ever make a go of their farms and ranches, and without the farms and ranches the town can't exist, can it?"

Longarm couldn't help but chuckle. "Those polecats who swindled the settlers here really did them a favor without knowing it. They can sell this land for enough money to start over someplace a lot better."

Matt Kincaid nodded. "That's a relief. I'd hate to think they were all going to lose everything."

"I hear that fella Lashley has vanished." Windy grinned. "I've got a sneaking suspicion he might've been working with the crooks who sent that wagon train here. Mayor Decker said their guide disappeared after they got here, and I'm wondering if that was Lashley, too."

"The law will catch up to them one of these days. I plan on giving a full report to my boss, Billy Vail. I reckon the Justice Department will be mighty interested in finding out what's been going on."

Kincaid leaned back in his chair. "That wraps it all up then. You can go back to Denver, Marshal, and my men and I can head back to Outpost Number Nine."

Windy laughed. "After saying good-bye to a certain blond widow, eh, Matt?"

Kincaid just flushed and looked uncomfortable.

John Fury drank the last of his beer and thumped the empty mug on the table with a frown. "That doesn't settle everything. If people come out here and start drilling for that damned oil, it's liable to stink worse than ever here in the valley, not to mention the racket."

Longarm shook his head. "That may not happen for years yet."

"Yeah, but it will sooner or later, and where will I live then?"

"No offense, old son, but . . . just how long are you planning on living anyway?"

"I don't rightly know," John Fury said.

* * *

A few days later, after Matt Kincaid and the soldiers had already pulled out and headed home, taking Windy Mandalian with them, and after John Fury had ridden off up the valley, Longarm got ready to board the stage and start back to Denver. Blind Pete was already on the box, and Jack Boggs had the coach door open so Longarm could climb in.

"Wait!"

Longarm turned to see Eileen Brewer hurrying toward them. She was dressed for traveling and carried a small valise. He stepped forward to meet her and take the bag from her.

"You're leaving, too?"

She smiled sadly. "There's nothing to hold me here now. The Bureau of Indian Affairs will send another agent, but there's no place for me at the agency."

Her brother had been buried on a hilltop behind the agency building. He had fallen in with owlhoots and made some mighty bad choices, but Longarm didn't believe he was truly evil. He hoped that El Señor Dios had some forgiveness in store for Allen Brewer.

"Well, then, I'm glad you'll be riding with me," Longarm said. "Let me put your bag in the boot."

Up on the driver's box, Pete spat. "We got a schedule to try to keep, folks."

Longarm grinned. "Hold your horses, old-timer." He stowed Eileen's valise in the boot and tied the canvas cover closed again. Then he helped her into the coach and followed her in. Jack Boggs slammed the door and climbed up next to Blind Pete.

As the stagecoach rocked into motion and rolled out of the settlement, Longarm looked across at the auburn-haired beauty. "Got any idea where you'll go and what you'll do?"

"Well, I suppose I could go back to Henrietta's."

Longarm frowned. "Henrietta's?" Suddenly, he recalled Bob Caldwell, the rancher who had insisted that he recognized Eileen, saying something about Henry. Caldwell could have been trying to say Henrietta's.

"It's in Wichita." Eileen looked embarrassed. "It's a house where I . . . worked. Custis, I'm afraid I wasn't *totally* honest with you about my background."

So she'd been a whore before coming out here to join up with her owlhoot brother. For a second, Longarm was angry at her for the lies.

But then he took a deep breath, shook his head, and chuckled.

"You're not too put out with me, Custis?"

"I reckon we've all done some things in life we ain't too proud of. You can't hold on too tight to the past. It'll drag you right down if you do."

She heaved a sigh of relief. "Thank God. I was afraid you might hate me if you found out the truth."

"I don't reckon I could ever hate you, Eileen."

He took a cheroot from his vest pocket and lit it as she continued to talk. Riding in the front seat and facing backward as he was, he could see the giant, pitted rocks at the mouth of the valley as the stagecoach passed them heading east. It seemed like the dark eyes in those skull-like edifices were watching him, and Longarm was glad when the dust from the wheels of the coach welled up and he couldn't see them anymore.

It took a while, though, before he could no longer feel them.

GIANT-SIZED ADVENTURE FROM
AVENGING ANGEL LONGARM.

BY TABOR EVANS

2006 Giant Edition:

LONGARM AND THE
OUTLAW EMPRESS

2007 Giant Edition:

LONGARM AND THE
GOLDEN EAGLE SHOOT-OUT

2008 Giant Edition:

LONGARM AND THE
VALLEY OF SKULLS

penguin.com

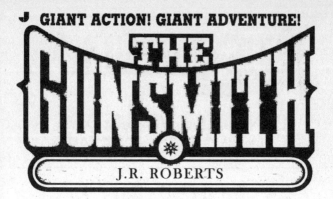

GIANT ACTION! GIANT ADVENTURE!

THE GUNSMITH

J.R. ROBERTS

Little Sureshot And
The Wild West Show
(Gunsmith Giant #9)

Dead Weight
(Gunsmith Giant #10)

Red Mountain
(Gunsmith Giant #11)

The Knights of Misery
(Gunsmith Giant #12)

penguin.com

M228AS1207

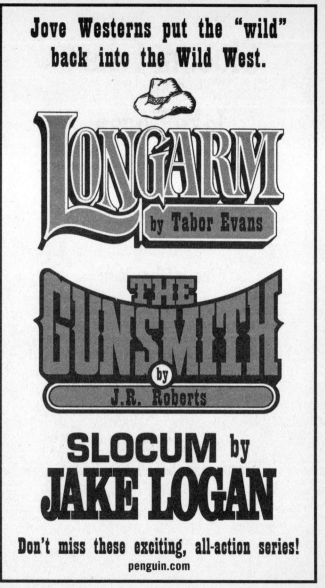